True East

To Jen,
Believe in magic!

Patty O'Hara

Patty O'Hara

outskirts
press

With love to Pam.
My sister, my shelter, my serendipity.
This one is for you.

*An absurd amount of gratitude to my family
in their order of appearance:*

*To Fred, a fantastic husband who shares responsibility for
the original seven of us: Deborah, Terry, Wendy, James, and
Christopher (aka) the kids. Followed by the grandkids: Liam,
Julian, Justin, Emma, Mary, Brianna, Ryan, Jack, Shane,
Hunter, Austin, J.J., Connor, Brooke, and Aidan.*

*There were legions of people who ultimately supported me and
encouraged me and I am thankful beyond these words for you
all, my teachers, my mentors my stalwart friends.*

Chapter 1

February 1990

There is magic in the past and not all of it is black. There are echoes of beach parties and the lingering taste of beer, sex, and snow. Soft, bled cotton from Madras made into shirts or shorts. Towels hung out to dry on a clothesline. Everything bleached by the sun and stiffened by the salt water. The smell of burning leaves. Dancing at the bottom of Cliff Drive to music coming from the car radio. Nor'easters, power outages, the Coast Guard coming to the rescue of those too proud or too foolish to leave. The requisite yellow oilskin slickers. Blizzards. Galoshes! Communion after confession. English muffins and vanilla cokes. Clam rolls and native corn. Sweet memories sit on her tongue and in her heart.

The plane banks too steeply to the left on its approach to Logan Airport and for one fleeting moment Mackie Kinsella holds her breath, waiting to surface from the depths of Boston Harbor, clutching her floatation cushion to her chest. She listened to the pre-flight spiel as if it was delivered by Sister Philomena, who ruled her world when she was in fourth grade.

"Must you fidget so, Mary Katherine? Jesus would be disappointed with your lack of attention."

Well, Jesus must be well and truly pissed off with her now. The prodigal widow. Richard not yet cold in his grave. Seven months of mourning and trying to avoid morning. Sleeping until noon. What must the neighbors think? Retrieving the morning paper from the driveway in her bathrobe at one in the afternoon. Putting the wine bottles in with the regular trash instead of the recycling bins even though she knows that she's polluting the planet.

The sun is just coming up when she hears the landing gear engage and she looks out and notices islands. She doesn't remember them and wonders if anyone lives there, wonders if she might someday build a nice cottage there with a screened-in porch. It would be a place for her to watch the children run through the sprinklers on a hot summer day. Of course, her children are grown. And she has no grandchildren. Emma and Eileen have failed to present her with children of their own and now Richard will never be a grandfather. But the girls are succeeding so well in other things. That must count for something.

Her teeth have grown an outer, fuzzy layer. She has had a cramp in her right calf for too many minutes, probably a deep vein thrombosis waiting to break off and swim to her lungs or brain where it will kill her. She craves breakfast or lunch or dinner, looks in her purse and finds only half a roll of Tums. Good for the bones. She would be happy to lie down or to be comatose.

Maybe someday, if she survives the crash, she will be a grandmother. Nana Mac. She likes the sound of that. Nana. Nana. Nana Mac. She and the grand boys will have a great time. Somehow she knows that they will be boys, the boys that she and Richard never had. She'll wear high top sneakers and they'll all go fishing off the town pier on Saturday mornings. She'll show them how to make drop lines out of Popsicle sticks and string and tell them that when night crawlers are scarce they can use bologna or bacon for bait. She'll teach them about the potential of sea glass and she'll learn how to play golf so that they won't miss Richard so much. They'll all wear Red Sox baseball caps and smile when the townies talk about them behind their backs. Mackie has been lucky enough to have a whole row to herself on this flight. She's finished off two little bottles of red wine, wondering why the red is always too cold and the white too warm. She skipped dinner, but devoured the triple chocolate brownie and a cognac. She wonders if they will check her blood alcohol level if she drowns in Boston Harbor when the plane crashes. Nana Mac, the lush, the family secret.

She is going to her mother's house by the ocean. It's the house where she survived her childhood. A weathered cedar shingle box, two stories high, plus the cellar and attic; it will need repairs. The front porch with L shaped rips in the screens. There is the loose board on the bottom step of the side door by the kitchen. The detached garage, big enough for one small car, will be full of cobwebs and spiders and dark. The lawn, dormant now in the bleakness of February in New England, is undoubtedly sheltering dandelions and crabgrass. The house, her only legacy when her mother died, has been vacant since the end of summer. She doesn't know why she is going there, but she doesn't know where else to go. All she knows is that she must flee California or die. Die like Richard of a broken heart.

In two days it will be Valentine's Day. She and Richard made love for the first time on Valentine's night. They were parked in front of her house, so many years ago. She had expected pain or ecstasy and gotten neither.

And now Richard is sleeping the big sleep. Maybe he has rolled himself into the fetal position. Birth and death, so closely linked, so goddamned fast. Had she remembered to tuck his pajama top into the bottoms? She likes to think of him that way, curled up and dreaming, his breath deep and safe within him.

The funeral director, and what a stupid title that seemed to be, requiring casting and rehearsals and sound and lighting engineers, had suggested a suit—did Richard have a gray pinstripe—and perhaps a nice paisley tie? He whispered that into her ear during the grand tour of caskets. He reeked of Listerine and cheap cologne as they inspected the wares, from the basic pine box to the Cadillac of caskets, hand-rubbed rosewood with an air mattress. She didn't know if Richard would sleep better on an air mattress in a rosewood casket, but in the end she opted for the oak, simple and dignified and closed. No Madame Tussaud's version of Richard for the grieving. Only Mackie knows that he is at eternal rest in his favorite jammies, soft, striped cotton with a drawstring on the pants.

Mackie also knows that passion might have died when he started tucking his pajama tops into the bottoms. Or maybe it was when he came home from the airport and started checking his voice mail after the regular mail and unpacking his suitcase, piling the stuff for the cleaners on the floor and not even realizing that she was in the room. Why did he not realize that she needed a hug?

Richard used to hug her freely. Rub up against her. Push her backward over the hood of his father's Chevrolet Bel-Air, all insistent manhood and promises. Those were the days.

They managed a marriage when so many of their friends had gone their separate ways, trading in their spouses like used cars, hoping for new and exciting unions, only to find themselves disillusioned when the novelty wore off.

Now Mackie is trying to get used to the idea that she is officially a widow. And now for the first time in a long time, she wishes that she wasn't an only child. She could use a big brother's arms, a younger sister's tears, something to make her feel more connected to the earth that she has just landed on.

⸺⸺◉⸺⸺

Leaving Hertz, Mackie heads out of Boston, feeling exhausted and exhilarated at the same time. She pushes the lighter in and fumbles in her purse for the Marlboros. She bought them on a whim. Mackie remembers the last puff on her last Newport menthol more than twenty years before.

Of course it's almost impossible to smoke anywhere in California now without feeling like a pariah. She wonders if

New England will be different.

One hand on the steering wheel and one lifting death in a package to her lips, she catches the end of the cellophane strip in her teeth and deftly pulls it around, spitting it out and flipping the box open—the gestures fly back to her. Just like riding a bike, one never forgets. The tobacco smells strong and familiar. Putting the cigarette in her mouth, she bites the filter hard, the way the tough kids used to do.

Mackie always had a small taste for the forbidden fruits. From the first, frightening drag (thirteen years old—under the pilings of Susie Torrey's summer house one cool Autumn day) it made her feel sophisticated. She used to imagine that she looked glamorous, desirable.

Both she and Richard smoked in the early days of their marriage—a shared pleasure not nearly as perverse as it now seemed to be. He had given it up long before she did, quitting when they moved to California. He loved being pissy and righteous. Educated by the Jesuits, Richard seemed to thrive on abstinence and penance. She had weathered it, sitting on her Bentwood rocker, rocking and puffing, puffing and rocking. Her ankle keeping time with Richard's admonishments as baby Eileen fed. She suffered Richard's evil eye. Finally it was easier to quit.

Richard continually cajoled her, often not subtly, and she had tried to adapt to the health obsessed, LA lifestyle. Richard jogged three times a week, but Mackie preferred reading to running. She adored food and hadn't fasted since Lent in sixth grade. Even then, she'd nibbled on Devil Dogs that she'd hidden between her mattress and box spring.

Until Richard died, Mackie spent three hours a month

foiling and waxing and trying, albeit half-heartedly to achieve the 'California' look. But they had made a bargain to share their lives and although she continually resisted his lead, a part of her had believed him. Thinking he was the strong one, the right one, she'd become a guilty liar.

"Yes, Rich—I jogged down to Safeway today, picked up some artichokes for dinner. And the salmon looked perfect. You know, Honey, you're so right, I've been feeling much better since I've been exercising. I've actually lost four pounds."

She neglected to tell him that she'd driven through Jack-in-the-Box for a Chicken Supreme and large order of fries and wolfed them down while driving home. Then she had spent the rest of the afternoon absorbed in her television soaps.

Richard all healthy lifestyle, riding the Tour de France on his exercise bike every morning, turning vegetarian, checking his cholesterol levels along with the Dow Jones averages. Swimming laps in the solar heated swimming pool. The whole damned yard was that pool and the concrete apron that surrounded it.

Mackie slows for a corner, picks up her mobile phone and calls her oldest daughter.

"Emma?"

"Momma?"

"The eagle has landed."

"Momma, where are you? You sound funny."

"I'm driving south to the old homestead. Say a prayer, kiddo. Who the hell said you can't go home again—Thomas Wolfe, Virginia Woolf, Wolfman Jack?"

"Are you crazy, Momma?"

"Maybe," Mackie says, feeling at least a little untethered.

"Are you telling me you're in Boston?" Emma says, sounding incredulous.

"Well, actually I'm on 93, almost in Shoreham."

"What's going on, Mom?" Mackie can hear noise in the background, the clatter of dishes, hushed voices. She can picture Emma behind the counter in her white jacket and baseball cap.

"I can't really explain it, Emma. I'm not sure I understand it myself."

"Momma, you sound too weird, but—I've really got to go. I've got a customer and he actually wants food not just the bathroom. Can I call you later?"

"Of course you can Em. I shouldn't have bothered you at work." Emma owns her little coffee shop, Regular Joes. It's just up from the beach in Laguna.

"I can't believe you're three thousand miles away."

"We'll talk later, sweetie. Go take care of your customers."

"Leenie is going to have fits," Emma says and hangs up.

Mackie inhales deeply, feels the rush as the nicotine hits home. Stifling a cough, she hits the right turn signal and maneuvers the car onto Three Mile Road and home.

Chapter 2

"You still like those peanut butter and jelly sandwiches?" A thick veil of smoke ascends to the acoustic ceiling as Boo Houlihan spoons coffee into the battered, aluminum pot.

Propping her chin on her hands, Mackie nods and watches the unfiltered Camel cigarette dangle from her aunt's lower lip in defiance of gravity and the Surgeon General. Boo is wearing her weekday outfit of housedress, rubber thongs and a bib apron. Although it's February, her dress is of a thin, white cotton material. Fields of poppies bloom across her back and derriere and peek out from her armpits. Her toenails and fingernails are painted the exact color of the poppies. Boo still dyes her hair the same unnatural sable color, but her scalp has begun to show through and Mackie feels a rush of sadness. Boo adds some crumpled egg shells and a pinch of salt to the pot and ignites Mackie's memory as she scratches a wooden match on the side of the stove.

"They do burials out in California same way as here?" Boo asks, tonguing her upper plate into place.

Mackie nods, "I can't bear to talk about Richard right now, if you don't mind Auntie Boo."

She doesn't want to think about the smell of carnations and the cold juxtaposition of concrete and earth. She feels as if she and Richard had been Siamese twins who were surgically separated. And now she is the lone survivor. Apparently they were joined at the heart and now there's just an endless emptiness inside her.

"Do you ever visit my mother's grave, Boo—or Uncle Buddy's?"

Boo tries to furrow her eyebrows, but since they are simply penciled arcs soaring above her soulful brown eyes, her success is limited.

"I never held much store in cemeteries, Baby girl," Boo says, invoking Mackie's childhood endearment.

Boo scrapes her chair back from the table and parks herself across from Mackie. The gray Formica table used to sport pink boomerangs. Now they look like wounded birds, one-winged creatures cross-hatched with knife scars and cigarette burns.

"And of course, our Buddy's around here all the time—so to speak."

Mackie looks puzzled, "Boo?"

"Ah—you think I'm going crazy." Boo chuckles. "I know he's dead, Mackie. He's just not dead to me, if you get my drift. Besides, I never go to cemeteries. They're no place for the living," Boo says, looking absolutely serious. Mackie laughs out loud, but stops when she realizes that Boo has missed the irony.

"I couldn't believe it when you called from Los Angeles, Mackie. Imagine getting on a plane like that. One minute you're in California and the next, Viola!" Boo says, throwing her hands in the air. "Here you are!"

Mackie smiles at her aunt's mangling of the language.

"You know, Mackie, sometimes I like to think that your Mama's going to walk right in that door and pull up a chair. Sit down with me and have a good stiff drink. You never get over losing a sister, Baby girl, let me tell you." Boo seems to drift off for a moment. "Sometimes I miss her even more than I miss our Buddy…if that's even possible."

"Mother drank? I never knew that. I mean I knew she had a beer every once in a while, but I thought she hated booze."

"Yeah, like Buddy hated his Budweiser. You know his nickname didn't come out of nowhere. And that belly of his—glory be to Roses Wharf!"

Mackie smiles as she remembers her uncle. He was a Buddha, as wide as he was tall. As a child, she sat spellbound and watched Buddy slick his hair back with Vitalis hair cream and shave with a straight razor and a mug of Old Spice shaving soap and natural bristle brush.

Reigning at the head of the kitchen table, Buddy drank beer from tall amber bottles. He was a truck driver for Sears and Roebuck. Smelling of beer, sweat, cigarettes, Old Spice and Clorox, he lifted Mackie as easily as he lifted the bulky appliances he delivered every day.

The last time Mackie saw Buddy he was dying of throat cancer. Sitting with three-month old Emma on her lap across the table from him, she watched him swig his Bud from the bottle as always. The suds leaked back onto his chin from a tumor that had grown too big to deal with. Blotting it with an immaculate handkerchief, he bestowed a blessing upon Mackie. Taking a puff of his Camel, his eyes showed unfamiliar tears.

"You done good, kiddo," he rasped before dissolving into a terrifying coughing spasm. Two weeks later he was dead.

———◦◦◦———

"You remember how your Mama used to make your sandwiches so special, Mackie, cutting off the crusts real dainty like?" Boo suddenly bows her head and whispers, "God rest her soul. And your clothes were always just right. She dressed you like a little rich girl. Velvet collars, expensive shoes. And she paid for you to go to St. Jude's, giving those piano lessons every week." Boo pours two mugs of steaming coffee and puts them on the table. "She had great dreams, your momma. Helen worked real hard for you to be special. To be what she never was—or never felt, anyway."

Mackie is stunned. Special is not a word that has ever been applied to her. For her entire childhood, Mackie had heard the disapproval in her mother's voice. Had taken the random slaps across the face as readily as she took elocution, dance and voice lessons. It was as if her mother thought that she might force her only daughter to somehow tap dance and enunciate her way into respectability. While other kids got to stay at home on Saturday mornings and watch cartoons and eat sugary cereal, Mackie spent the day locked inside St.Jude's Academy having lessons, being chastised for clumsiness, and being consigned to the back row at recitals. Confession had followed. And then the weekly eight o'clock

Children's Mass when Mackie implored God in Latin to save her damaged soul. 'Agnus Dei quitollis peccata mundi—

She had rebelled by not making her own daughters participate in such things. Baptized into the Catholic Church, but raised heathens, Emma and Eileen never received their first Holy Communion, nor were they confirmed. They simply went out to play on Saturdays and spent Sunday mornings watching cartoons on television while Mackie and Richard lingered in bed.

In fact, Mackie had been half-hearted at encouraging them to excel at anything. Lousy at making school lunches, she let the girls forage in the fridge for leftovers. Occasionally she took time to decorate their lunch bags with colored markers or tucked scraps of paper inside with scribbled notes. Cookieless fortunes. 'Happiness will find you in unexpected places—Beware of gifts bearing Greeks—It's never too late to have a happy childhood.'

"Want me to make you a sandwich now, Baby Girl?" Boo asks, shuffling over to the cabinet, scratching some phantom itch on her forearm and reaching for the Skippy without waiting for an answer.

"No thanks, Auntie Boo, I ate on the plane and I really should be getting over to the house. I came directly here from the airport—kind of postponing it, you know?"

"It wouldn't kill you to eat again, Mary Katherine. You're too damn skinny. Leastwise you didn't go turning into one of those bleach blondes out there in California. You always did have the most beautiful, thick auburn hair."

"These days this auburn hair gets touched up every four weeks." Mackie rakes her bangs back off her face, revealing green eyes that have faded like sea glass. "And, Boo, you can't be too skinny or too blonde in California." But her given name has sliced through the air and arrived at her heart, like a knife thrown in a carnival sideshow. Mackie feels herself revolve and end up upside down in a skimpy outfit with too many people watching. The knife has missed, but barely. It has cut through the air like an accusation. Mary Katherine. The old triple threat, Mary Katherine Swan. The ghost of Sister Philomena looms.

Mackie sees the disappointment on Boo's face and reneges. "Actually, I'd love a sandwich, Auntie Boo."

Besides, she has had a sudden, overwhelming urge for a peanut butter and jelly sandwich on soggy Wonder bread, cut into four precise triangles and neatly wrapped in waxed paper. Those sandwiches were one of the few ways her mother had of showing love.

The old thumb sucker needs a hug. She longs to abandon her chrome and plastic throne and embrace Auntie Boo.

"You okay, Baby Girl?"

She pushes away from the table, needing to stand, needing to feel the solid linoleum beneath her feet. Her linen trousers are rumpled beyond repair and now she realizes that the entire outfit is ridiculous for New England in February. She looks ready for a regatta in her navy linen blazer with its shiny gold buttons. The red silk t-shirt and winter white trousers. What in the hell could she have been thinking? Mackie Kinsella and her widow's weeds.

"I'll pass on the food, Boo," Mackie says and watches Boo frown.

"I went over and turned on the heat for you at the house,

— 14 —

Mackie. There's not much there, honey—not what you're used to anyway. But you're always welcome here."

Mackie hears the awkwardness in Boo's invitation. Knows that somehow Boo feels her ancient, mismatched dishes and cracked coffee mugs won't be okay.

"Thanks Boo, but I need to go." She longs to be anywhere but where she is. She wants to believe in the Father and the Son and the Holy Ghost. And she knows that she is now part of a trinity; Mackie, Emma and Eileen. Standing, she feels the ground move and thinks of earthquakes. Magically she finds herself in Boo's capable arms. "Sweet girl, you're okay now. You're home."

Dipping her head, she nuzzles the space between Boo's cheek and shoulder. She is too tired to think anymore. Taking a deep breath and stifling a sob, she inhales and smells Old Spice.

BOO

Boo pours a measure of bleach into the washing machine, glug, glug, glug. Satisfied, she adds just a half a cup of liquid detergent and tosses Buddy's clean underwear in as the waterfall cascades into the tub. Part of her knows it's ridiculous to do laundry for a dead man, but the bigger part of her knows that it feels good. Letting the lid slap closed she goes to the kitchen cabinet and brings down the bottle of Jim Beam and a Welch's jelly jar. Pouring a good measure, she sits down at the kitchen table and inhales before she drinks, loving the smell even more than the taste.

"You there, Old Fool?"

Smiling, she listens to the swoosh chug of the Kenmore's heavy-duty wash cycle. It sounds like a heartbeat.

"Never mind, answering—I know you're here. Just as talkative as ever, I see." Boo chuckles to herself, but then quickly frowns. "Our girl's in trouble, Buddy. She's come home."

As if Buddy had answered her, she replies, "Well, you know damned well she wouldn't be here if she wasn't in bad shape. You never could see the nose on your own damned face."

Swoosh chug—swoosh chug—swoosh chug—

"Well, Old Fool if that's the way it's going to be. You always were one for the silent treatment. You never could sling more than two words together on a good day." Boo takes another slug of the Jim Beam. "I couldn't give you babies, but lord, you always did have Mackie to love."

Boo feels the effect of the whiskey, warming her and

loosening her lips. 'Loose lips sink ships,' she thinks. Time to set up the ironing board and plug in the iron, turn on the radio. Oldies but goodies during the spin cycle. She pours herself another Jim Beam. Holy water. Ritual cleansing. Spin cycle to dryer. It all comes out in the wash.

Chapter 3

Mackie accelerates when she hits Three Mile Road, which is in reality only two and a half miles of treacherous winding blacktop. It runs directly into Shoreham Harbor and at the final crest drops abruptly onto Main Street. St. Gabriel's Church sits on one end of the street and the town pier on the other. In between, the post office and the cinema are surrounded by an assortment of stores and services. The Curl Up and Dye Beauty Shoppe, The Schooner Saloon, The Harbor Barber (where Mackie got her hair cut in front of the huge plate glass window until she was twelve years old and got tired of being teased by the boys.) There is one package store, a euphemism for liquor. Kennedy's has a drive up window for the ladies who don't want to be seen entering or leaving with their purchases. Bewley's Hardware anchors the north end of town before the pier and that is where Mackie heads after Boo's and before the package store where she will show just how evolved she is by walking right in; Widow's benefit.

She doesn't seem to know anyone who is working there. Years ago the Bewley brothers were always in evidence, Harry at the cash register and Johnny roaming the store, handing out advice whether it was solicited or not when he wasn't in the back room reading Playboy Magazine and jerking off. Mackie thinks that the boy at the register must be working part-time after high school, or might be one of the Bewley's sons—or God forbid, grandsons. The store smells exactly as she remembers it, a pungent mixture of solvents and wood, linseed oil and cedar or pine. The aisles are full of potential. She is on a mission. She needs to purchase a trusty hammer, nails and a socket wrench. Maybe a small, power saw. A box of screws and a Phillip's screwdriver and several sizes of regular, anonymous screwdrivers. She imagines that she is armoring herself. Pausing in the housewares aisle, she picks up sixteen soft, pink, 60 watt light bulbs and some all-purpose cleaner. A package of sponges, a squeegee, single edged razor blades, a safety knife, a five gallon container of antique white paint, drop cloths, painter's overalls and cap, brushes, rollers, a broom, a mop, a shovel. She is nearly orgasmic and exhausted by the time she reaches the cash register to check out. Handing over her Visa card, she signs the slip without looking at the total. She is spent by the time she walks into Kennedy's and locates the wine section. She selects a familiar Chardonnay from Sonoma County.

"I'll have a case of the Kendall Jackson," she says to the clerk—and a carton of Marlboros.

After he puts it in the trunk of her car, she tips him five dollars.

"Enjoy the party, Ma'am."

The house sits on a gentle rise just a few blocks from the beach and Mackie finds herself pulling into the driveway without any memory of the short drive from the harbor. Boo apparently has put on the outside light and one or two others inside the house. The front porch is unscreened for winter. It looks forlorn and forbidding and Mackie thinks that the house has shrunk in her absence. She is paralyzed, afraid to get out of the car. She sits with the engine running, smoking one cigarette after another although they are making her sick to her stomach. She wonders if she might die of carbon monoxide poisoning, although the car sits in clear, open air. Unfamiliar with the local radio stations, she surfs through and finally hears Eric Clapton and feels her pulse slow.

Slowly it dawns on her that she has completely forgotten food, milk, bread, butter, soup. She's not in the least motivated to eat, but anticipating hunger, her own as well as everyone else's, has become second nature. Often she plans dinner while eating lunch. She wakes up thinking of French toast and real maple syrup.

Finally, she turns off the engine. There is no way she's going to open the garage door and put the car away. That can wait until daylight. She decides that her purchases can stay in the car until morning, except for the wine. She opens the trunk, decimates the carton and grabs a bottle. She's working into hungry, but she's too tired to chew and the wine seems to have chilled perfectly in the coldness of the trunk. She grabs her hanging bag and carry-on, glad that she's packed lightly.

She takes a look around and sees Malone's house across the street. Light streams out from the windows and as she scans the neighborhood, she realizes that there are quite a few lights on. Houses that used to be occupied only in the summer months are now emitting life signs. She sits down on the front step for a minute to take it in and hear the roll of the Atlantic, smell the salt and seaweed. Good Atlantic Ocean smells.

Newport Beach, California where the ever-disapproving Eileen lives with her husband, Walter, an aspiring actor, and thousands of dollars' worth of electronic equipment seems to Mackie like a beach created with blue screen and technical wizardry. All the people have been sent in from central casting with their perfect tans and perfect bodies and perfect, white teeth. It is a beach as carefully groomed every night as the people who spread their blankets there each morning.

Shivering, she gets up, feeling a century old as she climbs the remaining steps and opens the storm door, bracing against it with her whole body as she slides the key into the lock and opens the front door.

The house smells stale and unfamiliar. Mackie has not paid attention to anything concerning this house since she left decades ago. She turned it over to a property management firm when her mother died and they send her tidy, monthly statements and she pays the necessary bills.

In her years away, she has forgotten that the floors are linoleum, now ancient and ugly as well as hard and cold. Most of the living room floor is covered with a sisal rug and the walls are dark, stained bead-board from floor to ceiling. The furniture is an odd mix of things; slip covered couches and wicker chairs, a glass and chrome coffee table and some cheap lamps. The whole thing is Early American Ugly. Mackie can't remember if any of it existed when she lived there. But she has not forgotten the piano in the dining room. No welcoming table and chairs for Helen, just the piano where her widowed mother gave lessons to legions of marginally talented or musically impaired town kids.

Flicking on the switch, the kitchen suddenly comes glaring into unforgiving fluorescent light. Mismatched appliances from several generations of Sears Roebuck—harvest gold refrigerator, avocado green stove and an old washer and dryer of once-upon-a-time white stand side by side. She sees the stove where her mother reigned, turning out predictable meals of overcooked vegetables and gray meat. Helen's idea of seasoning began and ended with salt.

She is far too weary for this. Opening the refrigerator, she puts the bottle of wine on the top shelf and smiles when she sees that Auntie Boo has not only turned on the heat, but also stocked the fridge; a gallon of full-fat milk, half a gallon of orange juice, a pound each of butter and bacon, a dozen eggs. Smiling, Mackie closes the door and spies a basket on the counter, a loaf of Wonder bread, Skippy peanut butter and Welch's grape jelly, a small jar of instant coffee. A survival kit.

Did she sleep or only dream of it? Sun streams through the window when Mackie finally opens her eyes. Last night, she begged off when Emma called back, promising to call later in the week and promising too to call Eileen. Too tired to think, she had peeled off her rumpled linen and collapsed on top of the high, spool bed that used to be her mother's.

And now she is freezing cold and desperate to twinkle. Eileen's leftover word from childhood flashes through her mind as she scuffs into the tiny bathroom across the hall, mounts the toilet and feels the pain of her full bladder ease. Tears of gratitude sting the corners of her eyes. Stopping to wash her hands, she sneaks a look in the mirror and groans when she sees the deep tracks left on her cheek by too many hours face down on the ancient, chenille spread. She has lines across her upper lip and accordion pleats by her eyes. Her face looks as if someone has driven a Jeep over it.

Is it any wonder Richard had a heart attack? He had been faced with this vision every morning. And she had taken him for granted. Had never stopped to think about what he must have seen in her. Oh, how on earth is she ever going to learn how to live with herself? What is she doing here and where does she belong?

Chapter 4

Mackie does not sleep well since Richard died and on the second night at home, she wakes up feeling her heart beating out of her chest. Richard simply refuses to stay dead. Sometimes he appears out of nowhere to share a sunset on the deck or Mackie feels him coming up behind her like he used to do when she was putting on her make up or brushing her hair. She senses him before she can feel him and turns, to embrace emptiness.

We interrupt this dream to bring you a news bulletin—Richard Martin Kinsella died at 6:43 p.m. on the fourth of July, Independence Day. The irony of it all is not lost on Mackie. She can still envision the awful turquoise and orange plastic chairs with cold, chrome legs. She could smell the fear in the waiting room where strangers share space but stay locked inside their own dramas. The small, Asian doctor, Chu? Woo? Fong? He seemed to be speaking some foreign language. His skin was silky smooth and he seemed hairless, like one of those odd Mexican dogs, although he wasn't bald. He was obviously far too young to be a cardiologist. He looked as young as Emma or Eileen. Mackie might fix him up. The good doctor and Emma that is, since Eileen had a perfectly good husband. She hoped that someone would be along soon to straighten things out. Let her know when they could go home again. She was getting very tired and she was absolutely sure that Richard was getting fed up with this, the machines, the wires, all the probing and checking, the monitors with their blips and green mountains.

Myocardial Infarction—arrhythmia—cardiac arrest. Those words had made no sense. Mackie needed to shop for the bonfire and beach party. Eileen and Walter were driving up from Newport and Emma and her date of the month would be waiting. She'd made Richard's favorite, pasta primavera, and she'd stop at Calareso's stand and pick up some tomatoes, butter lettuce, and an avocado for salad. Yes, that's exactly what she'd do just as soon as she spoke to someone about the awful fluorescent lighting in the waiting room.

———«(O)»———

The digital clock reads 3:23 in ugly red numbers. Mackie turns over and reaches across the bed, splaying her fingers, smoothing the sheets that are already smooth. The cotton is blended with polyester and is worn thin. She misses her own sheets and her eiderdown pillow. She is sleeping in a pair of Richard's unwashed sweats. A relic from her former life, they make her feel safe.

She is running on empty. She's disoriented, but magically finds a full glass of water on the bedside table and downs it in a matter of moments. She knows that she must have brought it to the room herself, before she climbed into bed.

"I am a highly functional drunk," she says, wondering if she should be checking into the Betty Ford.

She hears something in the backyard, the crunch of footfalls on frozen grass. It is a sound memory from the past. She hasn't heard the sounds of snow for years. Perhaps she'll just pretend to be asleep.

"I have nothing you want," she mumbles.

Besides, she doesn't know if she can move or speak above a whisper. Nevertheless, her legs swing out over the side of the bed and she reaches for her bathrobe, feeling like an actress in a B movie. Pulling it close around her and tying the sash, she goes to the window that faces the backyard and pulls the shade aside, expecting to see only moonlight and the shadows of the sparse bushes and trees. They make a kind of fence between her house and the house behind it. In southern California everyone is closed into concrete walls, the higher the better to surround the swimming pools and any signs of life. There it is possible to travel from house to market, school, airport and home again without actually having contact with another human. One has only to hit the electronic garage door opener and put the Lexus into reverse upon leaving. Upon return the door opens again to the mere push of a button and one is safely inside.

But this is New England and fences are not required. Mackie peers into the semi-darkness and sees movement, a bulky shape, sexless, but definitely human. Someone is pacing around the back yard and it is the goddamned middle of the night. She is frightened, but oddly controlled.

"I have nothing left to lose," she thinks as she dials 911.

Her voice is stronger than she would have believed possible under the circumstances.

"This is Mackie Kinsella. I think there's a prowler in my yard. I live at 82 Beachcroft. Can you please send someone right away?" She is polite even in crisis. Her heart shifts into a staccato mode and she feels like she might wet her pants, but she stays on the phone as instructed, waiting for the police to come. The voice on the other end is incredibly soothing.

"Someone is on the way. It won't be long. Stay on the phone with me if you can."

"I'm in my bedroom." Submerged under her comforter she whispers into the phone, "Should I lock the door?"

"Lock the door if it's easy, Mackie, but just stay on the line. Help is on the way."

Mackie loves the sound of those five words. Help is on the way. If she survives the night she will invite this woman over for lunch.

She hears a car pull up in front of the house and then another, sees the broad beam of a flashlight and then hears the small parade troop down the driveway and into the backyard. Then she hears muffled voices and the incongruous sound of laughter. She peers out the window and sees three red pinpoints of light. The backyard has somehow become the smoking room. She's indignant that there seems to be a party going on and that she hasn't been invited. Now, unafraid, she goes downstairs, turns on the outside lights and opens the side door yelling "Hello?" into the darkness. Her voice is not as loud as she thinks and her breath makes a puffy cloud in the freezing air. Louder, she yells, "Hello?"

"Well, hello yourself, Baby Girl," Auntie Boo says,

rounding the corner from the backyard and beckoning for the two men that are behind her to follow. One is in uniform. He is wearing one of those caps with fleecy earflaps and a bulky, navy blue parka. A badge that looks like a pretend one is pinned to his jacket. It flashes in the moonlight. The other man has apparently just stepped out of a Great Outdoorsman Catalogue. He is wearing one of those long coats with lots of mystery pockets and a corduroy collar. His head is bare and Mackie imagines that he must have left his cowboy hat at home. Even without the horse, he is graceful in a way that she can't put her finger on. She ushers them into the kitchen and quickly closes the storm door and then the inside one.

"Officer Duffy," the policeman says, nodding. "Colder n' a witch's tit, out there. You better get your Auntie a nice warm blanket."

She looks at Boo and realizes with horror that she is wearing only some worn, flannel sweats and her usual flip-flops. She has however, added a navy blue, knit cap that not only covers her hair but is almost obscuring her eyes. America's Most Wanted—right here in her kitchen.

"Boo! What on earth were you doing out there?"

"Well, I couldn't sleep. Thought I'd come by and see if maybe you were up."

Officer Duffy rolls his eyes.

"I don't sleep good at all anymore, Mackie. It seems like I keep falling into the dent that Buddy left in the mattress."

Mackie hurries out of the kitchen and goes upstairs where she pulls a well-worn sweatshirt out of the suitcase. She's been home almost a week and still hasn't bothered to unpack. She hasn't needed much in the way of clothing. Clean unders in case a car hits her. She still wears panties to bed. Richard used to make fun of her for it. She has tucked a photograph of Richard, the girls and herself into the mirror and it catches her eye. Richard has that half smile, but the girls and Mackie are beaming out at the photographer. They look like an advertisement for Florida orange juice.

Shaking her head, she pulls the spread off her bed, wondering if Boo is okay. After all, skulking around in the back yard in the middle of the goddamned night is kind of weird behavior even for Auntie Boo. But Mackie is so sure that she can't cope with one more awful thing that she pushes the thought to the back of her mind.

Back in the kitchen, the stranger from the yard is making coffee. He's lined up four mugs on the counter and looks thoroughly at home.

Pushing the neck of the sweatshirt over Boo's head and helping her put her arms into the sleeves, Mackie feels worry gnawing at her. Boo has always been her stalwart auntie, solid and dependable if eccentric. And now she sits, dazed and not smelling clean. Eileen's U.C.L.A. Law School logo is emblazoned across her bosom and she seems to be holding court with Shoreham's finest in attendance. Is Boo acting crazier than Mackie remembers or has her auntie been spending too much time in the company of Jim Beam?

"I'm Sully," the stranger says, his voice breaking into the hard silence, offering Mackie a warm hand. "I do some photography for the Beacon," he says, naming the local newspaper.

Mackie looks at him, not understanding what that has

to do with prowlers in her yard. What was he going to photograph? Suddenly she feels like an exhibit. She wraps the bedspread around Boo and Sully continues to talk.

"I keep the police band on twenty-four hours a day. There was an injury accident on Beaver Dam Road earlier tonight—nothing serious, thank God. When I heard this dispatch I got curious. I heard you were back in town." He takes a breath while Mackie absorbs this. "Coffee? Might warm everybody up."

Mackie is still speechless.

He has removed his coat and leans against the counter in jeans and a navy blue sweater that looks like cashmere. It has a V-neck with nothing underneath. Richard had owned several much like it. "You are Mackie Swan, right?"

She nods her head and then corrects him, "Kinsella. Mackie Kinsella now. I'm married—that is I was—I'm—" she feels the word catch in her throat and she tries to swallow and fails.

Mackie feels as if she is as old as Boo and she hates it. How have they come to be members of the same terrible club? The "widows club." Mackie listens to the sound of the teakettle whistling and wonders how she has come to be in this place where it feels as if life will never be normal again.

"Do I know you?" she finally asks Sully, sounding more accusatory than she means to be. He has a fine face, a sweep of flaxen hair that seems only recently to have been brushed with a bit of silver, eyes like polished mahogany. His mouth is a bit full at the top, his nose long and straight. He possesses an altogether pleasing arrangement of features and yet he seems completely unaware of his luck. Mackie, a person who has never liked her own face, might have garroted someone to have been given that blessed arrangement of skin and bone.

He moves to make the coffee as if he has been in this kitchen a thousand times. Following trails that he could not have possibly known, opening and closing drawers and cabinets, finding spoons, a sugar bowl, a chipped creamer.

"Shoreham High," he says. "You were a few years ahead of me. I had a major league crush on you. You haven't changed a bit. You probably knew my sister, Jannie Sullivan. She was in your class."

Crush? Oh my god, what century did that word come from?

He'd had a crush—on her? He slipped it in so fast that she thinks she misheard him. "Of course," she says, remembering a girl who was neither pretty nor particularly popular in those days when those were the only important things. Mackie finds the milk and pours it into the pitcher. "Wasn't she president of The Future Homemakers of America?" The very name of such a homespun club coming out of Mackie's mouth makes her smile.

All of a sudden Boo pipes up, "She's a lezbo, you know."

Officer Duffy chokes, spraying coffee from his nose and his mouth.

Sully bursts out laughing.

Boo throws her head back, opens her mouth and blows several, perfect smoke rings. Then she smiles and stubs out her cigarette in a beanbag ashtray that Mackie has never seen before. She has been using an old Diet Coke can for her butts.

"Jannie Sullivan. Queer as a three-dollar bill. Always was,

always will be. Glory be to Rose's Wharf, she was wearing men's shoes before it became the thing." Boo mimics quotes with her fingers.

Mackie feels heat suffuse her cheeks, "Auntie Boo!"

"Well, it's God's truth, Baby Girl. And it's not like she's the only one in town."

Sully nods, wiping the inside corner of his eye, "She's right, Mackie." He finishes his coffee and brings his mug over to the sink, rinses it and turns it upside down on the counter. Putting on his coat, he makes eye contact with Duffy and smiles at Mackie. "It's okay, really. I think we ought to call it a night and get out of here. Give you some space. I'm sure that Officer Duffy would be happy to see that your aunt gets home safely."

Mackie kisses Boo on the forehead and bids them good night although it is nearly morning. Too wired from the coffee and the impending sunrise, she pads into the living room where she tries to revive her old Girl Scout skills and build a fire. She makes a log cabin with kindling. Pushing twisted newspaper into the open spaces, she places one piece of wood across the top and strikes a match. The wood is bone dry and it catches fast.

She lights herself a cigarette and feels ashamed that she is smoking again and she promises herself that she will quit tomorrow. In the meanwhile, she pushes the old sofa over close to the fire and curls her legs up under her. She can hear the sound of the ocean outside her house. This is her house. Not anyone else's. How strange that seems. How lonely and terrifying and daunting.

But this is a new chapter, one that holds all kind of

potential. She searches her memory for an image of herself in high school, wonders what Sully saw way back then. A crush! She lets herself smile, lets her mind run free.

She has managed to replace all the light bulbs in the house with the soft, pink ones that she bought at Bewley's Hardware, but the rest of her purchases are piled in the back room off the kitchen. She was crazy to buy it all. She doesn't even know if she'll be staying on. There's the house in California, to say nothing of Richard's estate caught up in probate. They had never bothered about wills. She doesn't even know how much money they had. What she might now have. She knows that there were stocks and options and God knows she signed her name enough times without reading the documents. She needs to get a hold of Eileen and see what's going on. She'll leave her another message. She'll talk to her machine. But maybe tomorrow morning she'll begin painting the place.

That'll be something.

MACKIE

I am in the backyard tied to the clothesline post with a length of rope. It keeps me safe. I can hear the music from inside—the scales—E,G,B,D,F every good boy does fine. Over and over the notes ring out. I am three I think, wearing jodhpurs although the only pony I've ever ridden was gaily painted and permanently impaled on a post at Norumbega Park—a rictus for a smile. I have a jaunty cap with earflaps and although the air is cold, I feel the warmth of urine trickling down my legs.

Chapter 5

It is mid-March when Boo pulls her Plymouth Valiant into Mackie's driveway and leans on the horn. The front fender is crumpled, rust has eaten through the paint in many places and the car has over a hundred thousand miles on it. The front bumper is hanging off and nearly scrapes the ground. Boo is offering Mackie the use of the car for as long as she wants. She says it's no skin off her nose, she can walk just about anywhere in town and Charlie Pickett can come by with the town taxi if she needs to go further afield. Boo's driving license expired a decade ago but she has no intention of renewing it. She considers the DMV just one more bureaucratic, moneymaking scam. Besides, she informs anyone who will listen to her rant, her age excuses her from such technicalities. She's promised to follow Mackie to the car rental place by the airport. Maybe they'll get some lunch afterwards. Boo has a two for one coupon for Happy Hamburger.

Mackie bounds down the side steps from the kitchen and says, "Good morning, Boo." The back seat of Boo's car is littered with fast food wrappers, old newspapers and blankets and if Mackie didn't know that Boo had a perfectly good house three streets over, she'd have to assume that her aunt was living in her car.

"You look like two cents worth of God help us," Boo says, flicking ash from her cigarette out the window and onto Mackie's Doc Marten boots.

"Well, thank you so much, Auntie Boo. You look lovely yourself."

"When's the last time you got a dye job?" Boo asks. "You going premature gray?"

"It's hardly premature, Boo. I'm a middle-aged woman if you haven't noticed. Besides, I don't have the time or the inclination. I've decided to just be more natural, more myself."

"Then what the hell's with the overalls? Is this your farmer's daughter phase or something?" Boo asks, climbing out of the car and eying Mackie from head to toe with disdain.

Mackie has assumed a new look for Shoreham. It's been gloomy, cold or raining since she arrived and her California clothes have proven themselves totally unacceptable for New England. Last week she ventured into the harbor and purchased the necessities for her new life. Taking lessons from Emma, who has always been her practical daughter, she bought serviceable clothes that would withstand wear and tear and require minimal maintenance.

"The overalls are comfortable, Boo."

"So are pajamas, God damn it, but you don't see me running into the A&P in them."

"Whatever," Mackie says, smiling wryly and kissing Boo on the cheek. " I'm really trying here, Boo—you're going to have to cut me some slack." Mackie walks away and says, over her shoulder. "I'll try not to lose you, but if I do, I'll meet you at Hertz."

Auntie Boo, fashion maven of the world. Yeah. Today she is wearing a ratty brown coat with some kind of faux fur collar. A pink ski band covers her ears and God only knows what she's got on underneath the coat. But still, the bantering feels good. Almost like the kind of mother-daughter duo that Mackie always dreamed of having but never managed with her own mother. The garage door is cumbersome and she says, 'fuck it' as she yanks the handle and raises the door. She knows that if she stays, she'll invest in an electronic door opener.

She smiles as she slides behind the wheel of the Corolla, full of purpose. She is going to buy a car today. No way on earth she's driving Boo's wounded Valiant around town, even if it is a sweet offer. She has Richard's life insurance money and she's sure she can find some reasonable transportation. Besides, it's a necessity; she's probably already spent the equivalent of a down payment on the car rental.

Pulling onto the highway, Mackie feels a sense of renewal. She can't believe that winter is almost over. She keeps leaving messages on Eileen's voice mail and getting cryptic messages on her own in return. Eileen is busy working on 'Initial Public Offerings'. She's looking for someone who specializes in 'Wills and Trusts'. Apparently things take forever at Harmon, Hamill and Sedgewick where eighteen-hour days are the norm. Eileen is worried about her mother. Eileen still thinks that Mackie should return home immediately. Emma, who has moved back into the house in Citrus Valley, and is using Mackie's Lexus in her absence, thinks that things are fine just the way they are. And why shouldn't they be with Mackie paying half the mortgage and Emma getting to play pretend house?

Although Mackie has always driven Richard's cast-off cars, she has little problem deciding on the gently used Camry at the back of the lot. She's never bought a car of her own before and feels a sense of exhilaration as she finishes signing the paperwork. Taking the keys from the salesman, she tosses them in the air and catches them. Raising them to her lips, she yells, "Tell you what, Boo, I'm springing for lobster rolls! We'll have a celebration. To my new car and moving on."

"Suit yourself, Sweet Pea—it's six of one half dozen of the other to me." Boo climbs into her Valiant.

"I'll meet you at Anchors Aweigh. The take-out part is open and we can eat at your house, ok?"

"Whatever floats your boat, Sweet Pea." Boo peels out of the lot and Mackie says a silent prayer for her aunt's safety.

Sitting in Boo's kitchen, they devour the sandwiches, a concoction of chunky lobster thick with mayonnaise, crammed into a hot dog bun. They sit across from each other, chewing their sandwiches and gulping mugs of lukewarm coffee. Boo suddenly belches, breaking the silence.

"I think you'd like Emma's little restaurant, Boo. It only seats about thirty people and she can barely make a living, but it's hers. That's something for a change."

"What's it called?"

"Regular Joe's—for the coffee, Boo. She only serves breakfast and lunch. The coffee is the draw."

"Kind of like those Starbuck places?" Boo lifts an eyebrow.

"Kind of," Mackie says. "Only so not."

Mackie finishes her sandwich and starts clearing the table. "It's so strange to me, Boo. I always thought that Richard and I would be moving into a little condo somewhere, enjoying the grandkids. Or maybe we'd be traveling to Mexico or Hawaii, soaking up the sun. I just can't believe what's happened sometimes. Here I am." A wave of melancholy sweeps over her.

Boo gets up and goes over to Mackie, rubs her back. "I was just thinking, Sweet Pea. Maybe we should have a party. Invite some people over. Your place is looking real good. What do you think?"

"I think not."

"Well, how about here?"

"No."

"Why not?" Boo says. "Live a little. You might enjoy a bit of social life."

"Boo, I would think that it would be obvious to you. I'm still in mourning…"

"Buddy thinks it would be a good idea."

"Buddy is dead!" Mackie, disgusted, pushes her chair back and walks out to the back stoop and lights a cigarette. Boo follows.

"Well of course he's dead," Boo says in a maddeningly calm voice. "They're all dead, Buddy, your mother, Helen, even your own dear Richard. They're all saints and souls now, deader 'n door nails, the bunch of them. But, if you don't mind me saying so, it seems to me that it might be about time for you to start knowing that you're alive, Baby Girl. Besides which, everybody knows I'm the best fun in town.

Mackie can only sigh. "I have a lot to do, Boo. I'm not nearly finished being sad."

"Well, maybe you can just come over and play some poker tonight. There's me, Charlie Pickett, the Piper twins..."

"I don't think so, Boo."

"Well then, let's use that old barbecue in your yard and have a cook-out next week."

"Boo, it's freezing...its March for God's sake." Mackie shivers and goes back inside for her coat.

"A Saint Paddy's party?" Boo calls out cheerily from the stoop.

"Boo, please stop. Stop worrying about me. I'm going to be just fine. I'm going to be great even. I'm going home now. The only thing I feel up to right now is a long, hot bath and a good night's sleep. Thanks for everything. I love you and I'll call you tomorrow. I promise." Mackie buttons her coat and kisses her auntie's cheek.

"You know what you need, Sweet Pea...a good man."

Mackie feels the heaviness descend.

"I had one, Boo. Once upon a time."

MACKIE

I am five years old and in kindergarten at St. Gabriel's. I love my navy blue uniform with its sharp pleats and the crisp white blouse with its changing ribbon at the neck. It is red grosgrain for all the months except May. May is Mary's month. In May we wear light blue. I make my shrine with the little statue of the Virgin Mary and hope that I will be chosen to lead the procession. My altar in the bedroom is exquisite. I have cut lilacs from the garden and even brought my dolls to worship. Their permanents have achieved lovely, tight acceptable curls. My horrid, stick straight hair still refuses to curl. Mommy says it is stubborn—just like me. Despite the rotten egg chemicals that mommy has put on it, my hair hangs straight. A failure. The lilacs fade and I'm not allowed to light the candles and alas it is snotty Patricia Gaffney who gets to be the virgin.

Chapter 6

Mackie gets home from Boo's and finds the house dark, forbidding and cold. She immediately starts turning on lights and pushing up the thermostat to seventy-five degrees to take off the chill. She turns on the radio to an oldies station and fills the kettle with water while waiting to hear the familiar clank and clatter of the old oil burner in the cellar, but she is met with silence. The cellar is certainly not one of her favorite places, and she knows less than nothing about the mysterious workings of heating machines. Richard had always taken care of anything that hinted of electronics, nuts or bolts or they called someone in. Mackie shudders, knowing that she will just have to take yet one more leap into the single life. Opening the door to the cellar, she feels for the light switch on the right and takes a deep breath as she descends the stairs. The cellar is thick with cobwebs and smells like decaying frogs. She gets a 'Psycho' like feeling when she gets to the bottom of the stairs and halfway expects some boogeyman to pop out from a dark corner. But, she is alone as she goes to inspect the burner and finds the beast in the far corner, cold and dead. Fortunately there is a sticker with name and number of Hubbard's. Mackie has no idea how long the sticker has been there. Bob Hubbard used to live at the top of the street, but that was a long time ago. She remembers him coming out a few times when they were having a Nor'easter and the cellar was flooding. Mackie had loved those fierce storms when she was a child. Now the thought of one was terrifying. Several times in the past they had been evacuated and spent the night in the school gym. Then those times had seemed like grand adventures.

She checks her watch and sees that it is almost six o'clock and she says a silent prayer as she goes back upstairs. She hopes that Mr. Hubbard has not gone out of business and she hopes that he is still at work if he hasn't died or retired.

—》《《》》《—

"Most likely you're out of oil, Mrs. Kinsella. Or could be that the pilot's gone out on ya. Did you check it?"

"I'm afraid not, Mr. Hubbard. In fact, I'm not even sure I can find it."

"Best I take a look at it anyway. I can get you delivered in about an hour or so, okay? Winter sure seems to be hanging on this year. Used to have your mother on a regular schedule. But with the house being vacant in the winter, it hasn't been needed. We usually come and service the burner in September and that's done her."

"Do I need to be here for it?" she asks, thinking she might just head back over to Boo's until the heat is restored. "I can leave the kitchen door unlocked for you."

"Nifty. I'll just check her out and fill her. I'll leave the invoice on the counter, lock the house and leave the key in the usual place."

After thanking him, Mackie goes up to the bedroom, pulls on a heavy sweater and looks through the hope chest for a muffler. Her breath catches for a second when she finds the maroon and gold striped scarf from her senior year in high school. There are also yearbooks and photo albums and other bits of the past. Mackie can't believe her mother kept these things.

The snow is coming down hard and streetlights outside the door cast inviting halos of light on the ground. She heads out for Auntie Boo's, enjoying the sound of her feet on the snow and the puffs of breath from her mouth. The air is cold on her face, but she feels warm inside her clothes and somehow finds herself not at Boo's, but in front of Turner's Tavern.

The Tavern has been in existence since the end of Prohibition and the dining room is doing a brisk business when she arrives. There are only about twenty tables, and tonight few are empty. Lots of couples are taking advantage of the early bird meals. Increasingly it seems to Mackie that the world is made up of twosomes, a fact that she hadn't taken notice of when Richard was alive. She debates about grabbing some dinner, but decides instead to head down the corridor to the bar. Originally it had been a service porch, used mostly for storage, but now it is a small haven for the townies.

Alexandra Fletcher is polishing glasses behind the bar. The six o'clock news is muted on the television screen in the corner. World events for lip readers. Outside the mullioned windows fat flakes of snow float to the ground and stick. It is the kind of dense snow that is perfect for fort building and snowball fights but treacherous for drivers. Black ice. Skids. Airbags required. Mackie is happy that she has walked here. She has missed snow.

Tonight, Al is wearing a crisp white shirt with French cuffs, a black bow tie and black trousers. Huge shamrock earrings dangle from her ears and are echoed in her cufflinks. Her hair is a wild corona of silvery curls. She banters with customers as Mackie stomps snow off her boots and tries to fluff up her hair. Shrugging her way out of a navy pea jacket that she found in the hall closet, Mackie feels her cheeks flaming and her nose starting to run and searches fruitlessly for a tissue. She remembers when she was a kid and simply used her sleeve and she smiles.

Suddenly, a man swivels around on his barstool and offers her a cocktail napkin.

"Thank you," Mackie says, and then recognizing him, "Sully?"

"Guilty as charged."

She wipes at her nose and feels the blush move up to her forehead. So much for 'crushes' she thinks. High school is long over and she is just the new widow woman. And she notices again how appealing he is. He smiles and she adds dimples to his list of attributes.

You Can Call Me Al, is playing in the background as the lady behind the bar pipes up.

"And you can call *me* Al. Name your poison, Hon," she says. "Al Fletcher at your service."

Mackie looks at a blackboard propped at the end of the bar.

Wines by the glass:
Drinkable red $4.00
Better white $5.50
Pink if you insist $3.00
Beer and Ale: Ask Al

"I'll have a glass of white wine, please," Mackie says, settling into a booth by the window. There are hurricane lanterns on each table and a fire blazes in the fireplace. Delicious smells waft in from the dining room making the bar feel like a soft cocoon.

Al comes around from the bar and delivers her drink, "Well, You're certainly not a townie, are you, Hon? First time here?"

Mackie nods and looks around. "I used to live here. Ages ago—what's with the quote on the blackboard?"

"It's Simon and Garfunkel week."

"Really."

"Yeah. I play all their old songs all week. Change it every Sunday. Next week it'll be The Beachboys. We have trivia contests on Saturday night and the winner gets a free meal in the restaurant."

"Sounds like fun," Mackie says.

Al walks back behind the bar and Sully pivots off his barstool and stands before her. "Mind if I join you?"

"Not at all," she says.

"So, your Aunt's ok?" He asks.

Mackie smiles, "I think so. I've been away for such a long time, I'm not sure what's ok for Boo." She looks at him from lowered lashes. "I'm not sure what's ok for anyone for that matter. I'm not such a good judge of ok, actually."

He smiles across the table at her. "Stop being so hard on yourself, Mackie. It must be wicked hard coming home after all this time."

The accent accosts her and for a moment she can't believe she used to sound the same way. *Wicked hahd.* She wonders how long it will take before she sounds as if she never left Shoreham. And at the same time, it's kind of charming. She remembers all the clean-cut high school boys and their not so wicked ways.

"I've moved around a lot over the years. We lived lots of places, California was just the last stomping ground."

"California must be something," he says. "All that endless sunshine. I think I'd miss the change of seasons myself."

"Definitely," she says. "I loved all of that—except for February and March—and maybe the dog-days of August. Ooh, and of course the Nor'easters."

Sully raises his glass and clinks with hers. "I'll drink to that."

Sometime in between Mackie's second and third glass of wine, Al asks, "You hoofing it tonight, Hon?"

"Yes I am, Al."

Bridge over Troubled Water, starts playing and suddenly she can't swallow.

"How about a couple of bowls of our world famous clam chowder, kids?"

She is munching on oyster crackers and waiting for the

chowder to cool when the haunting lyrics remind her of Uncle Buddy and she misses him desperately. Her jaws ache and she knows that she has fallen into a deep well of sadness and won't be able to climb out. Coming to Shoreham was a mistake.

It seems as if all Mackie thinks about anymore is death. It's always lurking just beneath the surface, ruining her life.

"Sorry, I need to leave." Mackie slides herself out of the booth and fumbles her way into her pea jacket, wrapping her scarf around her neck. The hideous striped relic of high-school days makes her feel like a defrocked cheerleader.

Tears are brimming at her eyes when she says, "Goodnight, Sully." Pulling a crumpled, twenty dollar bill out of her pocket, she throws it on the table and says, "Trust me for the rest." Although to her ears it sounds more like 'truss me'.

And so she makes her getaway, leaving the tavern and heading up Turner Road, her head tucked in and her heart heavy. She is nearly home before she hears the crunch of snow under tires and sees the path of headlights sneaking up on her.

Pulling up beside her, Sully rolls down the window and asks, "Give you a lift, lady?"

"No. Thank you though." And again the tears appear. "I'm enjoying the walk. I'm fine."

Fine. It was such a useless word, such a fiction. She'd always hated that word. Richard had loved the word. He had used it all the time.

"How do I look, Honey?"

"Fine."

"Do you want to have dinner at Severino's?"

"Fine."

"How about a movie?"

"Fine."

Well, Richard is no longer fine. And she sure as hell will never be fine again.

Her stomach lurches and she runs to the side of the road and retches.

Suddenly Sully is with her and she is more mortified than ever. He stoops down beside her, takes his glove off and places his hand on her forehead. "Are you ok?"

She gets up, takes a few steps away and then scoops up a handful of snow and eats some. Taking a deep breath she says, "I'm okay. Really. I'm much better."

"Probably a bit of food poisoning," Sully says. "Got to be careful with those clams."

Since Mackie barely managed a few spoons full, she doesn't know if he is being sarcastic or not, but he smiles softly at her. Then he scoops up some snow and makes a perfect snowball, turns around and hurls it, hitting a tree twenty feet away. It breaks the tension between them and Mackie smiles, happy for the diversion. Not to be outdone, she makes her own snowball, winds up and pitches it, widely missing the mark. The contest continues for a few minutes until Mackie shivers and says, "I really do need to get home."

This time she takes his offer of a ride. "Would you like to come in for coffee?" Mackie asks as they pull up in front of her house and she opens the car door.

"How about a rain check?"

"Sure. Thanks again for the rescue, Sully."

"Nothing to it, Ma'am—just part of the service.

You'd better get out of those wet clothes before you catch pneumonia."

She is reluctant to say goodnight and surprises herself by saying, "I had fun."

"Me too. You've got a great throwing arm there."

"Goodnight, Sully."

"Hey, Mackie…You know I'm going to hold you to that rain check."

"I certainly hope so," she says, wondering for a moment if he might get out of the car and hold her.

She wraps the striped scarf around her neck one more time and watches him leave. The Jeep makes heavy tread marks as it rolls down Beechcroft Road and she watches until the taillights disappear.

Chapter 7

Mackie goes to open the door and finds it locked. Mr. Hubbard has come and gone and hopefully has fixed the heater, leaving the key behind in 'the usual place' whatever that might be. Checking over transoms and under rocks, shivering as she goes...she even braves the bulkhead to see if the cellar door might be open. She finally gives up and heads for Boo's. She knows that Boo has a spare key but she dreads needing to explain her evening foray and wants nothing more than the warmth of her house and the quick change into sweats and into bed.

Richard. What have you done to me? Mackie whispers the word and feels the ache as she walks the few blocks to Boo's house. She has become somewhat used to living alone but hasn't slept well since Richard's death. She still strains to hear him, imagines his breath upon her as she takes each long, cold journey into sleep. With Richard she had always found warmth in the center of his back. She had let him carve his name in her heart. She had let him own her. He had taught her so many things and they had taught each other. Making the girls from their passion. Making a life together.

How could she say goodbye to so many years of being with him? She felt him still inside her in the deepest parts. He was her youth, her middle years and her other half. He had filled her as surely as the girls. And they had left her, which was as it should have been…but Richard should have stayed.

And now she finds herself the sole creator of this new life.

It is a frightening collection of days and weeks in a place at once familiar and yet so full of mystery. Can there ever be room for someone like Sully who smells of expensive soap and winter air? His body is long and uncharted. The years he spent before she came back a vast blank to her. Should she feel guilty for even thinking of another man? Can a widow be an infidel after all?

As she approaches Boo's house she sees that every light is burning inside and out and there is a strange car pulled up in front. Mackie feels her heart accelerate and takes the front steps two at a time, crashing into the living room to find her aunt prone on the olive and green plaid sofa. She is covered with an afghan and lies, mouth slack, snoring loudly. A lanky, middle-aged stranger sits on the sofa beside her holding one of her hands in his. The other arm is wrapped and elevated on a pillow. He looks up, startled as Mackie makes her entrance. She looks from her aunt to the stranger beside her and back again to Boo.

Rising, he motions with a finger across his lips to be quiet. Walking into the dining room, he holds out his hand.

"I'm Graham Joy," he says with a voice as rigid as his posture. "I'm a friend of your aunt's as well as her doctor. And who might you be?"

"I'm Mackie Kinsella, Boo's niece." Mackie says as she feels her heart hammering against her chest. "What's happened? Is she all right?"

"First let me quickly assure you that your Auntie is quite fine. That is as fine as one can be after a fall. Especially at her age "

Dr. Joy sounds like he should be presenting an episode of Masterpiece Theater, not making emergency house calls.

"I've examined her here and see no need for her to go to emergency services. She seems well oriented and I'm quite certain there's not been a fracture. I believe she's just wrenched her wrist."

He is taller than Mackie by nearly a foot. The heavy-glasses magnify his eyes to an alarming degree and his baldness makes his face seem oddly vulnerable. He is wearing wool trousers with a knife pleat, highly polished wing-tip shoes and an impeccable white oxford cloth shirt topped with an old man's sweater vest, although he seems close to Mackie's age. He is completely out of place in Boo's dining room where the refuse of the poker party is overwhelming. Chairs are askew around the dining room table and beer cans, overflowing ashtrays and baskets and bowls cover the table.

Mackie looks around and starts clearing the table. She inserts her fingers into the openings of three beer cans, grabs a dish of congealing jalapeno bean dip and a basket of Fritos in the other. She furrows her brow and says, "So, doctors still make house calls in Shoreham?"

"Not exactly, Mrs. Kinsella."

"Call me Mackie, please," she says, "What on earth

happened anyway? How did you get here and where is everyone else? Is she really all right?"

"Let me see," he takes a breath. "We were having our monthly poker evening. The Piper twins were here and Charlie Pickett. The new school librarian was here as well, Doris something-or-other? Your Auntie had been losing all evening, but finally claimed a good hand. She insists that she was holding a strait flush before the fall. She was going for her 'stash' in her bedroom, upping the ante I think she said."

"Holy shit."

"Pardon?" Dr. Joy raised his eyebrows.

"And?"

"And she fell up the stairs."

"Well then, shouldn't she be x-rayed or something? Was she in a lot of pain? Frightened?"

"Actually, she was angry as hell. The crowd dispersed rather quickly, divvying up the pot before they left. Your aunt is quite sure she was robbed."

Mackie smiles despite herself and picks up a cigarette from a pack on the table and lights up. The good doctor scowls.

"I'm quitting next week," Mackie says, inhaling deeply and feeling her cheeks flame, she suppresses the urge to tap her foot. "I've only recently taken it up again."

"Listen, Mrs. Kinsella," he says. "I understand your concern, but I am your auntie's primary physician. I'm also quite fond of her. It is my best opinion that she has simply wrenched her wrist. I've given her something to help her sleep. We can certainly sort out x-rays in the morning, if you feel it necessary. That being said, would it be a terrible inconvenience for you to stay here with her tonight? I don't think she should be left alone."

"Of course not," Mackie says.

"Splendid." Heading back to the living room, he opens the closet and takes out a topcoat and a scarf, which he wraps around his neck before he opens the storm door.

"I appreciate your staying here. I'll ring you in the morning and in the meanwhile," he takes out a business card and writes his home phone number on the back and hands it to Mackie. "If you should need anything."

"Thank you, and good night, Dr. Joy. I'm sure we'll be fine."

"Good night, Mrs. Kinsella."

"And, thank you," Mackie says, wondering what fresh hell the morning might bring.

Mackie continues her clean-up operation to the incessant and reassuring snoring of Auntie Boo's unbroken sleep. When she's finally finished she looks for something to read and finds only some old Reader's Digest condensed books. Propping her feet up on an ottoman, she settles into Buddy's old overstuffed chair to read but almost immediately drifts into sleep.

⸻ ⦿ ⸻

She wakes up, stiff-necked to the smells of breakfast and the clatter of dishes from the kitchen. Ravenous, she shuffles into the room and tries to stretch out the kinks.

"Good morning, Sweet Pea!" Boo chirps, flipping a fried

egg over in a pan of sizzling bacon fat. She wields a spatula in one hand and her injured wrist hangs in a sling fashioned from what appear to be a pair of pantyhose. "Sleep well?"

Mackie stifles a yawn, "I'm supposed to be taking care of you, Boo. How are you feeling, anyway?"

"Fabuloso, Sweet Pea—but you look like who did it and ran!"

Mackie laughs. She hasn't heard that expression since she left Shoreham as a bride. "I love you, Auntie Boo, but are you sure you're ok? That was quite a fall you took."

"Of course I'm fine. You can't hurt an old ox like me." Boo slides the egg onto a plate that already holds several strips of bacon. "So you met the good doctor?"

"Dr. Joy, you mean?"

"Yeah, the Brit," Boo says.

"Yes."

"Well? What do you think of him?"

"He seems nice enough." Mackie takes a sip of her coffee, smiles and says, in a clipped accent like his. I found him splendid, actually! Bit stuffy though.

"Nah," Boo says. "Just British. They're all like that."

Mackie wonders when Boo became an expert on foreign relations.

"Is that right?"

"Yep. Remember David Niven?" And Cary Grant? It's the accent. Makes them all sound stuck-up."

"I see."

"Sweet Pea, you need to broaden your horizons. Let some fresh air in."

"Hmm," Mackie says, taking a forkful of egg and

following it with a bite of bacon, "about all I want to let in now is breakfast, Boo. Thanks for taking care of me." She licks grease from her fingers. "I can't remember the last time anyone did that."

"Makes me happy," Boo says, pouring the bacon fat into a coffee can on the top of the stove.

Mackie finishes in silence. Enjoying the way the light filters through the glass on the top of the back door. Enjoying the sound of the water running as Boo finishes cleaning up.

MACKIE

I am eleven years old and playing shortstop for our Shoreham Beach Bombers, an impromptu softball team thrown together by "big Julie Hanson". She will start college in September. She's about five foot two and weighs about two hundred pounds and I have a crush on her. My Uncle Buddy has not missed a game all summer and now he sits cross-legged on the burnt out grass cheering me on. I'm on deck practicing my swing and I watch him, his gray uniform growing damp moons under his arms. He winks at me and gives me the old thumbs up. When it's my turn to be up at bat, he stands up for a better view. I hit a line drive and he whistles through his fingers and lets loose with his Budweiser baritone, "Run, Mackie, run! Go, girl go."

The blood rushes into my ears, but I can still hear him cheer me on and my Keds grow wings.

Chapter 8

A week later Sully sits at the bar at Turner's Tavern having his usual Irish coffee light on the 'Irish.' Al mixes another batch of happy hour Mai Tais. It is Saturday night of Beachboys week and Al is wearing a Hawaiian print shirt in lieu of her normal starched white. She has managed to corral her springy hair in a high ponytail and has even applied a liberal helping of rouge to her face. A few of the patrons have gotten into the spirit and arrived with t-shirts and shorts under their parkas. Al has presented everyone with plastic leis and she wears four of them around her own neck. Little Deuce Coupe, plays in the background lending a surreal atmosphere to the bar as snow falls outside its windows. Thick coats and discarded boots drip water from the melted ice onto the ancient wood floor. The smell of wet wool permeates the air.

"You make up the trivia questions, Sully." She demands, handing him a pen and a yellow legal pad. They have added bar dice to the tavern and Sully has been shaking and rolling them over and over again, lost in his solo activity. "Make yourself useful."

"How long do women mourn?" he asks Al, shaking the

cup and rolling the dice onto the bar. "I mean, like widows? You know?"

"Any particular widow in mind, Sully?" Al says, tearing into a carton and pulling out colorful paper cocktail umbrellas that she begins to open.

Sully puts the dice back in the cup and rolls his eyes.

"Ah… the Widow Kinsella, perhaps?" Al says.

"She's…" Sully is lost for words.

"Pretty?" Al asks, followed by, "Lonely?"

"And sad." Sully says. "And maybe even kind of lost, if you know what I mean."

"Be careful, Sully. Wounded women aren't your specialty. Remember Olivia."

Sully stabs himself in the heart with his fist and says, "Yeah, Al. I remember her every month when I send the wee alimony check. You could say she resonates."

Now, Sully looks up at Al and says, his voice suddenly loud and pleading, looking like a lost boy, "Help me, Rhonda!" The guy sitting beside him joins in and soon the whole room is a chorus. Johnny Fitz, off- duty firefighter, leaps onto the end of the bar with the grace of a Bolshoi ballerina executing a pirouette and shouts out, "Next round is on me!"

It is at that moment that Mackie enters the room. She feels like the third runner up in the Miss Shoreham contest. The bar holds twenty-five people comfortably and Mackie has arrived as number twenty-six. It is a good thing that Fitzie is around, albeit dismounting the bar, for they are surely violating the fire code. Al comes around from her cash register and bestows a lei on Mackie, kissing her on both cheeks and saying, "Aloha, wahine. Mele Kalikimaka."

"Al?" Mackie says, raising her eyebrows.

"I think it means, hello, goodbye and merry Christmas," Al says. "I'll get you a Mai Tai…park it, Hon. There's seating available in the mezzanine." She gestures to an empty stool beside Sully.

"Hey beauty, what wave did you ride in on?" Sully says as Mackie plants herself beside him. She is still overwhelmed with the heat and the atmosphere and the fact that she is sitting beside Sully.

Mackie looks down and sees the pad of paper and pen in front of him and asks, "Homework?"

"Yep. And Al is going to make me stay after school and clean the blackboard if I don't finish."

Mackie looks up at said board to see:

BEACHBOYS WEEK
Beer by the case…price on request
Thunderbird coolers (free taxi to the E.R.*)
Boozy watermelon coolers
Please have a Mai Tai

*Courtesy of Charlie Pickett

Al delivers her drink and the music starts from a time out of place. Mackie looks down at the pad in front of Sully and sees:

#1. Who were the original Beach Boys?
#2. Who got sole writing credit for 'Surfin'U.S.A'?
#3. What was the group's name before they became The Beach Boys?

"You know the answers to these, Sully?" she asks.

"I do. In fact I'm the musical trivia expert around here, aren't I, Al?"

"Actually, Mackie, this whole trivia thing was Sully's idea. And I thank him for it...profusely even. It's increased the off-season bar business three-fold." Al bows a bit and takes the pad from Sully. "Now don't you go giving out insider information, Sully," she warns winking at Mackie and yelling down the bar to Johnny Fitz. " Hey, Fitzie you ready for another Mai tai?"

Sully whispers to Mackie, "The Wilson brothers: Brian, Dennis and Carl, their cousin, Mike Love and Al Jardine, just a friend. Chuck Berry because he accused them of stealing the harmonies from Sweet Little Sixteen." Sully raises his eyebrows like Groucho Marx . "Now ...say da secret woid and divide a hundred dollars."

Mackie giggles.

"And the Beach Boys were formerly known as The Pendletones," Sully proclaims.

"Is that right?

"Yep."

"Well, Mr. Sullivan, apparently, you will be buying my dinner now since I am disqualified from the contest," Mackie says, twirling her umbrella and sipping the Mai tai appreciatively. "I'll have you know that I am not a cheater."

"Name the place. Give me a time." Sully's voice has dropped. "I'm yours."

"Oh," Mackie blushes. "I wasn't serious, Sully."

"Well, I'm a man of honor, Mrs. Kinsella and I insist."

Mackie stammers, a "Well, fine— I'm busy tonight—but"

"Ah, a date?" Sully says.

"Oh, yes. It's a rather heavy one, actually. I'm making dinner for Boo. She hurt herself last week, but she's so fiercely independent that she hasn't let me do a thing to help."

"Oh no, is she all right?"

"She's fine just a sprained wrist. Thanks for asking."

"Most welcome. Mackie, have you ever thought that maybe she's not so independent?" Sully pulls on his earlobe and cocks his head.

"Boo? She's a force unto herself."

"Agreed. But just maybe she's afraid of your cooking," he says and Al turns around and gives him an evil eye.

"I'll have you know I'm an excellent cook," Mackie says defensively.

"Watch out or someday I'll make you prove it," Sully says.

Mackie hesitates for a few seconds and then, checking her watch blurts out, " Well, Sully, there's no time like the present. Let's say eight o'clock sharp at my place. Jacket not required."

Mackie says a quick good-bye to Al and makes a beeline for her car, pulling up at a payphone in front of the A&P. What in the hell has she done now? Her cheeks are flaming as she hits the speed dial for Emma and sighs relief when her daughter answers.

"Em, I need a goof-proof, fast cook recipe for dinner and I need it right now—the market closes in ten minutes."

Boo's favorite tuna casserole with potato chip topping that she'd made earlier would be exiled to the freezer or the trash can.

Chapter 9

Sully arrives before Boo. Opening the door, Mackie finds him standing there freshly scrubbed, hands behind his back like a schoolboy. He smiles and like a magician, presents Mackie with a bouquet of cattails.

"Good evening and wow!" he says surveying Mackie from head to toe. "Can we say metamorphosis?"

Smiling, she motions him into the house and he sets the cattails down and takes her hand, spinning her around.

"Wow," he says again.

"Thank you. Thank you."

Mackie has spent more time bathing and dressing than cooking thanks to Emma's advice to pick up some pre-cooked rotisserie chickens from the market and discard all packaging. Fresh vegetables are roasting in the oven and the scents of garlic and rosemary waft through the room. A pound cake from Svenson's Bakery, now anonymous awaits ice cream and hot fudge sauce. The pink light bulbs that Mackie has installed are benevolent. Dressed in black trousers and turtleneck sweater with her hair blown dry and gelled and a simple gold chain around her neck and gold hoops at her ears, she feels pretty for the first time in a long time. She feels pretty and somehow expectant.

Sully slips out of his coat and they both erupt into laughter. He is wearing the same outfit of black turtleneck and black jeans. "Oh, my," she says, taking his coat. "This is so L.A," Mackie says. "Black is the requisite evening thing there."

"We're practically twins!" Sully says smiling.

"Let me hang this up for you. Boo isn't here yet, but she's notoriously late."

Boo arrives fifteen minutes later, carrying a lime gelatin mold livid with fruit cocktail. It is in the shape of a fish and Boo has placed a maraschino cherry where the eye would be. Mackie takes it and the container of Cool Whip that Boo thrusts at her, muttering, "Thanks, Boo...you shouldn't have."

"Well, what else would you have after tuna surprise?" Boo says. "I didn't realize this was going to be a supper party."

"I ran into Sully earlier and just thought he might enjoy a good home-cooked meal for a change," Mackie says. She looks Mackie and Sully over from head to toe as she pulls off the hood of her less than clean pink sweatshirt and unzips it, revealing an even grimier jersey beneath and stretch pants that have been stretched to the outer limits.

"Well, you two look just like Tweedledum and Tweedledee," she says. "Mackie, you should have told me company was coming. I would of worn my black ensemble too. Are both you guys in mourning or what?"

Mackie rolls her eyes. She is still having trouble getting used to Boo's lack of guile. "Sit by the fire, Boo. Get warm.

I'll get you a glass of wine."

"Make that a Jim Beam on the rocks and you got a deal," Boo says, throwing her sweatshirt at Sully as Mackie goes into the kitchen. "Buddy sends his regards, Sweet Pea. I'm sure he would have come along if he knew you were having a party."

Later on, back from seeing Boo home safely, Mackie washes dishes as Sully dries. "She claimed I gave her heartburn," Mackie says. "I think she was upset that I didn't give her the tuna casserole."

"She pinched my ass before she left," Sully says, handing a glass back to Mackie for a rewash. "Do you think that's a good sign?"

"Oh my God," Mackie says. "I am so sorry. I really don't know what's going on with her. She's always been slightly—"

"Italian?" Sully says, grinning.

"Eccentric. But I'm beginning to worry. All this stuff she's doing—talking about my uncle as if he's still here—showing up in my back yard that night."

"You obviously care a great deal about her."

"She was more like a mother to me sometimes than my own mother was. I'm not sure what I'd do if something happened to her. She's fallen recently and she's just not getting any younger."

Sully takes Mackie's hands out of the water, dries them with his towel and looks her in the eyes for a long second.

"Maybe she's just losing her inhibitions." He runs the back of his hand so softly down the side of her face that it makes Mackie swoon. And he says softly, "After all this time." His hand goes lower, brushes across her breasts and ends up on the small of her back, pulling Mackie towards him. She leans into him and feels as if she is about to drown. Pulling her head up she finds not air, but his mouth on hers and his tongue... insistent and hot. She gives into the feeling, smells his skin and responds with her whole body as he draws her close. Suddenly the sensation collides with her memories of Richard, and she pushes Sully away, struggling for composure.

"I'm sorry." Turning away from him she says, "I don't think I'm going to be good at this."

"Good at what?"

"This—being with you. I feel as if I'm cheating somehow. I still feel very—married."

"Hmm."

"I am sorry, Sully. I think I've given you the wrong idea somehow. It's just too soon."

"There's no rush." Sully resumes drying the dishes. "I'm not going anywhere."

"I feel utterly ridiculous—kind of a born-again virgin."

Sully chuckles and he stares at her for a moment. "At least tell me you enjoyed it."

She smiles, plunging her hands back into the water. "It was good for me."

Sully laughs, deeply this time. "Well, okay then. We can go from there."

Chapter 10

At eight o'clock the next morning, Mackie is buried under the covers. She keeps replaying Sully's kiss taking it further. Just thinking about him brings a deep rush of longing followed by that sense of guilt. She supposes it's normal in one way; after all, Richard was not only her only husband but also her only lover. Can she be disloyal to his memory?

The doorbell rings, bringing her quickly to her senses. She puts on a robe and goes downstairs to answer the door. Eileen stands, shivering, wheelie suitcase at her feet and a look of resignation on her face. Her eyes are puffy and her face splotchy and naked. Her blonde hair, usually contained in a tightly controlled twist away from her face, hangs limply and her usual business suit has been replaced with sweats and an anorak that she must have borrowed from her husband, Walter. Her bulging briefcase is slung over her shoulder. Can this be her cool and ever sensible, professional daughter?

"Leenie, sweetheart. What is it?" Throwing her arms around her daughter and kissing her, Mackie feels her heartbeat get erratic, "Are you all right? Has something happened?"

"I'm fine, Mom."

"Is it Emma?" Mackie asks, trying to read Eileen's face for clues.

"Emma is fine." Eileen shakes her head slowly. "Can I come inside please, Mom? It's freezing out here."

"Oh my God, of course, Leenie—I'm sorry. I just had no idea—that is I never thought—why didn't you call me for heaven's sake? I would have picked you up at the airport." Looking around for a car and finding none, she says "How did you get here, anyway?"

"Lawyer's taxi, Mom—I get picked up in a Lincoln town car. We get spoiled rotten in this profession. Just bill everything out to the client—except in your case. You can't believe the perks we get. It's all just a phone call away. You wouldn't believe the power of the phone call; the best food, the plane protocols. But this ride will be on me, Mom."

"Honey, get in here," Mackie says, pulling her daughter inside. "You look exhausted."

"I look like shit."

"Let me take your jacket, I'll get you some coffee." Mackie is flustered, "I'll get a fire going for you."

"Mom." Eileen's voice is even.

"What, honey—what is it? Why are you here? Are you sick?"

"Please stop, Mom."

Light begins to dawn on Mackie. "Leenie—did you just call me your client?"

"Mohammed is coming to the mountain, Mom. Maybe you'd better sit down. I have some news and I'm afraid none of it is going to make your day." Eileen shrugs out of her anorak and hoists her overflowing briefcase up onto the coffee table.

"Why didn't you tell me you were coming?" Mackie feels a sense of impending fear. She doesn't think she wants to know whatever it is that has brought Eileen to her door in this state. "Let me fix us some coffee, honey." Mackie says, reaching for a cigarette and pulling a lighter out of her bathrobe pocket.

"What the heck are you doing, Mom?" Eileen says, clearly shocked. "You don't smoke!"

Mackie's cheeks flame. "I just started again. It's nothing. It's temporary. Just one more nasty habit." Mackie gets up and heads for the kitchen. "You just sit here and warm up, Leenie I'll be right back."

Eileen gets up and follows Mackie into the kitchen. Mackie reaches for the coffee grinder, pours in some fresh beans and presses down on the cover hearing it whir into motion.

"Mom, just how well did you know Daddy?"

Mackie stops, turns around, folds her arms protectively across her chest. "What?"

"I asked how well you knew Daddy," Eileen says, sighing.

Mackie turns on the water and turns her back on her daughter. Her heart is now pounding. She fills the pot, adds the coffee and turns on the switch. Taking down two mugs from the cabinet she puts them on the counter and says, "What do you mean? We were together for a long time, Leenie. I guess I knew him as well as I ever knew myself."

They walk back to the living room together, the unspoken thing growing between them, taking up room. Mackie is having trouble breathing.

Eileen sits down on the couch and crosses her legs and her arms at the same time. Mackie thinks somehow this is aggressive behavior—something she has perhaps read about in one of the monthly magazines that now fill her empty evenings.

"He was my husband." Mackie says, and adds. "Your father."

Eileen raises her eyebrows.

"We were together for decades, Honey."

Eileen starts twirling a piece of her hair around in her finger, a habit that takes Mackie hurtling back to the past where she envisions Eileen in her fleecy footed pajamas in front of the television watching Sesame Street. And now the reality begins to hit her. This is her daughter the lawyer. She has arrived unexpectedly, laden with briefcase and little else.

"Does this have to do with the estate?" Mackie asks, knowing that it must.

"Just how much did you know about your investments, Mom? Your assets?"

"That was pretty much Daddy's arena, Leenie. After all, he was the one earning the money. Money that put you through the best schools I might add." Mackie feels suddenly defensive. She never begrudged the girls their education, but has always felt the lack of her own.

"I was afraid of that," Eileen says. "I suppose you just signed on the bottom line when Daddy told you to."

"I trusted your father."

"Yes—I imagine you did, Mom." Leenie clears her throat and says carefully, " I think you may be over estimating your reserve."

Mackie furrows her eyebrows, "But we had lots of investments—stock and—and things. We were getting close to retirement. Daddy had a plan."

"Daddy invested heavily. There was a time when you might have been set for life if he had pulled money out and diversified." She stands up and paces. "Unfortunately that wasn't the case."

Mackie chews the inside of her cheek. "Well, okay—lots of people have been losing money. At least we had no outstanding debt."

Eileen stops and locks eyes with her mother, "Oh Mom— I so wish that were true," she says.

Mackie does not want to hear this. "I think the coffee's ready." She goes to the kitchen, opens the refrigerator and takes out the milk. Crosses to the counter and pours the coffee into the mugs. Leenie reappears. Mackie hands her the coffee and takes her own.

"Mom—I need for you to listen to me."

"Let's just go in by the fire, honey. No need to stand here in the kitchen."

Mackie feels as if she is trapped in some bad movie. Everything seems forced and she doesn't know her lines. They sit beside each other on the couch in front of the fire. Not touching not talking.

Finally Eileen speaks. "Without going into a lot of boring detail—the new bottom line is that you really don't have much money left."

Mackie feels her world shift. She wants someone to call, "CUT"

"Do you remember the home equity loan you took out

last year?"

"Of course I do," Mackie says. " It was for the kitchen remodel. But we couldn't even decide on a contractor. So that money is just sitting in our account." Mackie looks beseechingly at her daughter ... "I think it was a hundred thousand dollars."

Eileen doesn't speak for a moment and then says softly, "It's gone."

"Don't be ridiculous, Eileen."

"Daddy made several trips to Las Vegas last year, Mom."

"But surely he couldn't have lost—those trips were business. Daddy's company was looking into relocating there. Some tax benefit or something." Mackie gets up, she feels as if she is going to erupt out of her skin. Pacing in front of the fire she says, "He was working, Eileen"

Eileen gets up and kisses the top of her mother's head. "Apparently he was playing too, Mom."

Mackie grabs Eileen's briefcase and starts shuffling through the paperwork, trying to decipher the legalese. "Well, there's the California house. I'll just have to sell it and keep living here. I'll get a job. I'll figure this out."

"Mom, the documents are confusing. It's taken me this long to figure out what's happened."

Mackie has a hundred questions and doesn't know where to start. She looks up and sees Eileen sitting behind the piano in the dining room. She is fingering the keys as if there is some secret hidden there. When she looks up at her mother there is great sadness in her eyes but there is also anger.

"There must be some mistake here, honey. I can't understand all this stuff, but things will be fine. Everything will be ok. You'll see."

Leenie stands and her voice is strong and venomous. "Daddy was a bastard. But then, all men are bastards."

"What are you talking about, Leenie?"

"Oh for God's sake, Mom—wake up! It's about time you took responsibility for yourself. Daddy's not here anymore to take care of your world."

Mackie slaps her daughter hard across the face.

Eileen shakes her head slowly from side to side. Tears well up in her eyes.

"Leenie!" Mackie reaches out and Eileen steps back away from her. She picks up her papers, shoves them back into the briefcase.

"I'm leaving now," Eileen says putting on her jacket, putting the briefcase over her arm, pulling the suitcase behind her. She opens the door walks outside and closes it.

"Leenie!" Mackie's voice is a whisper. She needs to run to her daughter. She needs to make things right. But she cannot move. When the tears come they erupt from someplace deep inside her. The sound is visceral— a hideous, primal moaning that hovers somewhere between birth and death.

MACKIE

It's the summer of my thirteenth year and mother's new boy-friend has arrived on the scene along with my 'friend' (which is what we call our monthly period—in a code that fools no one). I am not overjoyed with either of them. He is the third in a series of men who are becoming more serious by the minute. He has begun staying over on the weekends and there is talk of 'making things permanent.'

I don't like the way he smells of whiskey or the way he tickles and wrestles with me on mother's bed when she is not here. Today he is teaching me the 'scissor hold'. I am in my pajamas and he is in his underwear with the gaping front. His legs are wrapped around my middle and I cannot breathe. I think we will not do this again soon. Soon I will be fourteen and old enough to go to the high school dances and flirt with boys. Then I will find a steady boyfriend and then, just like in the song—first comes love and then comes marriage and then comes Mackie with the baby carriage.

BOO

"Well she's gone done it up good now, old fool." Boo is at the ironing board, steam hisses a bit as she takes the shirt by the horizontal seam across the shoulders and lays it across the board. "It ain't easy being a widow, Buddy—I guess I know that better than most. But Mackie went and slapped that poor girl for telling God's own truth. Her own flesh and blood. You know our Mackie's always felt inferior like. Miss Eileen graduating from U.C.L. and A. Magna Cum Loudy and all that stuff. The only mistake that child ever made was being too damned smart."

Boo takes a healthy slug of Jim Beam and scratches her right breast. "I don't imagine Mackie knows what it musta cost that baby to come on out here." Boo turns the shirt and pulls the front side with the buttons over the board. She spits on the iron to see if it's still hot and says, "Leastwise, Emma has the good sense to screw up occasionally.

But you know what, Buddy? I don't think those girls know their mama at all." They grew up all over the place. Mackie just kept moving to keep up with Richard. It was like we just stopped existing after she met him. She never once brought them back here. Except when Helen died of course. It was kind of like she just drew the curtain on this act and took the show on the road. Just my opinion."

Boo's ironing board sits in front of the TV and freshly ironed uniform shirts are on hangers on the doorknob. A cigarette burns in a Ball jar lid and has grown a two-inch ash. She shakes her head. "Seems Mr. Perfect wasn't as perfect as Mackie thought he was. Seems her Richard just went and spent the family fortune."

The cigarette falls out of the lid and Boo scoops the mess up and lights a fresh one. "Now Leenie has hightailed it back to California." Boo takes a deep drag and goes into a coughing spasm. "Maybe it's good I didn't have our baby, Buddy. I think it must hurt something fierce. All that innocence and beauty at the beginning and no fixing what happens after."

Boo turns the shirt and irons one sleeve and then the other. Done with her chore, she sighs, loops the hangers over her thumb, and turns off the television.

Walking out of the room she mutters, "I am not watching too much Phil Donahue, old fool."

Chapter 11

There is nothing of me left to love, Mackie thinks as she drifts into morning and wants nothing more than to go back—to bury herself under the covers. To return to the sleep that brings her to the closest thing to comfort that she can find. The good doctor Joy (and how fitting that name seems now) has prescribed some lovely pills to help her sleep and now her dreams have taken on a life of their own. Comfort and Joy.

After midnight, she cavorts with celebrities. Bette Midler meets her at a beach party and they form an immediate bond. Bette loves her style and starts wearing the same Doc Marten boots that Mackie favors. Bette introduces her to her own inner circle and Mackie ends up throwing wonderful house parties. They end with bonfires on the beach where everyone cleans up not only their own trash but everyone else's before leaving for coffee and omelets made to order.

In another dream, she and Elizabeth Taylor are sharing a hot tub. Liz's Pekinese sits blissfully on the edge eating caviar and licking Liz's fingers that have been painted lavender to match her eyes. One night she gets up to twinkle and returns to sleep to be joined, rather quickly by Harrison Ford who kisses her deeply. She tugs at his earring before he can return to his senses.

But morning comes and Mackie is alone. Damaged goods. She is why Richard is dead. She should have known that he was working too hard. She must have missed the signs. She cannot begin to fathom this nonsense with the money and Vegas. Richard had been true and steady, hadn't he? Surely Leenie has jumped to the wrong conclusions. What had she said, "All men are bastards?" What is that about anyway? Is there trouble with Walter, always auditioning for some new dream role, Leenie under so much pressure to succeed, putting in those outrageous hours, bringing home the bacon. This thought stops Mackie cold.

"Oh my god, I slapped her! What have I done to my sweet and brilliant baby?" Mackie reaches for the phone, dials and gets Eileen's machine. "It's, Mom, Eileen. I'm so sorry, honey," Mackie says —call me, please." And then she realizes that it is four a.m. in California and she is on the other side of the damned country. Sighing, Mackie puts on her robe, walks out of the house and down the driveway to pick up the morning paper. Back in the kitchen, she makes a pot of coffee, lights a cigarette and sits down to read. She feels hung-over, although she has followed Dr. Joy's instructions and not mixed her pills with wine. (If she doesn't count the one or two glasses to wash them down).

When she gets to the classified ads she takes time to read about the available rental properties, the various garage sales and reluctantly arrives at the job offerings. There are only a few listings and Mackie looks first at the ones in boxes. She reads only the bold type: DELIVERY DRIVER FURNITURE, ICE CREAM COUNTER, LOAN PROCESSOR, and SECURITY OFFICERS. As she reads through the ads, most positions require resumes and just a few of them state the pay.

She can make minimum wage as a telemarketer. The family of a stroke victim is offering a small salary along with room and board for a kind, dependable non-smoker. Well, Mackie takes a drag, I guess that leaves me out. She has worked occasionally over the years, getting her real estate license when they lived outside Chicago. But she had only done that because the girls were in school all day and she had been bored. And it had been decades ago. Of course she has many years of volunteer experience that might be useful. She has most recently collected and sorted clothing for homeless families, appalled at what people think is 'useable and clean'. But, good grief, how on earth is she going to put together a resume and more importantly how is she going to make a living for herself when she's never really learned to live by herself?

Hands shaking, Mackie abandons the classified section and moves to Arts and Entertainment. She goes to the Horoscopes, finds CAPRICORN (Dec.22-Jan.19) and reads: Be upfront in organizing priorities. Criticism may occur, pay it no heed. Highlight original thinking, take initiative. Watch for financial bonanza. Then she looks at the date at the top of the page and bursts out laughing. She has lost all track of time. The days just run one into the other and weekends are different only because of the Sunday comics and the distant sound of church bells. It doesn't seem possible to

Mackie that the Ides of March have past and she is sitting in this kitchen, her own kitchen, in Shoreham, Massachusetts.

She is three thousand miles away from her other life, the one she used to have. It was the life with the successful husband and two grown daughters. The one with the Lexus in the garage and calendar full of seemingly important engagements. It was the life she didn't understand and couldn't quite figure out. It was the life she railed against. The designer houses she spent her hours and days and years in and never felt at home. Mackie thinks of all the homes she has made over the years. She thinks of all the compromises. And she doesn't even know what it is that she compromised. She knows she made a bargain. She knows she must have had other dreams, separate dreams, and yet she has no idea what they might have been. Who might she have become? And more importantly, had she accomplished anything at all? Mackie folds the paper and wishes that she had a birdcage she could line it with. Life can be such a joke. It is April first.

Chapter 12

On Monday Mackie phones Emma and asks her to get a market analysis on the house in California. She has decided to sell. She has no idea how much money it will bring in, but it will certainly buy her time. Let someone else do laps in its solar-heated swimming pool. Let someone else live behind those requisite gates and walls.

Boo keeps dropping in unannounced. Mackie makes a great pretense of being all right for her aunt. "I'm fine, Boo. Trust me, she says," feeling anything but fine or trustworthy. Sometimes she pretends she isn't home. And then she feels guilty.

The good doctor Joy has refused to renew her prescription for the lovely pills unless she comes into his office. Her sleep is erratic and some mornings she wakes up finding herself in the same sweats she thinks she must have been wearing the day before the day before yesterday. She and Boo—god help them both.

Mackie calls Eileen every day and leaves a message. The last is a whittled two words, "Please call." But Eileen does not return Mackie's calls and Emma doesn't seem able to or is unwilling to let Mackie in on what is happening in California. She craves this connection with them. She is adrift.

Restless and fortified with coffee, Mackie sits down on the bedroom floor before her mother's hope chest, ready to mine its contents. It is a guilty pleasure. Helen Swan had been a private person in her life and Mackie doesn't feel totally comfortable going on this excursion now. But if not Mackie, who?

She opens the yearbook from her senior year of high school, turning the pages until she comes upon her own picture. Mary Katherine Swan is on same page as Richard Riordan, Alan Silver, and Janice Sullivan. Obviously Shoreham was not the Mecca of independent thought in the good old days. Mackie next reads what is written under her name: "It's nice to be natural, if you're naturally nice." Library, 1,2,3; Junior Prom Committee3; Shoreham Harbinger 1,2; Cheerleading 1,2,3,4; Yearbook Committee 4. Good grief, she had actually been on the committee that assembled this testimony to youth. She remembers going through books of quotations to find a fitting phrase for everyone. How insipid I was thinks Mackie. How uninspired and unambitious. She looks under Jannie's picture: "She is of herself, the best thing, a collection." Future Homemakers of America 1,2,3,4; Field Hockey 3,4; Basketball 1,2,3; Glee Club 4.

Mackie's book has been signed from front to back by classmates that she barely can summon to mind—only aided by their photos and their words. It is full of 'remembers' and 'I'll never forgets' but Mackie has forgotten. She cannot summon the CYO skating party that Bob Hubble mentions nor the 'infamous afternoon at Galavins' that Faith Wescott goes on about. She cannot remember those halcyon days. She cannot remember being a ' real great girl with a wonderful personality'. And when was she ever a 'hot ticket?' And why didn't she know that she had a 'terrific personality?'

Why is memory so damned selective, she wonders. She goes to the section for sophomores, remembering that Sully said he was a few years behind her in school. In these sections, the kids are all lined up on the gym bleachers and identified only by first initial and last name, a Yankee economy, Mackie thinks. There are about a hundred kids in each class. There is an M. Sullivan in Row three and Mackie runs her finger across the row to where Sully should be to find a plump-ish girl. Then she checks juniors and there is no Sullivan at all. She locates the boy who must have been Sully in the freshman class. A. Sullivan is in the back row center and al-though he has not yet attained his adult height, the smile is unmistakable. And the haircut is definitely from the Harbor Barber.

Mackie puts the book aside and finds a shoebox tied with grosgrain ribbon. The ends are snipped in a way that is at once familiar: part of her uniform at St. Jude's. The ribbons were worn at the neck of the girl's white blouses. She had gone to there from kindergarten to eighth grade when she joined the Freshman class at Shoreham High.

The first thing she pulls out of the shoebox is a scapular, two small brown wool squares attached with braided string. Pictures of the Blessed Virgin Mary are on each piece. The weird necklace was hand-made by the Carmelite nuns.

Mackie was supposed to wear it day and night, under her undershirt, with one side touching her heart and the other touching her back. Rumors were that it guaranteed a place in heaven. But at the very least it was supposed to keep her safe from harm and make her more like Mary. But Helen made her hang it on the bedpost at night because she was afraid it would strangle her. The box also held a rosary made with shamrock beads. It had an ornate, Celtic crucifix at the end and Mackie had no memory of her mother ever using it. Helen didn't practice the faith, and yet she had paid for Mackie to go to parochial school all those years. And she had insisted on Mackie going to Sunday Mass and to Christian Doctrine classes. A St. Joseph's Daily Missal that contains the order of the Mass in both Latin and English shares the space. Had her mother become a closet Catholic then?

Mackie lived at home for all those years and yet she hardly knew her own mother. Knew even less about the man her father might have been. And she never asked questions. She just accepted her life as it was. She stayed at home, the good Catholic daughter until she was old enough to leave. And then she found Richard and entered her own sort of bizarre witness protection program, fleeing Shoreham all those years ago as she ultimately fled Citrus Valley.

Mackie puts the missal, the rosary and the scapular away. These are the artifacts of her mother's past.

Chapter 13

Mackie wakes up disoriented. It is either a dark, forbidding morning or it is late afternoon. She leans over to turn on a light and whispers a quick 'damn it' when nothing happens. The clock is also blank. She must have blown a fuse somehow. She walks over and opens the shade. Wind is whipping the trees and something that is either sleet or snow or a combination of both lashes across the windows. And it is freezing!

Grabbing her robe, she stops to pick up her watch on the dresser and notes that it is nearly eleven thirty. Well, at least she has a point of reference she thinks, teeth chattering, as she goes downstairs. It is not yet afternoon. The house is a disaster. Mackie's clothes are hung on chairs or thrown on the floor. She doesn't bother to do the dishes anymore and never makes her bed since she is apt to crawl back into it anytime day or night. What difference does it make, she thinks, picking up the remote. She tries to turn on the television. Again there is nothing. Realizing that all the power must be out due to the storm, she walks into the kitchen and lights the stove, thanking god for gas cooking and for the promise of hot coffee. She rummages in the kitchen drawers for candles and matches in case the power is not restored by nightfall and feels a sense of excitement at the prospect of a good storm.

She remembers the Nor'easter that took place in March in 1962. That year they had been evacuated by the Coast Guard and the house had suffered hundreds of dollars' worth of damage. When the seawall failed, the Mulroney's house had floated right out to sea, bobbing along like a buoy. And over the years, her mother had sent her newspaper clippings of the worst storms. The horrific blizzard of '78 had put Shoreham right on the front page of the Boston Globe. That one had been in February and had completely destroyed almost a hundred homes. Dozens of boats had broken free of their moorings and were thrust out of the harbor to splinter like matchsticks on the shore. Mackie remembers reading that several people were killed in that one; a young girl and a neighbor trying to rescue her were drowned when the skiff they were in capsized. She seems to remember that someone died of heart attack too.

Mackie decides to call and check on Boo and discovers that the phone line is also dead. She curses herself for giving up her cell phone as an economy move. The wind has picked up and the sky is an ominous shade of green. She definitely doesn't want to go out in this weather and reassures herself that Boo will be fine. After all, she's lived here her whole life and survived quite well without Mackie's help. And her house is further uphill from the beach than Mackie's is. Further than the water has ever risen.

Mackie, dressed in overalls, a layer of sweaters, and heavy

sweat socks is still cold. Although the fire is going, it only gives off warmth when Mackie is practically sitting on top of it. So, armed with a bottle of cabernet, some catalogues, a book of crossword puzzles, several novels, a flashlight, candles, two tuna fish sandwiches and half a package of Oreos, Mackie goes back to bed.

Night falls early. Thunder claps and the wind howls. A shutter bangs noisily against the house. The candle goes out and it is pitch dark. She lights another and goes to the window and sees eerie flashes of lightning and hears the pounding of the surf. It hasn't occurred to her to be frightened until now, but she tastes fear collecting at the back of her throat. She grabs the flashlight, turns it on and goes downstairs. She is sure that by now the basement must be flooding. She looks out the windows and sees few signs of life. She opens the front door and braves her way onto the porch, feeling the wind bite through her clothing, looking down she see waves whipping at the stairs. Her heart lurches as she realizes that the tide has risen that far. My god, why hasn't she bothered to make friends? Where has everyone gone and why has no one come to see if she is safe?

She goes back inside and feels an overwhelming absence. She has no Richard, her daughters are not even speaking to her and she has never in her life been so alone. She hangs her head and weeps.

Chapter 14

Sully is out riding shotgun with Duffy when the storm turns potentially serious and the tide starts rising. All of the families in the low marshlands by the North River have moved to high ground and the fire department has seen to setting up emergency shelter at the VFW Hall. A check with the National Weather Service confirms that the storm is likely to veer off before midnight.

"Late in the season for a bitchin' storm," Duffy says.

"You saying that New England weather is predictable?" Sully says, punching Duffy good-naturedly in the arm.

"Yea, right," Duffy says. " Predictably lousy—predictably unpredictable"

"At least I got some good shots," Sully says, patting his camera. "That surf must have been twenty or thirty feet out by First Cliff. But the beach is going to be a goddamn mess in the morning."

"Can I drop you home, Sully?"

"Nah—you can drop me at Turner's and I'll take a taxi from there. I'm starving."

"And dying of thirst, too I suppose?"

"That too."

"You want some company? It's just not healthy for a man to drink alone."

"Aw, thanks Duff. I'll be fine though." Then Sully thinks of Mackie. He thinks about her all the time now. He hasn't talked to her since the night of the kiss. He doesn't want to rush her.

"The wife's likely got supper up. Beef stew night. She wouldn't throw you out, Sully."

Sully smiles. "Thanks for the offer, Duff, but I'll take a rain check."

"Ha,ha,ha—a photographer and a comedian," Duffy says.

"Hey, do you mind driving by Kinsella's house on the way? I'd like to make sure she's high and dry. She's probably forgotten what weather is. All those years away in the land of sunshine."

"Sure thing."

They make it halfway down Beachcroft Road and see that it is flooded. Duffy pulls the car over. "Thank God for hip boots," Sully says, swinging his long legs out of the car. He pulls on his oilskin slicker and hat and turns on his flashlight. The wind is dying down and the rain has almost stopped.

"You going to be ok? Duffy says.

"Fine, Duff."

"Want me to wait?"

"Nah. Thanks for the lift."

"Ten-four", Duff says and reverses up the road.

There are flickers of candlelight and the glow of one or

two fireplaces as Sully wades down the street. When he gets to Mackie's it is pitch dark. He sloshes up to her house and climbs the steps. The front door stands open and he steps in and yells, "Mackie?" No one answers. He walks, swinging his light around the living room. The house appears to have been ransacked. Magazines are scattered on the floor, the couch cushions are awry and various articles of clothing are draped here and there. He walks through the dining room, past the piano and into the kitchen. Swinging his flashlight he illuminates the kitchen. It looks like it has been hit by a Nor'easter. The counters are covered with open jars of peanut butter, jelly, and mayonnaise. He smells tuna fish and other things not as nice. The sink is full of dishes. There are pots and pans and dirty skillets on the stove. He begins to worry about foul play.

He calls her name again and heads up the stairs. "Mackie?" he calls again, not wanting to frighten her if she is indeed here. "It's Sully. I've come to see if you're ok." He flashes the light into the first bedroom he comes upon. It's empty and then he hears whimpering. He crosses the hall and finds her. She is sitting in the middle of her bed swaddled in blankets, surrounded by books and magazines, dishes, glasses and boxes of food. She has created an island.

"Sully" she sobs.

He crosses to the bed and takes her in his arms. "Well, I have to admit I imagined getting you in bed," he says. "But this isn't exactly what I had in mind."

"Oh, Sully. I've been so scared," Mackie says. "I'm so tired of being alone."

Sully slips out of his coat and hat and leans back against

the headboard, pulling Mackie close. "Shh. It's ok. I'm here now." She lays her head against his chest and feels his heartbeat, slow and steady. Her own breathing slows. She thinks that being held is perhaps the most wonderful thing in her world now.

"I was out riding with Duffy. Checking out the beaches and some of the marsh areas. I just thought I'd come by and see how you were weathering your first storm after so long. I'm glad I did." He gives her a reassuring hug. "It's gone out to sea, Mackie. It's over now."

"I don't know what's happening to me," Mackie says, "Freaking out over a little storm. I've always been capable— dependable. I raised a family, for god sakes. Ran a household. Now I'm just a mess. I cry all the time. I don't seem to be able to cope with the smallest things. I just want it to stop. I want my old life back."

"I don't think that's going to happen, Mackie," Sully says. "There's no going back. I think you're just going to have to find a way to live this life." He kisses the top of her head.

Suddenly the lights come back on. Startled, Mackie pulls away and surveys the room, realizes what a mess it is. What a mess she is.

"I was going to ask you if you were hungry," Sully says, "But by the looks of this bed—I'd guess not."

Mackie is mortified. He must think that she is a hysterical psycho to say nothing of a total incompetent and possibly a glutton. Maybe I'm having a nervous breakdown, she thinks, getting up and starting to clear the debris from the bed. How does anyone know if they're losing it when they're actually losing it?

"Have you had your dinner?" Mackie asks. The digital clock is flashing and she realizes that she doesn't even know what time it is. " I can fix you something—after all, it's the least I can do."

Sully looks at his watch. "Look, it's almost eight o'clock. I'm going to walk over to Turners and grab a bite. Would you like to come along?"

"Oh, thanks, but no, Sully. I think I'll just get things picked up here." She is stacking the magazines and catches a glimpse of herself in the mirror. "And get myself pulled together. Her hair is wild and she is braless, swathed in sweats with her hair limp and needy. "You go on though, you must be starving." She makes shooing motions with her hands. "Besides, as you so cleverly pointed out, I couldn't possibly be hungry."

Sully smiles and Mackie just wants him gone. She feels her humiliation growing with every minute he lingers. She is going to get her act together. Whatever it takes. She will get some lovely little pills from the good doctor Joy.

"Thank you, Sully. Thanks so much for coming by."

He squints, tips his head as if assessing her and kisses her forehead before he walks out of the room.

Chapter 15

Graham Joy's office is located in his house in an exclusive section of Shoreham known as Indian Creek. It backs onto the North River and most of the homes there were built in the mid-eighteen hundreds when four and five-acre lots were the norm. Mackie has always been somewhat intimidated by doctors. Now that she sees the expansive Cape and the luxurious grounds, she is terrified. She drives her Camry up the circular drive and between towering oaks, wondering if it's too late to back out of the appointment.

She has slowed the car to a crawl, taking in the pale yellow house with its assortment of windows, doors and balconies. There are also several out buildings and Mackie thinks maybe his office is in one of them instead of the main house. Then she sees a discreet, wrought iron sign directing her to the side of the house and a small parking area. Here, an entrance with a small brass plate reads simply: Graham Joy, MD.

Mackie parks the car and gets out. She is freshly showered, has on clean underwear and a real pair of slacks with a belt and a good cashmere sweater under her tweed blazer. Her legs and pits are shaved and she has pulled back her hair and plaited it, successfully hiding the infringing gray. She is even wearing lipstick and eyeliner for the first time since her dinner with Sully. She thinks that she should feel accomplished, sort of Town and Country but, instead, she feels inadequate and incorrect. She feels as if she is about to undergo her junior high physical and she is the only girl wearing a training bra. She is about ready to flee when the door opens and rotund middle-aged man with a face so shiny it appears polished, emerges holding the hand of an exquisite child. She looks to be about four or five years old, has hair only a shade or two away from being blonde and the most amazing huge, dark eyes that are just slightly almond shaped.

He smiles at Mackie and prompts, "Come along, Daly. What'll it be, the park or the beach today?"

When she smiles, Mackie sees that the child has huge dimples. "Both, you silly goose!" she says batting her eyes first at him and then at Mackie.

Catching the smile, Mackie steps into a foyer that has a slate floor. An office is immediately to her left and no one is sitting at a huge, leather desk nor on any of several, upholstered chairs. A coffee table holds not the usual outdated magazines, but new issues of Architectural Digest, Time, People, G.Q. And there is an Oriental rug on the wide, pine-planked floor. Another door opens and Dr. Joy emerges wearing a different version of the sweater vest, starched shirt, bow tie and neatly pressed trousers. Unfortunately he is also wearing saddle oxfords. She has never trusted men who wear these throw-back shoes.

"Ah, Mrs. Kinsella. I'm afraid I'm navigating on my own this afternoon. Nancy, my nurse, lives down by the marshes and she is consumed with cleaning up after last night's storm. Did your place come through it all right?"

"Well, the basement flooded but the sump pump is running now that the power is back on, so, all in all, things are fine." Mackie wonders if she should take a seat or do something besides stand there. "I had forgotten that storms aren't nearly as much fun when you are a 'grown-up'," she says making quotation marks with her fingers.

"So true. Of course, Daly thought the thunder and lightning were magical. She was over the moon—I would have been happier under the bed, but I try not to warp her with my phobias."

"Did you say, Daly? Is that the beautiful child that just left here?"

"My daughter." He says, barely concealing his pride.

"Your daughter?" Mackie tries to wipe the surprise from her face, but is unsuccessful.

"Luckily, she takes after her mother."

Now Mackie is blushing. "I'm so sorry. I didn't mean—"

"No worry. I'm often mistaken for her grandfather."

"Daly Joy?" Oh my goodness."

"Indeed. She is all of that and more." Dr. Joy takes a breath and almost smiles.

"Now then, if you don't mind, shall we step into the examining room so I can get a brief health history and check your vital signs—etcetera."

"Do you have to weigh me?" Mackie asks, eyeing the dreaded scale. "I don't want to know what I weigh."

"Well, hop up then and close your eyes. I shan't tell you the numbers."

Mackie slips off her shoes and does as told, listening as he adjusts the counter weight.

"Done," he says and she gets off the scale. "Now then, shall we get on with it?"

"Do I need to disrobe?" She asks.

"I don't think that will be necessary—unless it would make you feel more comfortable of course." The enigmatic doctor is ever serious and Mackie doesn't quite know what to make of him. And so she giggles nervously.

"I don't think so."

"Mrs. Kinsella, I realize that you are only here temporarily. If you decide that you are going to stay on in Shoreham we can discuss my being your primary care physician. My practice is quite small. For now, I think it would serve you well if we just deal with your current complaint."

"My current complaint, as you classify it, is that I wish you would just call me Mackie—or at the very least, Mary Katherine.

"I shall do my best," he says.

"And I've just discovered I have no health insurance so I'm going to have to pay you for the visit."

"Not to worry. I shall have Nancy send you an invoice."

He takes a brief history and Mackie realizes that she has not had much luck in the heredity department. She has no siblings, and a deceased mother and father He cuffs her, cradling her arm as he pumps the sphygmomanometer and frowns as he looks at the numbers. "Your pressure is a bit on the high side, I'm afraid. Of course it could be attributed to 'white coatitis'."

Mackie looks questioningly at him.

"Fear of doctors or the procedure—although I'm not wearing my white coat at the moment. There are some people who react with a temporary rise in pressure. I think we might recheck it in a month or so. Or you might purchase one of those handy home monitors or even check it at Alexander's Pharmacy. But let's just keep an eye on it shall we?"

He asks her to pull up her sweater and then blows on the stethoscope and warms it between his hands before he proceeds to listen to her heart and lungs. As he moves from her front to her back her nerves take over and she babbles.

"Is your daughter's name Irish, then?'

"Actually it's Korean, as is Daly's mother." He spells D-a-l-y. "Her mother took great pains with naming her. It was never to be my choice. Among many other philosophies, her mother believed that a name influences character. The name Daly implies a quick mind and an independent spirit. Ironically it suits her perfectly. Take a deep breath, please."

Mackie does and waits.

"Again."

He fixes her sweater and makes a few notes on her file.

"She is a stunningly beautiful child. How old is she, anyway?" Mackie asks.

"Not quite four, but she is tall for her age. And Herbie tells me she is quite bright."

"Herbie?"

"The gentleman you saw her with. Herbie is her nanny/tutor for lack of a better term. He is also our cook. A true Renaissance man—but enough." He slings his stethoscope around his neck and walks over to a small desk in the room and beckons Mackie to sit down across from him. Mackie hops off the table and tucks her sweater back into the waistband of her slacks. She wishes she could check herself in a mirror but there is none.

Crossing his legs and lacing his fingers together he says, "Now, what is it that is wrong, Mary Katherine?"

She cannot speak. He sits quietly for some moments, staring at her through those thick lenses. His eyes seem enormous and knowing.

"It's just—I wonder." Mackie stares at her hands. "Do you think you could recommend a good shrink?"

"Are you talking about a therapist?"

She nods her head.

"I most likely could," he says. And leaves a silence. When he speaks again it is to ask, "Why is it that you feel you need to see a therapist?"

Mackie sighs. Her mouth is as dry as Melba toast. She picks up a paper clip from a little jar on his desk and begins bending it and unbending it. " I just don't seem to be doing very well. In fact, I feel like I'm about to fall off the world. If I don't find someone to talk to soon I'm going to be known as the crazy widow Kinsella."

The doctor takes off his glasses and rubs his eyes. He studies Mackie for a moment and then gets up from his side of the desk, scrapes his chair around and sits down beside her. He takes her hands in his own and says so softly that she hears it as a whisper, "You can talk to me."

"I slapped my daughter," she says, feeling the tears start. "Well, here I go," she says, trying to blink away the tears, covering up with a smile.

"Well, not a great thing, I'm sure. But surely not unforgivable?"

Mackie fishes a tissue out of her purse and blows her nose, "I'm sorry, Dr. Joy, I just find myself crying all the time. It's just ridiculous."

"Who says it's ridiculous?" he asks.

Mackie thinks a moment. "No one, really. Just me—it's just what I think. I should be handling things a lot better than I am."

"Why?"

"My husband died," Mackie counts back, "ten months ago. That's almost a year."

"Yes," he says. And leaves a huge silence.

"Well, you would think I'd get over it and on with things. Stop feeling so sad—so helpless."

"I wasn't aware that there was a designated method of mourning. A schedule." But he pronounces it 'shedjool' and makes Mackie smile.

"Did I say something humorous?" he asks.

Mackie blushes. "No, not at all. I'm sorry."

"Aha, first you're sorry for crying and now you're sorry for smiling."

Mackie shrugs and Dr. Joy gives her hands a squeeze. "I think you are being too hard on yourself."

He gets up, takes off his glasses and pinches the bridge of his nose. "There is no proper way to do these things. There are no rules. You must learn to let yourself feel what you feel. Crying can be cathartic, as can laughter. They are each, in their own way, coping mechanisms. Honor them. Honor yourself, you've had a hell of a year."

Chapter 16

Mackie leaves Dr. Joy's office with a sample of mood levelers—she does not care what they are called but she secretly wonders if they are placebos. He doesn't feel she needs them but has compromised, giving her a 'fortnight's' supply. He has also suggested that it would be wise to give up the wine and quit smoking immediately. And, not unkindly, he tells Mackie that a 'regimen' of exercise might be helpful—that it might, in fact help her more than the pills will do. The handholding has touched her heart. Dr. Joy might be a bit pompous, but he has gifted her with a glimpse of his humanity. She might even have to forgive him the saddle shoes.

Later that afternoon she walks briskly to Boo's house. It is only half a mile but Mackie feels that it is a beginning. The Valiant is parked in front of the house and the driveway is littered with an assortment of rusty tools, an ancient bicycle, and piles of books, boots and oddments. Boo comes out of the garage pulling a Radio Flyer that is loaded with old Mason jars, tackle and fishing nets. Buddy's old wooden dory has been 'parked' on the side of the garage since the year he died and now it sports a sign: 'make me an offer'

"What's going on here, Boo?"

"Well, hello Mackie. I'm going to have a garage sale. I figure it's about time to get rid of all this old junk. Maybe someone can find a use for it."

The sun is going down and Mackie shoves her hands deep into her pockets. "Does Uncle Buddy approve?" Mackie asks.

Boo shakes her head. "He's dead, Sweet Pea. Don't imagine it matters much to him." Boo unloads the wagon and heads back into the garage.

"But you still talk to him, Boo, don't you?" Mackie asks, following her aunt.

Boo shrugs and pulls down an oilskin slicker from a hook and holds it up for Mackie to see. "You think this would go?"

Mackie shrugs. "I don't know, Boo."

Boo throws the coat into the wagon. "You could give me a hand here, Sweet Pea."

"What do you want me to do?" Mackie asks, watching Boo coil several lengths of heavy rope.

"Ah, nothin'. You can just keep me company, Sweet Pea." Boo carries on, pulling tarps and paintbrushes along with assorted cans of what must be ruined paint and stain down off shelves. She picks up a stack of National Geographic Magazines, blows the dust off them and throws them in the wagon.

"Do you know anything about my father, Boo?"

Boo looks around at her belongings, ignoring the question. "You got any junk of your Mama's that you want to get rid of, Mackie? That way we could make it a regular estate sale." Boo chuckles.

Mackie shakes her head, "No I don't, Boo. But what about my father, did you know him?"

"Why are you so concerned about history all of a sudden, Sweet Pea? Seems to be you'd be better off thinking about now."

Mackie crosses her arms and shakes her head. She's not ready for a lecture. "It's just that my mother never talked about my dad. Really all I know is that he died before I was even born. He was a rich summer-bum, wasn't he, Boo? They fell madly in love in June, got married and he was killed when his car went off Three Mile Road after a Labor Day party? He was driving friends home and sober as a Mormon, but the car went off the road and hit a tree?"

Boo starts adding numbers on her fingers. She closes her eyes, shakes her head and says, "Enough."

"What, Boo?"

"It's history, Sweet Pea. He wasn't perfect. You're mother never wanted to talk about him after. He's gonzo—that's it." Boo picks up three nested pans, "What do you think about these old cast iron skillets?"

"Two bucks apiece. Emma would pay ten times that for a seasoned skillet, but that's ok she's not here."

Mackie, who has never seen so much as a photograph of her father asks, "Was he handsome, Boo?"

"He made you." Boo says.

Mackie doesn't even know where to look. She finds an old vanity in the corner of the garage. Cobwebs have made a lacy mantle over it and the mirror is crazed. She thinks with a coat of white paint and new hardware it would be a great piece. She sighs. History 101 is clearly over.

"I think I need to head home, Boo. I have a lot of work left in the house."

"Keep up your damned painting and scraping, but stop trying to make everything bright and clean. You always did look for the better part of it all, Mackie. I swear you could make seaweed look like roses."

"Good grief, Boo!"

"Ain't much good about grief if you ask me. Just my opinion—for what it's worth."

"I'm going home now, Boo," Mackie says. "Good luck with the sale."

Boo fires a parting shot, "Alexander's is looking for counter help, Sweet Pea!"

Mackie just raises her hands in surrender as she stomps off, thinking that maybe she'll jog the half mile home.

Chapter 17

On Monday morning the doorbell rings and a UPS delivoryman hands Mackie a dwarf orange tree. The next day she finds a crate of artichokes on the front porch. And the day after that a basket of nuts and cheese is delivered. All are gifts from an Aemon. Mackie feels the joke of her life continue. She knows no Aemon. However, if she had a libido, she might find the U.P.S. deliveryman appealing despite his ugly brown uniform. He is one of the few people she is in contact with these days.

This morning he has delivered two bottles of excellent Cabernet from a vineyard in the Napa Valley. Aemon strikes again. Mackie consumes half a bottle with her lunch of grilled cheese sandwich and chicken noodle soup, feeling somehow that it is medicinal. The gifts all arrive with only the card saying Aemon, no message.

"Do you have a secret admirer or are you opening a business?" The UPS guy quips, his curiosity peaking as later that day he delivers a package from, *GO SOAK YOUR HEAD*, spa indulgence.

Of course it too is from Aemon. And now, Mackie knows

it must be her daughters morphing their names, sending her these lovely bits of California. She carries the carton, grinning from ear to ear as she sets it down and opens it. She feels a shiver of anticipation and a warm glow building. This must be her girls way of taking care of mom, missing her.

What looks like a gallon of paint is tucked into a nest of excelsior. Mackie pulls it out, walks into the kitchen, rummages in one of the many drawers where she keeps her tools and pulls out a screwdriver. Prying the lid off, the first thing she finds is a CD Soothing Sounds of Nature. 'a perfect partner to meditation, massage or stress-relief'. Feeling relief building already, Mackie uncorks the remainder of her wine from lunch and pours herself a glass. Deciding that this is a gift that deserves a bit of time and ceremony, she picks up the bucket and, swinging it, walks into the living room to light a fire. She will pretend that she is a goddess. She will savor. She will relax. Slipping the CD into the player, Mackie hears the sounds of birds chirping and perhaps a waterfall in the background. She pulls out several small bottles of oil. One is clove, peppermint, ginger and rosemary follow and Mackie doesn't know if she is supposed to put these in the tub, rub them on her body or cook with them. Another contains jasmine, frankincense and sandalwood. Mackie has never thought of frankincense as being anything but a gift for baby Jesus. The birds have stopped chirping and now it sounds as if the house has a tin roof and rain is falling on it. She pulls out a loofah, a pair of white cotton gloves, and a tube of frangipani body lotion. There are also floating, mango butterfly candles. By the time Mackie finds the pumpkin papaya face-mask, it is almost dinnertime and she is getting hungry. Perhaps she'll treat herself to a delivery pizza from Abbadessa's. After her bath that is. I will wallow in pleasure, Mackie thinks. She runs the tub as hot as she can stand it, adds a few drops of the clovey, minty oil and sinks down into the water. Tiring of the Sounds of Nature, she is now listening to Sinatra. She lights her butterfly candles but is afraid that if she drifts off, somehow they might ignite the oil. Perhaps they are not meant to be in the tub with her? She blows them out. The phone rings and she ignores it. Let someone listen to my recorded message for a change she thinks. Anyway it's probably Boo calling.

She is beginning to feel a bit tense. The water starts to cool and Mackie decides to climb out and get dried off and in her pajamas although it is not even seven o'clock.

She calls Abbadessa's and orders a medium vegetarian pizza in homage to California. Knowing they run consistently late on delivery, she figures she will have a good half-hour before it arrives. She decides to try her papaya, pumpkin facemask in a quest to unclog her pores and ward off wrinkles as it promises. She pulls her hair up into a topknot and starts applying the mixture to her neck and face in upward, circular motions, she watches in fascination, as her face turns orange.

She feels the mask tightening and drying and thinks, what the hell, in for a penny, in for a pound, and so she slathers her hands and arms with the frangipani lotion. Then she slips on the cotton gloves. Remembering the missed call she sees that the message light isn't flashing. Boo would have left a message—damn telemarketer, thinks Mackie. Dialing Eileen's office number, she gets the usual recording.

"It's mom, darling. I've figured it out and I want to thank you so much. I can't tell you how you girls have brightened my week. I'm trying out everything from the spa kit as we speak. In fact, if I sound funny, it's the mask—I feel like my face might crack—don't make me smile. Oh well, I'll try you later. Hope everything is okay, Leenie. Love to Walter."

Next she phones Emma at home. Getting no answer at the house, she tries work.

"Regular Joe's," says Emma.

"You're working late, honey."

"Well, I'm short of staff. Actually I am staff. Sam gave his notice a couple of weeks ago. He's going back to school."

"Oh, Em, I'm sorry that's good and bad news I guess. I know how much you relied on him."

"I didn't realize how much," Emma says. "And to tell you the truth, Mom, I can't really afford to replace him."

"I just wanted to thank you." Mackie says, listening to the clatter of dishes and running water; the background noises of the coffee shop.

"Well, don't thank me, Mom. I haven't gotten around to it," Emma snaps. "I'm just trying to keep this place afloat."

"What on earth are you talking about, Em? I just called to thank you and Eileen for the lovely gifties."

"I have no idea what you're talking about, Mom. I thought you were calling about the house." Mackie hears the sound of something breaking and Emma's, "Goddamn it all to hell."

"Is everything OK?" asks Mackie.

"Actually, nothing is OK. It is so not OK I can't even tell you. But listen, Mom, someone from Caldwell Banker is supposed to come out to the house next week."

"To do the evaluation?" Mackie asks.

"Yes. To do the damned evaluation," Emma hisses. "And why on earth would you think we would send you something? Eileen is still furious about what you did to her. Talk about killing the messenger—I can't believe you actually slapped her. You and Daddy never hit us."

"You mean all this stuff isn't from the two of you?"

"Well, no!" Emma says, sounding too much like a Valley Girl. "Listen, Mom. There's a lot going on here right now. Not all of us can just take leave of our lives and run away. Even if we'd like to."

"Emma—what is going on?"

"Look, Mom, I really need to go. I've got to do inventory, wash the floors and be back here by four a.m. to start the baking for tomorrow. I don't know who's sending you what but you can't just dump this whole mess on Leenie and me—it's not fair." Mackie hears Emma's voice crack. "Why can't you just come home?"

"Em, I'm sorry. I've been so self-absorbed, really. I love you. You know that."

"Ya, fine, Mom—me too." And the line goes dead at the same time the front doorbell rings.

Mackie grabs her wallet and goes to open the door, even though she has lost her appetite. She is peeling off her gloves when she looks up and realizes that it is not a delivery person standing there. That is, unless Sully is moonlighting. Seeing her, he breaks into a huge smile and then starts laughing, holding his sides and shaking his head. "I see you got your presents," he says.

"You?" Mackie says. "You're Aemon? I don't believe it!"

"Aemon Xavier Sullivan to be exact," he says. "I'd kiss you—but"

Mackie realizes how she must look. "I thought you were the pizza," she says.

Sully looks himself over, "Nope. I'm definitely not pizza. You, on the other hand smell a great deal like a fruit cocktail."

Flustered, Mackie says, "Well, come in and let me wash this stuff off." She peels the gloves off and says. "Just wait here—and can you pay the pizza guy when he gets here? There's a twenty in my wallet."

"Sully?" Mackie says as she heads up stairs.

"Yes."

"Thank you for the presents."

"I enjoyed doing it."

"It was far too extravagant, but incredibly sweet of you."

"It was worth it if it made you happy."

"And, Sully?"

"Yes."

"I'm afraid I have to go back to California for a while. There are some things I need to take care of."

"Ok," he says, frowning. "How long do you think you'll be gone?"

"I'm really not sure," she says.

"When are you leaving?"

"Tomorrow," she says, not even realizing that she has decided it.

"Tomorrow?" he says incredulous.

"Yes," she says. "My girls need me."

Chapter 18

The smell of ozone and the hard glare of concrete assault Mackie the minute she emerges from the terminal at LAX. She paid a premium for the fast flight and now she stands on the curb, carry-on bag at her feet waiting for Emma to collect her. It's four o'clock in the afternoon and she knows that it will take them two hours to get to Citrus Valley on the traffic clogged 405. She can't believe she's done this again. She knows that Sully is hurt just as she knows that she is becoming a flight risk, but Emma needs her and she prays that she'll be able to make things right with Eileen.

Mackie sees the Lexus rounding the curve, going too fast of course, Emma is notoriously lead footed and an aggressive driver. She feels a tug as Em pulls up to the curb. Three months is a long time to have been away. Emma pops the trunk and hops out of the car, comes around and hugs her mother.

"Mom? You look so different," Emma says, beaming, holding Mackie at arm's length. "Your hair, your clothes—well, everything."

"And you look wonderful!" Mackie says, meaning it.

Emma, dark eyed and athletic, favors Richard's side of the family. She seems to be aglow. Coming directly from work, she is wearing her chef's jacket and baggy, cow-print trousers. Her hair is cropped to an inch around her head and she has let it go back to her natural brunette shade. "I thought you said you were stressed, working yourself to death?"

"Well, I am, stressed and tired—all that. The restaurant has been hell. But never mind now." She throws Mackie's bag in the trunk. "We better get going. The 405 is going to be a parking lot."

When they finally exit the highway and turn onto Beach Boulevard, Mackie frowns at the ugliness of the strip malls, fast food restaurants, and continuing traffic. The road is a sea of BMW's and Saabs mixed with Mercedes and the SUV's. Sport's utility vehicles that will never go further off road than the local pre-school. And God, she had forgotten the noise, the side-effect of too much suburban commerce.

They pass housing developments of increasingly expensive property and eventually pull into their own community of custom-built homes. Theirs sits at the crest of a cul-de-sac and is distinguished from the other white stucco, red-roofed structures only by its elaborate, leaded-glass front doors, Richard's idea. As they approach the driveway, Mackie has palpitations. The bougainvillea is violently pink and has grown wild. The front lawn is overdue for mowing and the flowerbeds are overrun with weeds.

Emma sees her mother's face drop and says, "I fired Francisco."

Mackie raises an eyebrow.

"Two hundred dollars a month, Mom! I planned on

handling the yard work myself, but with the restaurant keeping me so busy, I just haven't had time. You have green thumbs. Now that you're home, you can do it. Can't you?"

Mackie bites the inside of her cheek, gets out of the car and goes to retrieve her suitcase. Emma precedes her into the house. "I kept the sprinklers on the timer at least mom. Nothing's dead!"

Mackie follows and breathes a sigh of relief to see that the kitchen is clean and tidy. Emma is a fabulous cook but is not known for her housekeeping skills. Her relief is short-lived though as she glances out the back window to the pool. It is growing algae. The hibiscus that camouflages the pool equipment has grown unchecked and the planters that once were full of colorful and hardy flowers and trees hold only plant skeletons. Even the lavender, one of the sturdiest, has succumbed to neglect

"I take it you cancelled the pool service too, Emma?" Mackie says, hearing the tension in her own voice.

Emma is opening cabinets and drawers, pulling things out of the fridge; a head of romaine, a cucumber, some mush-rooms. In what Mackie sees now as in a proprietary manner, Emma gets out a cutting board, grabs a knife from the block and starts preparing a salad. She sighs, "It was another hun-dred a month, Mom. No one is using it anyway."

Mackie is beginning to feel like a guest in her own house.

"Look, Mom, you just took off. You didn't want to know what was happening here. You told me where the checkbook was—told me to take care of the bills, and damn it, I've been doing my best."

"I know." Mackie hears the hurt and then sees the tears

in Emma's eyes. Sweet, tough, Emma, her stalwart girl.

"Leenie is always too busy or too worried about Walter and his ever-fragile ego."

"Oh, Emma."

"I know she's the golden girl, the winner, Mom. I'm not trying to be critical—honestly. She's my little sister. I love her."

"Of course you do, Em."

"Mom, I've been trying so hard to keep things afloat here. I'm sorry if you think I've let you down."

"I'm sorry, Em. I know it's been hard. It's been pretty awful for everyone."

Emma turns inward, a turtle under her protective shell and says, "Ok. I thought we'd eat in the dining room. Make it kind of a festive occasion," she says. "I asked Eileen and Walter over for dinner." Emma looks up at the clock. "They'll be here in half an hour."

"Oh, Em—I wish you hadn't."

"Mom, you have got to clear the air with Eileen, and the sooner the better. All this unresolved crap is unhealthy. It's bad for the digestion."

"But, I'm not even hungry, Em."

"Well, you will be when you taste my food. I splurged on beef tenderloin and some killer shrimp."

"I'm tired, Emma," Mackie says, holding her head.

"Well, join the club, Mom."

"Oh, Em. I'm just so sick of stress and bad news. I never thought it could be so hard to get from one day to another. I miss your father terribly, regardless. I'm still not sure what he did or didn't do, but I'm sure he loved me. And God knows I loved him. And you know he was a wonderful father to you and Leenie."

Emma nods, puts the knife down and walks to Mackie, hugs her and kisses her cheek. "You know what Mom, I was going to wait for a better time, but I just can't."

"What?" Mackie says, steeling herself, trying to read her daughter's face.

"Momma, you're going to be a grandmother."

Mackie feels her knees buckle and swells with a sense of joy for the first time in so long. It's all going to be right now. She'll usher in the new generation and although Richard won't be there to welcome the baby, a sense of order will be restored.

"Oh, Emma, they've finally done it—Leenie and Walter are going to have a baby!"

Emma shakes her head, and a grin spreads across her face, "Not Leenie, momma me. I'm pregnant—isn't that wonderful?"

BOO

Light filters through a grimy attic window where Boo sits, sorting through a stack of photo albums. "Well, Buddy. Our girl got up and went." Boo lights a cigarette and sips her Jim Beam. She's gone back to Citrus Valley. Going to make things right there, tie up loose ends, so to speak." Boo smiles as she looks at a picture of Buddy and herself taken decades ago on Larson's Pond. Both bundled up in heavy sweaters, hats and scarves. They had spent the day ice-skating. Boo remembered it like yesterday. "We were a damned cute couple," she says. "Damned cute. Just my opinion."

Boo turns a few more pages and says, "She left this morning." Taking a drag of her cigarette she exhales, blowing a smoke ring.

"Of course she's coming back, Old Fool." Boo gets up and stretches, arching her back. "She just needs to make things right with Eileen. Plus she has to sell the house. She's practically broke, you know." Boo spots some old Sears Roebuck catalogues and says, "These are great!" She picks them up and adds an old Brownie camera to the pile.

"I did so tell you. Why do you think I'm having the garage sale? Glory be to Roses Wharf! I swear sometimes you're as thick as a plank, Buddy."

Suddenly, Boo sees a sheet covering something in the corner. She knows what it is before she uncovers it. It is the hardest pain.

Tugging at the sheet, she sees the slats and she longs for the prison she has never known. Rock maple. Most likely today's safety police would condemn it. There is more than enough space to pass a soda can through. It is just two sides and two ends. How could something so insubstantial be designed to hold such precious cargo? She is no longer an old woman. She is a barely more than a girl. She is all of life's expectation and fear. And more than that she is, for one brief moment, the promise of what might have been.

She was not even showing. Two months pregnant and they were both so excited. They knew that they would have the perfect baby—be the perfect parents. He was concerned and involved at a time when that was an oddity for men.

"This is a fine crib, he said. Top of the line." He was so solicitous it was almost funny. He bought her maternity clothes. He painted the nursery a soft yellow. When Boo was queasy, he threw up. When Boo miscarried, Buddy all but bled. When the doctors removed the possibility of her ever having a child, Buddy wept when Boo could not.

"Don't you worry, my sweet. This crib is not going anywhere." Boo can hardly see through her tears. For Boo, crying has always been an indulgence. An indulgence and a handicap. And Boo has learned about being strong. It is her wish for Mackie.

"And don't you worry about Mackie, Buddy. No one's going to hurt that girl." Boo smiles through the tears. "Not as long as old Boo Houlihan is around."

She switches off the light and thinks she hears a baby crying. And then feels the memory of his kiss on her neck, hears the echo of forty years of banter, and smells the Old Spice. "Now don't you go getting frisky on me, Old Fool."

Chapter 19

Mackie is awash with emotions: joy at the prospect of being a grandmother, fear for Emma and her future, and sorrow that she has drifted so far apart from her daughter that she is now being presented with this fait accomplis. But it is obvious that Emma is happy and excited.

"It's wonderful, Em! A baby— I can't believe it. My little girl is going to be a mommy." But Mackie is not sure it's wonderful at all. She wants more time to get used to this idea. "And me a grandmother," her voice, unsteady betrays her.

"I thought you wanted grandchildren?" Emma says. "God knows you've hounded Eileen and Walter about it for years. Why not me?"

"Well of course you! I guess I just thought maybe there would be a courtship, then a wedding—and then a baby."

"How traditional," Emma says, slapping plates onto the table. She pulls out the drawer of the sideboard and grabs napkins and napkin rings. She opens the doors of the china cabinet and grabs water goblets that Mackie doesn't remember owning. "Things don't always work out according to your plans, Mom. I'd think you would have learned that by now.

"This baby is not an accident," Emma says emphatically. "And I am not a child."

"Of course not," Mackie says. "But you're always going to be my little girl. I'm just worried about you and what's going to happen."

"I know you are, Mom, but honestly, I'm going to be fine. I'm going to be a great mother."

"And the father?" Mackie asks.

"Yes, Mom. The baby definitely has one of those." Emma smiles and walks back into the kitchen and starts mincing garlic. "I think he's going to be thrilled."

Mackie follows. "You mean he doesn't know?"

"It's early days, Mom. I wanted to make sure I didn't miscarry. The first trimester can be iffy. And I needed time to think things through."

Mackie stares at Emma and sees the woman she is becoming. "It must have been so hard for you, honey, keeping this all to yourself."

Emma shrugs and Mackie looks up and sees Eileen and Walter coming around the side to the French doors. "Do they know, Em—about the baby?"

"Yes. They know, Mom."

Mackie walks out onto the patio, holds Eileen at arm's length and looks into her eyes. "I'm so terribly sorry, Leenie. Slapping you was hateful. I'm going to try to figure out this business with the money—and everything."

Eileen nods and Mackie pulls her into a hug but Eileen just stiffens. The unspoken distance between them is palpable.

"Well, Mommo," Walter says, his perfectly modulated

words erupting into the air, "welcome home." He hands
Mackie a bottle of Perrier Jouet Champagne and plants
a kiss on her cheek. "Congratulations!" His cologne over-
whelms Mackie. His eyes seem to have turned a startling green when she is sure that she remembers them as
brown. And she is quite sure that his hair has never been
quite as blonde as it now is. "Or should we start calling
you Grandmama?"

"Hello, Walter," Mackie says. "It's good to see you."

"Always good to see you. I know Lee-lee and Ems are
thrilled to have you back."

"Well that's kind of you to say, Walter, but I'm not sure
that's true." Mackie looks at Leenie. "Come on inside you
two. Emma is fixing us a feast."

⸺◈⸺

"To the next generation," Walter says, lifting his flute and
waving it toward Emma. "May our tribes increase."

Emma's flute is filled with water in deference to her pregnancy. Eileen downs her champagne in one swift gulp and
Mackie takes a sip. "We didn't worry about drinking when
I was pregnant with you two," Mackie says. "But we had no
money for such luxuries then anyway. It's wonderful champagne, Walter. Thank you."

They sit around the dinner table, oohing and ahhing over
the beef, which is superb and the shrimp—how huge and
tasty. Walter is up for a part on one of the few soap operas
that shoots in LA. He is going for a second reading in the

morning. Mackie watches Eileen watch Walter and sees the love in her eyes. She looks younger when she is with him, her face softer, her cheeks flushed. It is a look so close to worship that Mackie feels uneasy. She wonders if Walter deserves her daughter, prays that he won't let her down.

"There should be enough equity in this house for me to find something smaller...more manageable.

Emma's face drops. "You're really serious about selling the house then?"

"It's the only sensible thing to do," Mackie says.

"She's right, Emma," Eileen says. "She can downsize. Interest rates are amazing right now. I was thinking a town-house might be nice and definitely more secure. Plus there would be less maintenance for Mom."

"They're building some nice ones in Newport—by the marina," Emma says. And of course all the shops are there. Plus it's only about half an hour away."

"That's the Gold Coast," Eileen says. "Mom needs to conserve her assets. This is the time to be practical. There are some nice units going up right in town."

"Everything is happening too fast," Emma says, her eyes filling. "I thought I'd be able to stay here until I get things worked out. I don't think it's going to be much fun to be homeless and pregnant."

"Maybe you should have thought about that before now, Emma," Eileen says. "Speaking of practical—getting pregnant wasn't the brightest move in the world. Have you thought about who will run the restaurant while you're in labor and delivery? And who's going to take care of the baby after that? Being a single mother won't be easy."

"Who says I'm going to be a single mother?" Emma says, her voice quivering. "You don't know any such thing."

"Well," Eileen says, "Where is ghost-daddy?"

"You're just jealous, Eileen, and I think you're being hateful. You wish it was you and Walter who were having the baby."

"Whoa," says Walter. "Ladies—let's be nice."

Mackie has been quiet. Watching her girls snipe. She is exhausted from the trip and overwhelmed. She sighs, pushing her chair back from the table. Standing up, she says, "This is still my house, girls. I want you to stop talking about me like I'm not even in the room. I want you to stop taking pot shots at each other. I am perfectly able to take care of myself. Believe it or not, your father and I managed to build this life together. We raised the two of you, although, at the moment I'm not sure how proud that makes me." She wads up her napkin and throws it on the plate.

"And now I'm going to go to bed before I say something I might regret. Things always look better in the morning." Mackie turns away and mutters, "Please, god." She stops in the doorway, clears her throat "And, Emma—please try to find a way to share this with me—with all of us." Her hand sweeps the room. "At least I'd like to know who this baby's father is—and I imagine he'd like to know too."

Chapter 20

Mackie retreats to her bedroom, bewildered and weary. She loves this room with its stone fireplace, French doors, plush carpeting. The furniture is a mish-mash of early hand-me-downs and later acquisitions. It contains pieces that moved with them from house to house, offering a sense of stability. They lived in Illinois, Virginia, Pittsburgh and New York, even Las Vegas before they landed in California. Corporate gypsies.

Suddenly she misses Richard and, just as suddenly she realizes that she hasn't been missing him as much lately. The difference is almost imperceptible—but there is a difference. Sometimes days go by and she doesn't think of him. She looks now at the photos that parade across her dresser, so many reminders. There are the baby pictures and the birthdays, the proms, graduations, vacations, weddings and anniversaries. She smiles at the young Richard and the younger Mackie and the older versions too. She feels as if she is looking at all those years of living from the outside in.

There is so much happening and so little that she can do about it. The decision to sell the house seems a good one. He's not here, she thinks. He's within me. Perhaps, if we hadn't been such vagabonds, I would feel more grounded here. But it is a house. It is only a house, she thinks as she drifts into dreamless sleep.

The sun is just rising when she awakens and her first thought is that she is going to be a grandmother. Life is moving on despite her. She stretches, just savoring the feel of the sheets against her skin, noticing the way the light and shadow play in the room. She can hear a chorus of birds outside the windows and she starts to do a mental inventory, deciding which things she will send to Shoreham, wondering what the girls might like to have and what should be relegated to the dump. I have purpose, she thinks, rolling out of bed. It is time to move.

She walks down the hallway to peek in on Emma. Although it's not even six a.m. she's gone. Mackie remembers Emma saying that she starts the baking for the restaurant at four. Mackie is still on East Coast time and craves coffee. The kitchen is immaculate and a thermos of coffee is sitting on the counter. Beside it a note from Emma: Good morning, Momma. I'll be home by three. We'll talk.

Mackie picks up a pack of cigarettes and stares at it. She's cut down to one in the morning and a few more during the day. This will be my last one she thinks, tapping it out and lighting up. Nana Mac needs to stay healthy. There will be lots of trips from coast to coast. This is a new beginning. I will be Nana Mac.

Mackie finishes the whole thermos of coffee and puts a call into Caldwell Banker. She sits on the patio, soaking up the sun and making lists. She intends to get the house in order as quickly as she can and to price it reasonably. Despite Emma's reluctance, Mackie wants a quick sale. Even with a short escrow, she will probably be looking two months down the road before she sees the money. She refuses to think about what she's lost; instead she's determined to concentrate on what she still has left. And that is considerable. For the first time since Richard died, she feels as if she has direction.

She calls Francisco and he tells her that he will come by on his way home from work. He's been their gardener for several years and Mackie is sad that Emma took it upon herself to let him go. She will give him some severance along with the fees for cleaning up the jungle that the yard has become. Mackie doesn't know a lot about him, but she remembers that he takes courses at USC and hopes to get a degree in horticulture. He is handsome in an Antonio Banderas sort of way. Or maybe it's just the black hair and ponytail that makes Mackie think so. She remembers him saying that he can only handle one or two classes a semester and might not graduate until he is eligible for an AARP card.

By noontime, the boy from the pool service arrives. Mackie watches him from the kitchen as he takes vials out of his kit and uses an eyedropper, testing things. He is wearing only baggie, flowered shorts and a pair of flip-flops and Mackie watches the muscles ripple on his upper arms and back as he runs a skimmer over the surface of the pool. He hasn't introduced himself, but periodically he looks over and smiles at Mackie. She doesn't know if he is the usual pool person because, frankly she has never paid attention to who performed the service. She does remember blonde boys but has no idea if they were a series of boys or simply the same boy week after week.

By the time Emma walks in the door, Mackie has filled four trash bags with outdated food, old newspapers, and assorted garbage. The bags now sit by the door to the garage. The windows sparkle and there are fresh flowers that she's cut from the garden.

Today there are smudges of fatigue under Emma's eyes and her chef's jacket is filthy. "Hi, Momma. What are you up to here? The house looks great."

"Let me make you some tea, Em. You look beat."

Emma takes off her jacket and clogs and fills the kettle herself while Mackie gets the mugs and the tea bags.

"Honey, everything is going to be ok. I've phoned the real estate people and their regular open house day is tomorrow. They've agreed to come by and have a look even though I haven't officially listed it yet. So I need to make it sparkle plenty. This reminds me of a lot of our moves—you know Daddy would get a few days' notice and be gone."

"I remember, Mom. You'd always go into manic mode, trying to keep the house clean. Eileen and I used to hate it so much—people coming through in the middle of dinner and stuff."

Mackie nods, "Oh yes, those were the days."

"And all those schools." Emma shakes her head; "We were always the new kids on the block"

"Did you mind so much, Emma?" Mackie thinks, how odd it is that she has never asked her girls something so basic.

"Oh, Momma, what difference does it make now? It's ancient history."

The kettle whistles and Mackie pours their tea and says,

"We always thought we were making those moves for your good, Em—for the family."

They stand side by side and sip their tea. "It was mostly good, Momma, honestly. I think Leenie and I both learned a lot from those moves. I think it made us pretty independent. I guess we also relied on each other a lot when we were younger."

"And now?" Mackie asks.

"Now we're grown up, Mom." Emma kisses her mother on the cheek. "I'm going to take a speed shower. I'm dead on my feet."

"Okay, honey. I'll forge ahead here. The pool service came this afternoon and I was lucky enough to get a hold of Francisco. He'll be by in a little while to take a look at the yard."

"You called Francisco?" Emma pulls at what there is of her hair. "Oh God, Mom, please tell me he's not coming here."

"Yes, he's coming, Em. The yard needs attention before the open house tomorrow. Why are you so upset?"

"Because I'm not ready to see him, Mom. That's why."

Mackie has a sudden sinking feeling, "Emma—what on earth is it? What did Francisco do?"

Emma takes Mackie's hand and puts it on her abdomen.

Mackie whispers, "Francisco?"

Emma nods.

"Francisco is the baby's father?"

"Yes, Mom." Emma tears off her chef's coat and runs out of the room, calling back. "And now that you know. I guess it's time to give him the news too. What time did he say he'd be here?"

"Around four," Mackie yells.

"By the way, Mom. I love him—and he loves me."

"Oh, Emma," Mackie says, "That's wonderful, Emma, but is it enough?"

She hears the water start and the shower door shutting and knows there is no answer for that question.

MACKIE

We have been living in Illinois for five months and Emma has just come into the world. She is surprisingly alert and funny, teaching me about herself with a clever series of gurgles and grunts and the occasional smile. Between working and commuting, Richard is gone fourteen hours a day and I feel a profound sense of loneliness.

I loved being pregnant, even though the first few months were full of nausea and nervousness. Money is tight so I bought almost all of the nursery furniture from a second-hand shop and refinished it. I also made yellow seersucker curtains for the small window in the nursery and matching bedding for the crib. I didn't have a baby shower because I don't really know anyone here yet. Well, that's not true; there is June who works behind the counter at the drugstore where I have my tea every morning.

I was hoping that my mother would come out to be with me for the birth, but instead she sent a package of diapers and three each of nightgowns, terrycloth suits and receiving blankets. There was a beautiful card and a crisp hundred-dollar bill. It was a nice practical gift.

Chapter 21

Sully takes it upon himself to drive by Boo Houlihan's house every few days. It's not that long he thinks since Mackie's been gone, but he thinks that Boo must miss her as much as he does.

Boo's been getting ready for her first 'annual' garage sale and Sully finds her in precarious positions more than once. "Glory be to Roses Wharf!" comes echoing out of the trees, followed by wildly wiggling strands of lights.

"What the hell are you doing up there, Boo?"

"And good evening to you too, Sully. Skip the lecture; Buddy's already done that. Just get your butt up here and help."

The next night Sully hauls an ancient Victrola down from the attic. Boo follows with stacks of albums that she's held on to over the years and enough books to fill the Shoreham Public Library.

The morning of the sale, he turns onto Driftwood Avenue and finds a carnival atmosphere. The four Garagliano kids, oldest seven years, have set up a lemonade stand at the top of the street. Bright, neon signs mark the way to Boo's house where huge bouquets of helium balloons levitate from her mailbox. A table sits at the edge of the driveway and boxes of Dunkin' Donuts share space with a huge carafe of coffee. The Christmas tree lights are hanging from every tree, shrub and bush and music mixed with static blares from one of the original boom boxes. It holds a price tag of $2.00 or best offer.

Sully spots Boo, carrying what looks like an aquarium down the stairs to the driveway. She looks like some kind of feminine Russian astronaut. A flowered bubble cap sits on her head trailing a flexible tube. He looks around, sure that this has got to be someone's recurring nightmare. There is a claw-footed bathtub in the middle of the front lawn. It is filled with everything from hotel soaps to rubber duckies and frog candles. Boo has arranged things in her fashion. A holiday section displays everything from small American flags to turkey platters and shamrocks. A plastic Santa with an illuminated bulbous nose flashes, begging attention.

"Good morning, Boo," Sully says, helping himself to a cruller and filling his travel mug with coffee. He puts a five-dollar bill in the jar for donations and looks around. "Wow," he says. "This is really something."

"You want change for that fiver?" Boo asks, clicking out quarters from the metal change keeper that is hanging from her belt. Sully remembers the Good Humor man having one quite like it, neat rows of nickels, dimes and quarters dispensed with the click of a thumb.

"Nah, Boo, you keep it." He takes a sip of the coffee. "If you don't mind my asking, what the hell is that thing on your head?"

"It's a hairdryer of course," Boo says. "You can have it for a buck."

Sully chuckles. "No thanks, Boo. I think I'll take a look around though—take a few pictures if you don't mind. I think Mackie would love to see this whole thing. It's such an extravaganza." He aims his camera at Boo.

"Cheez Whiz," she says putting on a really cheesy grin. Sully takes three or four frames in rapid succession.

"You might just make the front page of the Beacon, Boo."

"You should stick around until the cheerleaders show up, Sully," Boo says, taking a marker and drawing a line through the price tag on a pair of hockey skates. She marks them down from three dollars to two. Looking up at him she says, "Folks just love a bargain."

"Please tell me you're kidding about the cheerleaders, Boo," he says.

"Nope. Be here about noontime. It's just the junior varsity squad. They're going to have a little show. I tried for the high school band, but no go. Jimmy Murphy's kids are going to play though. They've got some kind of garage band—good for a garage sale, right," Boo grins. "I think they're called the *Cockroaches*—or maybe it's the *Centipedes*—some kind of damned bug anyway."

Boo sees some people approaching and goes to greet them. "If you see something you like, make me an offer, folks. Got a little bit of everything here. Have some java and just take your time. Look around. Donuts are fresh this morning. I got up at four a.m. to bake 'em."

Sully thinks that Boo could sell prime rib to vegetarians. He walks around, looking at tags. God love Boo, he thinks.

Not much is priced over five dollars and although there is
fifty years accumulation of treasures and trash he doesn't see
how she's going to make more than a hundred bucks for all
of her work. Still, she's having a great time and so is everyone
else by the look of things. Cars are now beginning to line the
street and there is a great feeling of camaraderie in the air.

"Hey, Boo," he says, coming close before he leaves. "Have
you talked to Mackie? Do you know when she's coming
back?"

Boo puts some singles in her cigar box and looks up at
Sully. "I haven't heard squat, Sully. Our Mackie has a way of
keeping her life in separate drawers. Even when she was little
she didn't want her peas touching her potatoes." Just then a
child approaches Boo, hugging a vintage teddy bear to his
chest.

Sully starts to leave, giving a wave of his hand.

"Why don't you call her?" Boo yells. "She's listed. Kinsella
in Citrus Valley, Californ-I-A!"

Sully stops and turns back to Boo. He watches as the
child holds out his fist and slowly opens his hand to reveal a
crumpled dollar bill. Boo looks at the child and then at the
money and then at the mother standing behind the child.
"Smart kid. Good shopper," she says, winking at the woman.
Taking the money from the child, she places the bear in a
paper bag and pushes her thumb down three times on her
change machine, releasing three quarters which she hands
back to the boy along with the bear in the bag. "He needs a
lot of hugs" she says. The child nods, mute.

Sully takes the lead, grabs Boo in his own bear hug and
whispers in her ear, "Don't we all, Boo. Don't we all?"

Chapter 22

Emma knocks on the door and without waiting for a response, walks into Mackie's bedroom "Hey, Mom, just exactly who were you thinking might be the baby's father?" Emma asks Mackie. She seems mildly amused, not hostile, while Mackie is still trying to process the information. Francisco has come and gone. Mackie had explained what she wanted done in the yard and then sequestered herself in her bedroom while Emma and Francisco talked. She has been trying desperately to find a way back to Emma. She has passed grief and gone on to anger, resenting that Richard is not here to deal with this latest situation. She wonders how he might have handled the news and wonders how she feels about it herself.

While Mackie was the volatile, mouthy one, every one saw Richard as a sea of calm. It added to the shock of his death. Responsible, solid, steady old Richard navigating crisis after crisis at work and dealing with family life with aplomb. Only Mackie knew that his initial reactions were often irrational, his outlook instantly pessimistic. "Jesus, Mackie—they want me to relocate to Pittsburgh again. It's going to be a disaster." "How the hell are we going to pay for Eileen's law school with Emma still drifting around? You know we're going to have to help her with her loans from culinary school, or she's never going to get ahead."

But situations deemed 'disasters' turned into triumphs and they acted as filters for each other's emotions. They learned to discuss situations, turning them this way and that, projecting possible outcomes, figuring out plans of action and in the end it was Richard who would sit down, take charge and be the arbiter of common sense and wisdom.

But Richard is not going to discuss anything ever again and Mackie is just going to have to deal with life on her own.

"Momma?"

Mackie comes back into focus and looks at Emma who is waiting for an answer.

"Well, I certainly didn't expect to come home and find you playing house with the family gardener," Mackie says, smiling and then wishing she could retract the words as soon as they fly out of her mouth.

Emma's mouth drops open. "Is that what you think?" Emma shakes her head and Mackie sees wet steel in her eyes. "For your information, Mom, 'the family gardener' has been a part of my life since just after Daddy died. You were just a little self-involved, too busy hiding the wine bottles in the trash and sleeping twenty-four/ seven to notice what I was doing. You didn't ask and I didn't 'share' as you put it."

"But, Em!"

"But, Momma," Emma parrots, "You're always so ready to bail me out. You're the first one to understand when I screw up—but you never seem much interested in the rest of my life, in all the happy parts. It's always, good old mom to the rescue."

Emma flops down onto the end of Mackie's bed.

"The only thing in the world I want is for you to be happy, Emma. You and Eileen mean the whole world to me. How could I not want for you to be safe?"

"But I don't need rescuing, Momma." Emma crawls up toward Mackie at the head of the bed.

Mackie, scooping Emma into an embrace, doubts the truth of this. "I just wish you could have told me sooner, Emma."

Emma tucks her head into Mackie's shoulder. "I didn't want to tell you over the phone. And I knew you'd jump to the wrong conclusions. Look, Momma, I know it's been a shock. And I did think I'd be able to stay here for at least a while. Maybe until Francisco finishes school."

"And when is that going to be, Emma, about the time the baby starts school?" Mackie bites the inside of her cheek. She has got to get the sarcasm under control, but it's too late.

Emma throws her hands up in the air and gets off the bed. Pacing the room, she says, "Momma, you are just plain nasty these days. What's happened to you anyway? Since when did you get so damned judgmental?"

"I'm sorry, Emma, I am!"

"You are so not sorry, Momma. I'm not even going to try to talk to you now. You don't want to know what's happening anyway. You're so much happier just living with your preconceptions and your misconceptions." Emma waves her off, going to the door, shaking her head, she gives the parting shot, "But just to soothe your mind, Mom, we never made love in your bed." Emma slams the door.

Mackie can't breathe properly. She yells, "Emma, this conversation is not over!"

Chapter 23

Juggling her mobile phone and a glass of chardonnay, Mackie straddles the diving board and squints into the setting sun. "Well, it's nice to be home," she lies. She swings her legs above the pool, which is clearing up despite its neglect. The cloying scent of hibiscus permeates the air around her. "It's ironic that you called right now because I've been thinking about you, Sully. I feel badly that I didn't get to thank you properly for my wonderful week of presents."

"No thanks needed, Mackie," Sully says.

"Well, it was totally sweet of you to do that for me."

"How are things going there?" Sully asks. "Is everything all right? You sound as if you've been crying."

"It's the damned hibiscus," she says, unrolling coils of toilet paper and pulling them off. She blows her nose, snuffles and tries to stop crying. The sound of his voice has set her off again. She's been crying non-stop since Emma slammed out of her room. Trying to figure out her life and return to the point that everything went so scuddingly out of control.

"Do you want me to come out there, Mackie? Is there something I can do?"

"No, Sully, but thank you. I know you care."

"I don't like to think about you being alone out there," he says.

"I'm hardly alone. I have my girls and we're just trying to get reacquainted."

"Okay, Beauty, but you were in a hell of a hurry to get out of here."

"I know I was. I'm sorry I left so quickly, Sully. I just thought it was what I needed to do." She sniffs again. "So here I am, sitting out by the pool, three thousand miles away from you. We seem to have lost our gardener and the flora is growing wild." She blows her nose.

"Are you sure you're not crying?"

"I guess I've developed allergies."

"I hear they're going around," Sully says. "I went by Boo's today. The garage sale was unbelievable. What an event!"

"I can imagine," Mackie says. "I think Boo has the first Sears Roebuck catalogue ever issued, and God knows what else. Did she manage to sell Buddy's old dory?"

"Everything but I think. I'm telling you Mackie, it was like a carnival."

"I miss Boo. I don't think I've spent enough time with her. That garage sale sounds amazing, I wish I could have been there."

"I took some pictures for you. It's too bad you missed it."

"Oh, thanks, Sully. It just seemed like such a crazy idea, although I guess it's a great way to get rid of half a century of god knows what."

"It was a circus. I think Boo had more fun than the cheer-leaders and the bands."

"What?" Mackie says.

"You really had to be there, Mackie"

Feeling guilty because she wasn't and guilty because she still is not there, Mackie asks, "How does she seem to you, Sully?"

"She's good, Mackie. She says that she hasn't heard from you. I think she's wondering when you might be coming home, coming back?"

"Well," Mackie says, I thought I might be coming sometime next week—but now I don't know. It seems we're going to be having a wedding here, Sully and I'm going to be a grandmother. Emma is pregnant, Sully. God, she's making me the mother-of-the bride and a grandmother all in one year. And I'm putting the house here on the market. God help me," Mackie shudders.

Miles away, Sully feels the tension in her voice. "That's wonderful, Mackie. Isn't it? I always did peg you as an overachiever." He's talking into his cell phone as he walks. "But you're going to be a damned cute Grandma. Although I'm not sure I'm ready to see you in orthopedic shoes with those little blue, gray curls around your head."

Mackie finally laughs. "Well, these days Nanas come in all shapes, sizes and varieties." Mackie swings her legs up and walks off the diving board, feeling connected, but lonely. "What is the noise I'm hearing, Sully? Where are you calling from anyway?"

"It's the seagulls. I'm home, Mackie. You know I live in the old Cedar Point Lighthouse, don't you? I'm out on the jetty. It's one of those amazing spring nights. I was up in the tower earlier but now I'm out on the jetty, way out by the bell buoy."

"That was one of my favorite places when I was a kid," Mackie says.

"Come back. Come home," Sully says.

"I don't know where that is." She says and walks across the patio. Tears run down her face as she walks back into her kitchen. She pulls the slider across and says, "I can't do this. I need to call you later, Sully."

"No! Talk to me, Mackie. Tell me about your daughter and the boy. Don't hang up. Don't leave me."

"I just can't do this now, Sully. Good-bye."

"Shh."

The whisper comes through the phone like a caress. Like his breath on her neck, his hand upon her breast, his arms holding her. She feels it, remembers the way he smells and feels. She remembers the smile, his eyes, his touch. And in the midst of this life that she is trying to make orderly and manageable, she wants nothing more than to be back with him. She wants to start all over.

Chapter 24

"What are you doing up, Momma? It's not even four o'clock." Emma is making her 100 proof coffee when Mackie shuffles into the kitchen, waving what she thinks of as a white flag of surrender. She hands Emma a check for five thousand dollars. Emma looks at it and arches one slender eyebrow and looks back at her mother.

"What's this for?"

"Honey, I'm sorry if I was out of line about Francisco. I've always been fond of him you know. It's just that this whole pregnancy and everything has come as such a surprise." Mackie pours herself a cup of coffee and says, "It's funny, Em. I had this vision of you getting married at St. Jude's. But of course you won't want a church wedding, will you?" Mackie thinks suddenly, "But Francisco, might—right? Is he Catholic?"

"Momma?"

Mackie's thoughts are tripping over themselves, "Anyway, I've been thinking about it, honey, and although I can't afford to do much of a wedding, I thought we might have a nice little reception here at the house, especially since it's in such good shape now that it's going on the market—and you could do the food, no?"

"Momma?" Emma hands Mackie back the check. "You still don't get it, do you?" She sighs, "Francisco and I will decide about the wedding, that is if there's even is going to be a wedding."

"You're not seriously thinking about not getting married are you, Em?"

"Francisco and I are discussing all the options. We think we're going to wait until after the baby's born."

Mackie's mouth drops, "But—

Emma picks up the car keys and her backpack and shakes her head. "Look, Momma I don't have a lot of time for this right now. I've got to get to the restaurant. I'll get your car back to you about ten o'clock if that's ok."

"Fine," Mackie says, "I'm just trying to help here, Emma. "Maybe we can talk when I drop you back at work for the lunch shift."

"No need, Momma. Francisco will be here at about eleven. His sister, Laura, is covering for us while we go apartment hunting." Emma walks back to Mackie, beaming and kisses her forehead. "Cisco and I are moving in together. Isn't that spectacular?"

Mackie's head feels as if it will explode. Moving in together? Mackie immediately thinks of the horrid old term, 'shacking up'. Even though she knows it is ridiculous, she feels proprietary to Emma. Just when did Francisco's family get into the picture? And just when did Emma's little restaurant become a joint venture? She knows that Emma is grown up and about to become a mother, but she still thinks of her as her little girl.

"I didn't know that Francisco had a sister," Mackie says, realizing that she knows next to nothing about Francisco.

"Actually he has three, Momma. Maria is a paralegal at Eileen's firm, Susana does the books for Francisco and Laura is going to culinary school next year."

Mackie feels her misconceptions gather and retreat as she crumples the check in her fist and says, "Drive safely, Em."

"Of course I will. Just take care of yourself for a change, okay? I'll see you later."

It is late afternoon and Mackie is lost in her own world, on her knees in the library when she hears Eileen call from the entry. A crumpled pack of Marlboros is by her side and the room is redolent with smoke. There is a small mountain of boxes forming in front of the bookcases.

"Mom? Are you here?"

She has been dusting books and sorting them into piles, running a constant litany of her errors and omissions as she works. Is she failing Emma? Has she damaged Eileen? Is she doing the wrong thing selling the house? Where does Sully fit in? Does Sully fit in?

She has made several tall stacks of books targeted for Shoreham; some simply because the bindings or the colors please her, some because she wants to reread them and others because they have been signed by the authors and savored by her. There is a pile of children's books that she is setting aside for Emma's baby.

"In here, honey, Mackie calls. I'm in Daddy's library."

She looks up to see her daughter waving away smoke,

framed in the doorway. Eileen stands on three-inch heels with her arms crossed, leaning against the doorjamb. As always, Eileen's hair is perfect and her tailored suit does nothing to disguise her femininity. Mackie thinks for the first time that her daughter must be an awesome opponent in the courtroom or the boardroom. "Shouldn't you be at work?" Mackie asks.

Coughing, Eileen says, "I'm on my way to take a deposition and thought I'd stop by."

"Sorry about the smoke, Leenie," Mackie says, stubbing out her cigarette.

"Your lungs," Eileen says and adds, "Daddy's library?" Squatting down beside Mackie she says, "That's such a joke, Mom. I know you decorated it for him, furnished it and all—but face it, he was never in here, you always were. We'd find you in here curled up in that old leather chair, reading or sleeping."

The memory tickles Mackie.

She picks up a battered copy of Amelia Bedelia and starts thumbing through the pages. Holding it up to Eileen she says, "Remember me reading this to you, Leenie? It was one of your favorites. She moves over and puts her arm around her daughter. I think it appealed to your literal mind." Mackie wants the moment to expand.

"This was Emma's favorite, Mom."

Mackie feels Eileen stiffen and retreat. "I'm sure you don't remember mine, Mom. But then you also had no idea I was headed for law school until I graduated from college."

"Eileen! That's just not true."

"Whatever you remember, Mom. It's fine."

"Was I such a bad mother? Am I such a bad mother?" Mackie does not know if she can bear to hear the answer.

Eileen rolls her eyes in that unmistakable don't go there way. Shaking her head she picks up a stack of Nancy Drew Mysteries. "Is it okay if I take these, Mom?"

"Leenie, take anything you want. Please."

But Mackie knows that somehow she has not given Eileen the one thing she came for.

"So it's definite? Shoreham?"

"At least for now, Honey. Yes."

"What about Emma and the new baby?"

"I guess I'll be a commuter," Mackie says. "She and Francisco have found an apartment."

"They're moving in together?" Eileen says.

"Apparently so."

"Really?" Eileen drags out the word. "And how do you feel about that?"

Mackie unbends and gets up. "You know what, Eileen? I don't think it really matters. How I feel. What I feel. I think you're both grown up now. I'm getting resigned to that. Seeing you with Walter, seeing Emma with Francisco, I think that you're all going to be okay somehow."

"You never really have understood what I see in Walter, have you, Mom?" Eileen says standing.

"I'm not sure what you mean, Leenie. "I don't know Walter very well, but it's obvious that he loves you. And that means a great deal."

"He keeps me from boring myself to death, Mom." Mackie sees Eileen's face light up. "And he's incredibly thoughtful. When we're alone he's not nearly as self-absorbed as he usually seems."

Mackie smiles.

"We have our fights, of course. He was furious when I flew out to see you in Shoreham. He just didn't get it. He thought it was a huge waste of money, but never mind." Eileen waves the memory off.

"I'll never forgive myself for hitting you, Eileen. I was so out of line."

"Mom, that one second doesn't change all the years of other stuff. All the good stuff and happiness."

Mackie nods, "I guess not."

"I've got to get to work, Mom."

Mackie surveys the room and opens another carton, puts in a stack of books. This packing up of her life is becoming an all too familiar thing. "Me too, Leenie." Eileen turns in the doorway and blows her mother a kiss. Mackie catches it and holds it to her heart.

Chapter 25

Seeing the For Sale sign pounded into the lawn in front of the California house, overseeing the last of her shipment and watching the rest of the furniture being loaded into the van to be sold at an estate sale has given this trip a sense of finality. Both the girls were eyebrow deep in work and Mackie, still feeling on shaky ground with the girls, opted for an airport limo.

The flight is absolutely full and Mackie, in a middle seat, sandwiched between a sumo-wrestler and a college kid who sleeps and drools through the flight arrives back in Shoreham having lost three hours.

She drops her luggage inside the door, thinking she'll unpack it later. Jet-lagged and emotionally drained, she pours herself a glass of wine and begins to pick through the stacks of mail that Boo has been retrieving and putting on the kitchen counter in her absence. She thumbs through junk mail, ads and catalogues, knowing that there is not likely anything worth reading.

As tired as she is, the house seems to envelope her with its lingering warm scents and peace. She can't wait to undress, take a bath and get reacquainted with her surroundings.

She'd rather do anything but talk, but feels that she must call Boo right away and at least let her know that she is back home.

"Welcome home, Sweet Pea. I was wondering when you were coming back"

"I just got in Boo. Thought I'd have an early supper and crash. Can I see you tomorrow, though? I've missed you."

"Just wash that cute face of yours and meet me at Turner's Tavern at six o'clock."

"Oh, Boo," Mackie sighs, feeling older than dirt. "Why don't you just come on over here and I'll fix us something."

"This is my treat, Sweet Pea. And I have a little something for you—a surprise."

Mackie gets to the bar at a little after five-thirty. The place is empty of customers except for two old men sitting at the far end of the bar. They are so alike that they might have been cloned and Mackie thinks immediately that they must be the Piper twins. She hasn't seen them for decades. She doesn't know whether it's the fact that they are wearing identical overalls and hip boots or their age that makes them an oddity. Hector and Hughey have run the bait and tackle shop at the town pier with their father since the forties.

"Welcome back, Hon!" Al says. "Grab a seat. I'm building the boys a couple of martinis? Can I get you one?"

"No thanks, Al. I'll stick to wine, but no hurry. I'm meeting my aunt here in a while."

"Is that you, Mackie Swan," one of the 'boys' asks. squinting across the bar. He sounds like Judge Roy Bean.

"It is," Mackie smiles. "But it's Kinsella now. Mackie

Kinsella. And I'm sorry, but I don't know whether you're Hughey or Hector." The vague smell of mackerel wafts across the bar.

"Well, we answer to most anything," one the "boys" says.

"Just don't call me chum," one of them says and they high five each other, laughing hysterically.

"Hector's the good looking one," Al jokes, taking a cocktail shaker, filling it with ice. She adds a few drops of dry vermouth, tops it with gin and starts shaking it rhythmically.

Lining up two stemmed glasses on the bar, she takes twists of lemon and runs them around the rim of each glass, pours the drinks and then picks up olives on toothpicks and drops them in.

"Age before beauty," she says, deftly placing one drink in front of Hughey and the other in front of Hector.

"You have beautiful hands, Al," Mackie says looking at Al's long, slim fingers and impeccable manicure.

"Why thank you, Hon!" Al says, "They're the tools of the trade. A girl has got to take care of her tools, you know." She goes to the wine cooler and pulls out a bottle of Sancerre. Uncorking it, she asks, "This ok with you?"

Mackie smiles, "That's hardly the house wine, Al."

"The house wine is panther piss," Al says. She fills the glass and hands it to Mackie.

"Cheers!" Mackie says, lifting her glass and the Pipers lift their glasses in salute.

"Cheers, Mackie Kinsella," they say in unison.

"What happened to the trivia contests, Al?" Mackie asks.

"We had the last one last weekend, Mackie," Al says. "We did a grand finale and everyone came dressed as their favorite silly song. You should have been here."

"I can imagine it," Mackie chuckles.

Al bends down and rummages under the bar. When she gets up she is wearing one of those Aussie outback hats. Corks dangle and bob, almost obscuring her eyes. "G'day mate," Al says with a broad and hilarious accent.

"Oh my," Mackie says.

"Tie Me Kangaroo Down Sport," Al says and adds, "You can see why we have to stop before the summer folk arrive. They already think we're crazy for living here year round."

"Do you like tending bar, Al?"

"It pays the bills," Al says. " My oldest two are in college and I've got another three in the wings."

"You have five kids?" Mackie says.

"That I do," Al beams. "A true full house; three girls and two boys. They are the good news in my life."

"And the bad news?" Mackie asks.

"Bad news is that their collective fathers aren't always on the beam with the child support." Mackie nods and sips her wine.

Al, in perpetual motion behind the bar, starts uncorking bottles of wine and arranging bottles, turning them just a fraction this way or that. "My customers tip good and this gig beats the heck out of some of the alternatives."

"Such as?"

"I drove a truck for a while," Al says, "long distance. God how I hated it, thought I might die from the pain of it."

"The loneliness?" Mackie asks.

"Nah, the hemorrhoids," Al whispers, "you don't want to know."

Mackie almost spews her wine out, laughing and then says, "I've never had to support myself, let alone my girls. It must be daunting. I can't imagine raising five kids."

"Never been any different for me," Al says. "I finally wised up and realized that I kept sleeping with the enemy. Ah, but God, Mackie, I loved those men at the time. I guess I'm just your basic serial monogamist." She throws the bar towel over her shoulder.

"But, I've been single for a couple of years now and I'm pretty happy. And the tavern is kind of cozy. A lot of good people stop by to pass the time." Al smiles warmly at Mackie.

"I think I'm going to have to get a job myself," Mackie says. "Or maybe start up some kind of a business. I'm not at all sure what, but I think I'd like to be my own boss. I'm not afraid of work."

Al smiles. "What sort of business are you thinking about, Hon?"

"This sounds silly," Mackie says, "but I've been thinking I might start some sort of decorating business. I used to hang a lot of wallpaper and I'm pretty good with color. Richard and I moved around all the time and every house was a challenge." Mackie lights up a cigarette. It feels good to be talking to someone who feels simply like a friend. She inhales and closes her eyes. "I think we must have lived in more than a dozen houses over the years."

"Wow," Al says. "I can't imagine. I've lived in Shoreham my whole life. I've been in the same house now for twenty-five years."

"Boo!" the Piper twins shout in unison, as Boo enters the bar.

"Glory be to Roses Wharf," Boo says. "It's old home week at the OK corral. What the hell are you boys doing here?"

Mackie gets up to hug her aunt, "It's wonderful to be home, Boo. I've missed you!"

"Well, ditto, Sweet Pea." They embrace as Hughey and Hector stand up.

"Care to join us, boys?" Boo asks, slipping out of her jacket and sliding into one of the booths. She is clutching a shopping bag and her face is flushed and her eyes sparkle.

"Aww, our backsides are out of here," they say as they walk by. "But remember, Boo, it's your turn to bring the sandwiches for poker."

Mackie is amazed that they speak in unison as they do or one starts and the other finishes a sentence. "And no more of those damned 'fluffernutters," they say and drift out of the bar.

"Go sit with your Auntie, Mackie," Al says. "I'll bring your drinks. Do you know what your Aunt will have?"

"Jim Beam for me and don't be shy," Boo yells.

"You've got it!"

"You look good, Sweet Pea."

"Thanks, Boo."

Al delivers the drinks and the dinner menus, "You ladies need some time?"

"Please," Mackie says. She wants to give Boo some time. Doesn't feel the need to rush.

"So, you take care of business out there?" Boo says.

"Yes."

"I can't believe that you're going to be a grandma," Boo says sipping her drink. "Imagine that."

"I'm trying to do that," Mackie says.

"You'll be great, Sweet Pea

Without saying a word, Boo smiles and slides the bag across the table to Mackie. Intrigued, Mackie peeks into the bag and sees money; some five, ten and twenty dollar bills, but mostly ones. Mackie shakes her head, bewildered. "What is this, Boo?"

"Money," Boo says. "It's for you Sweet Pea, and don't you go trying to push it back at me, Missy. Buddy and I want you to have it."

"I can't take your money, Boo!" Mackie says, horrified. Knowing that Boo surely cannot afford this sweet generosity.

"Of course you can, Sweet Pea. It's from the garage sale. Buddy says we done real good."

"Boo?" Mackie is so touched that tears appear at the corners of her eyes.

"Guess how much is in there?" Boo says.

Mackie breathes in deeply, "It looks like a lot, Boo, hundreds even."

Boo whispers, "One thousand, four hundred and sixty-seven smackers."

"You've got to be kidding," Mackie says.

"Nope." Boo is radiant. "If I could of sold that damned dory we would have doubled it I bet."

"I can't possibly take this, Boo."

"Well, I ain't taking it back so you better figure out something to do with it, Sweet Pea. Don't you go looking an old gift horse like me in the mouth."

"But, Boo—" Mackie pleads.

"That's the end of it." Boo makes washing motions

with her hands.

Al arrives with huge bowls of salad and a basket of rolls. "Refills, ladies?" she asks.

"I think I need one, Al," Mackie says.

"How is it that you and my mother ended up being so different, Boo?"

"Ditto on the James, Al." Boo pushes her glass across to Al and takes both of Mackie's hands in her own. "You mean different like your Emma and Eileen, Sweet Pea?"

"Yes, I guess so. Only more. Mother was always such a perfectionist. Nothing was ever quite good enough. Not me, not the men she dated. I guess maybe my father was lucky he died in that accident. At least he never got to see that kind of disappointment in her eyes."

"Don't be so sure you know who you're momma was, Sweet Pea. Or who I was, who I am for that matter. I reckon you're born with a lot of what you end up going through life with. It's kind of the luck of the draw if you get my drift. Some of us are smart and some not so. "

"But Boo, you always look at the bright side. I can't remember you being unhappy."

"Don't be foolish. No one alive gets away with that." Boo shakes her head, "You know better than that."

"But mother was always so angry. There was a kind of bitterness about her all the time."

"She had disappointments, Sweet Pea. We all do."

"Why couldn't she love me, Boo?"

"She did love you!" Boo reaches across the table, grabs both of Mackie's hands. We all always loved you. You were our girl. You still are, Mackie."

Mackie sees that Boo has tears in her eyes.

"I'm sorry, Boo. This is such a wonderful, generous gift from you." Mackie pats the bag and Al arrives with the drinks.

"Have you two young ladies decided on dinner yet?" Al asks.

Boo takes the unopened menus and hands them to Al. "We'll have the lobster, and the Brownie Sundaes to start. Double whipped cream and don't be shy."

Al jots down the order and smiles from ear to ear. "You two are my kind of ladies!"

Boo lifts her glass and Mackie lifts hers to it and clinks. "Life is good, Sweet Pea."

"Life is good."

Chapter 26

"Okay. I've been good. I haven't bothered you, intruded on your space or whatever the jargon is."

Mackie feels arousal at the sound of Sully's voice on her answering machine. He could seduce her with a whisper.

"I want to see you. I can cook. Come for dinner tomorrow. Please—I've missed you Mackie."

She takes the grocery bag, puts it on the counter, and sighs. Welcome home, she thinks. He cooks. She remembers him. Lurching for the phone book at the bottom of the pantry, she punches in his number before she can change her mind.

"Hello," he says.

"Sully—it's me, Mackie," she feels the tremor in her voice. "I'm back, but of course you know that—"

"I'll be right over," Sully says.

"No!" she panics.

"Kidding," Sully says. "Although I'd be there in a second."

"Well," she collects herself. "It's your turn to cook so I thought I'd accept your invitation for dinner tomorrow. Is that all right?"

"That's terrific."

"What can I bring and what time should I come?"

"You. And whenever you're ready."

She doesn't know if he means the double entendre or not, but she blushes and says, "Seven o'clock?"

"Great," he says.

"Great," she echoes.

"I take it you don't need directions. That's the joy of living in a landmark," he adds.

"I'll find you," she says and hangs up the phone.

Mackie's anxiety peaks at five the next day. She has not really looked at her body since Richard died. Well, that is not totally accurate. She's looked at bits and pieces of it, feeling quite removed; her legs when she remembers to shave them, her armpits, the creases that seem to have taken root around the outside edges of her eyes. Occasionally she will brush her nipples accidentally and feel something that stirs memories of arousal. Sometimes she acts on that impulse, but always in the dark and under the covers.

After bathing, she stands naked in front of the full-length mirror in the bathroom with her eyes squeezed shut. When she dares to open them she looks and gasps, "Dear God, who is this who stands before me?" Body parts seem to have shifted and she is pasty white. One of the few good things about living in LaLa land had been a sort of perpetual tan. And, she supposes the inability to hide beneath heavy sweaters, overalls, and such. She flicks off the lights, leaving only one of the scented candles burning and looks again. If she squints it's not so dreadful. She has, after all given birth twice and will soon be a grandmother. That gives her a sense of satisfaction. "I have a good, useful, sturdy body she thinks." Besides, no one is going to see it—possibly ever again.

She is now grateful that she made a quick visit to her hairdresser, Young Ran when she was back in California. Young Ran is an ageless Korean woman whose name suits her perfectly, thinks Mackie. She is beautiful in the most natural way and she overrides Mackie constantly on her choices. She had gone in for just a trim and simply for the joy of having someone wash her hair. The sensual pleasure of closing her eyes and laying her head back while someone lathers, massages, rinses and conditions.

"No color, today Young Ran, I've decided to go 'au naturel'.

"Oh, no good for you to be old gray, mare," Young Ran says sweetly. "I just do a little bit of color—and maybe a fast wax?"

"Just a trim."

Young shakes her head, "I trim a little and just a little color. You have no tan now. I fix it, ok?

Mackie relents, as she always does, the power of a hairdresser being only slightly less than that of a doctor or a cop.

"What's it like being a hairdresser?" Mackie asks as her color cooks. Her chin has been stripped of whiskers and there is a halo of tinfoil around her head. She thinks she might be picking up signals from someone in Abu Dhabi. She hates seeing herself in the mirror and contemplates plastic surgery—just a tiny little wattle lift—and maybe the eyes.

"Do you like doing this?" Mackie asks, wondering if there is satisfaction in spending one's days making others look good.

Young Ran, always enigmatic says, "When I took over the shop it was hard. Lots of weekly wash and sets. And they all so lonely—but I not good with them. Too high-maintenance." She shrugs. "Eventually they stop coming, but I always feel a little guilty. Someone needs to take care of the blue ladies."

Mackie looks in the mirror before leaving, seeing once again a younger looking version of herself sporting a sophisticated auburn bob instead of a braid or ponytail. Hugging Young, she says, "Thank you for saving me from myself."

"You gonna have to come back here in a month you know, if you wanna keep looking this good."

———◦((◦))◦———

Frantically pacing in her bedroom, Mackie calls Emma at noon and leaves a message on her voice mail. "I have a date."

Two hours late Emma calls back. "Tell me you're kidding, momma!"

"I'm kidding."

"But you're not, are you?"

"I'm not."

"Is this the guy who came to dinner before, the photographer?"

"The same."

"Go buy expensive underwear, Mom. Not that stretchy stuff you usually wear."

"Emma!" Mackie shrieks through the phone. "We are

just having dinner. Actually he's cooking."

"Mom, I'm just telling you that great underwear will give you confidence. I am not talking about sex. It's good advice, trust me. Eileen told me about it and she bills out at three hundred an hour. I'm giving you this pro-bono or whatever that free stuff is."

"Ok, Em—how are you feeling, honey?"

"I'm great but lunch rush is on and I'm about to get slammed."

"You're feeling ok?"

"Second trimester is a piece of cake. No more vomititis. And Cisco is so excited now that he can feel the baby."

"I wish I could be there, Em."

"Me too, Momma."

"It sounds ridiculous, doesn't it? I'm a soon to be grand-mother having a date? Oh my God."

"It sounds kind of nice, Momma. I'm happy for you."
"Chicken, avocado, jack hold the sprouts, great—beverage? Iced tea? You've got it."

Mackie listens to Emma and pictures her behind the counter of her little shop. Sees that smile and wishes she could reach through the phone to hug her daughter. Put her hand on that warm belly that harbors her first grandchild.

"Thanks, sweetie. I miss you. I miss my good girls."

"We miss you too, Momma." Double Latte? "Oh, Momma?"

"What, Emma?"

"Just be yourself."

Mackie stands in front of the mirror, savoring the feel of the expensive, lacy lingerie against her skin. After talking with Emma, she drove out to the new mall in Quincy, feeling only marginally guilty when she handed over her credit card for the splurge on the bra and panties. Eileen is right, she thinks, feeling better about herself already. Staring at the outfits she has laid out on the bed she realizes that her California clothes are making more sense in Shoreham now that summer is approaching. Still, she can't decide between the cream, linen blouse and trousers or the long chambray skirt and silk sweater. She has a giddy flashback to her high school days, dressing for the dances and the inevitable Saturday night dates. An ascension of butterflies almost sends her to the phone to cancel the date. What on earth am I doing? Her mouth is dry and she slips into her bathrobe, stalling for time.

She goes to the kitchen and figures a glass of wine will help her decide what to do. What to wear? How to act? Unfortunately, the only bottle she has is in the house is the one she bought to bring with her to Sully's. It's a pinot noir, one of her favorites. "What the hell," she thinks and uncorks it, pouring one glass. "I'll pick up a new bottle at Kennedy's"

Mackie decides on the skirt and sweater and does her makeup, "Good God, it's nearly seven," she mutters looking at the clock. Less is more, she thinks, blotting her lipstick. Now she has a choice; be close to on time with an open bottle of wine or be late. She is usually chronically early. She hates waiting for anyone, finds latecomers somehow flawed or at the very least inconsiderate.

She cannot believe that she is on her way to Sully. She cannot ever remember a time when she might have been en route to anyone. So she sticks the cork back in the bottle and lays it on the front seat of the car thinking that it will be a good icebreaker if nothing else. Although she thinks she clearly remembers the way to Cedar Point and can, in fact see the lighthouse beacon in the distance, she misses the turn off and slams on the brakes. Putting the car into reverse, she peers out the windows into pitch black for a glimpse of the driveway.

The lights take her by surprise and then she feels instant fear as she realizes that there is a police car behind her. She brakes, puts the car into drive and puts her foot gently on the gas pedal, pulling over to the side of the road. She hasn't had a ticket for twenty years and she knows that the one glass of wine she had can't be a problem, but she feels as if Sister Philomena is about to chastise her from the grave. She opens the driver's side window and gropes in the dark for her purse, ready to produce her driver's license.

The flashlight beam hits her in the face and she knows it is Officer Duffy by his voice although she can't really see his face.

"Ma'am? I observed you driving in what could be considered an unorthodox direction. May I see your license and registration, please?"

"Of course," Mackie says, handing it out the window while she leans over to open the glove compartment.

"Well, this is a nice card, but I need to see your driver's license and registration, Mrs. Kinsella." He hands her back her Bloomingdales charge card.

Mackie, now totally flustered starts shuffling her cards and finds her driver's license and hands it over to Duffy along with her registration.

"Is that a bottle of wine on your passenger's seat?" Duffy asks.

"It is. I'm bringing it to Sully's house."

"Are you aware that it's illegal?"

"Sully's house?" Mackie says, momentarily confused.

"That open bottle of alcoholic beverage," Duffy says.

"Oh, good grief, Duffy," Mackie is suddenly annoyed, " I had one little glass of wine over an hour ago. If you want to use a Breathalyzer on me, go right ahead."

"Now don't go getting all techy, ma'am." Despite the uniform and the years of training, Mackie sees the smile tickle the corner of Duffy's mouth.

"I'm sorry, officer," Mackie says. "I had no idea I was breaking any law and I promise that I'll be more careful from now on."

"Do you need a police escort to the Sullivan estate?" Duffy asks.

"Oh, please not," Mackie says. "I'm truly sorry. I was not aware of that particular ordinance."

"Well, I know you're from California, Mrs. Kinsella and I'm sure a lot of things are done different out there," Duffy says. "I'll just lead you down the drive," he says, returning her license and registration. "It's tricky if you don't know it. Especially after dark."

"Thank you, Officer Duffy," Mackie says, cheeks flaming, thinking to herself, there's nothing quite like arriving late for a dinner engagement with a police escort and an opened bottle of wine. "That would be kind."

The driveway is densely overgrown and pitch dark and Mackie is actually kind of glad that Duffy is leading the way.

He turns off his colored lights and makes a U-turn when he gets to the lighthouse, saluting Mackie as he leaves.

The door to the little house opens before Mackie is ready. She feels her heart lurch when she sees Sully standing in the doorway, his shadow filling the space, haloed by soft light. She gets out of the car, clutching the bottle of wine. The wind has picked up and she hears the surf hitting the rocks. She remembers the jetty, huge rocks breaking out into the water—a giant's path. How many hours had she spent at the end of that magical causeway? When it felt as if she had nowhere to go, no safe place, she had ridden her bicycle out to the lighthouse and traversed the jetty. She would sit huddled, sweatshirt pulled over her knees, arms pulled out of its sleeves, sheltered in the warmth of her own skin. The house had been abandoned in those days and the kids found easy entry. Mackie had climbed the tower to the top many times, feeling brave circumnavigating the upper deck—the little house closed below. It had seemed a small, deserted kingdom. How could she have forgotten the geography?

"Hello, Lady," Sully says. Squinting into the distance and pointing at the retreating taillights of the squad car, he says, "Did you bring a friend?"

"That was Duffy," Mackie says, holding the bottle of wine aloft, pulling out the cork. She feels as if she is seventeen again, about to embark on something illicit and frightening. Taking a sip, she swallows and says, "Apparently I'm a felon."

His laughter is deep, rich. "Oh, goodie," he says picking his way gingerly across the gravel. He is barefoot, wearing a chambray shirt unbuttoned over jeans. "I've always wanted to consort with a criminal."

"Officer Duffy felt I needed an escort."

"Ah, and isn't Duffy a wise man indeed." The distance between them disappears and Mackie finds herself in his arms.

"I'm sorry I'm late. I hate being late. I hate people who are late. And now I am one of those people." Her breath is coming faster. She is blathering and suddenly feels embarrassed, awkward in his arms. "I can't believe I missed the turn getting here."

"Well, you're here now," he says, pulling her closer against his smooth, bare chest. Mackie feels as if her nerves are outside her skin. "That's all that matters."

"I used to come out here all the time," she says, pulling away, folding her arms and looking up.

"And just what did you do out here?" Sully asks.

"Dream, stargaze, try to figure out the meaning of life," She says. "Look, there's Orion." She points out the three stars that make his belt.

He takes her hand and raises their arms together. Pointing up he says, "And right there, is Cassiopeia." He spins her around, "God, I've missed you."

"Me too," she says, "It's good to be here." She couldn't imagine that she would visit this place again. She couldn't remember that sweet safety of being so embraced.

"Let me run into the house and get some shoes. We can go out on the jetty if you like."

"No," Mackie says quickly. She wants to slow things down as her emotions start to collide with her memories. "Not now. I want to see your house. And I'm starving, she says sniffing the air. "What is that awesome smell?"

"Osso Bucco," he says, taking the wine from her and pulling her into the house. "And the wine will be great. What's left of it that is." She punches his arm playfully.

Mackie hesitates when they get to the door. "I've never been to a man's house before."

"And I've never entertained a criminal."

Her laughter breaks the tension and he pulls her inside the little house. "Welcome to my humbleness," he says.

Mackie looks around, sees huge black and white photographs covering the walls. The furniture is sparse and seems almost Nordic in its simplicity. A braided rug over wooden floors, a small wood fire, a sofa, a worn, leather rocker, a steamer trunk that has been set with plates and wine glasses.

"Would you like the grand tour now or later?" he asks, "And would you like a glass or does Madame prefer to swig from the bottle?" He doesn't hesitate to pour two glasses and hands her one.

"Tour later please." Mackie says sipping.

"The ladies' choice." Sully says. "Would you like to know a bit about the place?"

"Yes." She can't take her eyes off the photos and is immersed in the warmth of the place.

"It was built in the early eighteen hundreds," he says and dips his head, "I feel like a damned docent."

"Go ahead, she says," loving this side of him. She can see the pride he takes in the place—in his home.

"It was derelict when I bought it, believe me. I had to evict quite a few unwelcome roommates."

Mackie looks at him, "Squatters?"

"Bats and rats and alley cats," he says, smiling. "The place smelled like an abattoir."

"That's hard to believe looking at it now, Sully. It's lovely."

"Thank you," he says and bows. "When I bought it there was no insulation and we won't even talk about amenities. I cooked on a two burner stove and kept food cold in an Igloo cooler."

"Really?" Mackie says. "You know I used to come out here as a kid, but the cottage was always boarded up. I felt like I owned the tower and the jetty of course, but the house was always a mystery."

"Well, Mrs. Kinsella, let me demystify this wonderful place, if I may." He takes her hand and kisses her right by her ear. She can feel his breath and hears a murmured, "Hmmm." She feels wonder in being so close to someone. She can't remember the last time—or doesn't want to.

"This is the living room," he makes a quarter turn and points through a doorway, "the kitchen," turns again, "the bathroom," and then he points to a narrow staircase, "and above, my bedchamber." She laughs, suddenly too aware of his maleness, the maleness of the place.

Seeking safe ground she walks over to the photos and asks, "Is this your work?" She looks at majestic seascapes hanging beside landscapes. She scrutinizes close ups of marsh grasses, cattails and cranberry bogs.

"Mostly."

There are photos that document the renovations that Sully did to the keeper's house. He's made a collage of them. "I'm impressed," Mackie says. "Did you do all the work on the house by yourself?"

"Yes. It took a while, mind you. These beautiful hardwood floors were quite hidden and neglected beneath shag carpeting."

"These are wonderful," Mackie says, sweeping her hands over the pictures.

"Thank you."

Finally her eyes rest on a photo of a lighthouse. Not Cedar Point, it stands on a cliff, a tall concrete tower with a Victorian cottage attached and a series of outbuildings beyond. Surf crashes against the cliffs as it does in the aftermath of a storm. "I love this one," Mackie says. "It's so Rebecca-ish. You can just imagine some grand tragedy happening there."

Sully walks over to her. "It's one of my favorites too." He grins broadly. "You have excellent taste. I've always loved that shot."

"It is yours?" Mackie asks with a sinking feeling.

Sully just shakes his head slowly from side to side. "Tom Harper, a fine photographer—does a lot of calendar work."

"Oh my," Mackie bites her lower lip. "I'm sorry."

"Don't be silly," he says.

"So you only like the black and whites."

"I find them less distracting," he says.

Mackie sips her wine. "You're quite the renaissance man, Sully, artist, chef, renovator."

He bows. "On that note, let's eat."

Sully tosses a Caesar salad and opens another bottle of wine as they sit down to eat. The veal is tender, simmered to perfection and they have devoured most of a loaf of crusty bread by the end of the meal. "You enjoy cooking?"

"I do," he says. "I try to keep myself civilized. Sit at the table for meals—even if it is just me."

"I'm afraid I've taken to grazing since I've been single," Mackie says. "After all those years of cooking and entertaining, it's kind of fun to just have cheese and crackers and call it dinner."

"Have you ever been married, Sully?"

"For one, brief excruciating moment," he says, smiling. "There's not much to say about it, so I don't," he says, closing that avenue.

"I'll just clear the dishes for now," he says, taking her plate and his own into the kitchen. She picks up napkins and glasses and follows him.

"I'll help you clean up she says."

Turning around he puts his hands on her shoulders. "It can wait until morning. Let's go sit by the fire and finish this wine." He steers her through the tiny door. "Maybe we'll even have some cheese and crackers," he says, and stoops to kiss her.

They move from kitchen to living room in a dance. Melded, he tucks her inside his arms. "You look incredibly fine here, in my little house."

"I should be going, now."

"Can't let you do that," he says, thickly. "We have no designated drunk driver. It's my job to take care of you. I don't want Duffy on my case."

"Shall I make some coffee?" she asks, but he is kissing her and she doesn't want coffee. She doesn't want anything more than to be right where she is in his arms.

"I'll be right back," he says, kissing her forehead. But

he goes into the bathroom, not the kitchen. Moments later when he emerges, the top snap of his jeans is undone and his shirt is off.

"I want to show you the rest of the house," he says, leading her upstairs. His room is heavily shadowed and she can just make out the bed. A small oil lamp glows on the bedside table.

"I modeled this after a ship's cabin," he says, and they collapse on the bed together. He pulls the sweater over her head and unhooks her bra and pulls her close.

Taking one of her nipples in his mouth he circles it with his tongue and she thinks she might climax right then and there. Every part of her body is wired to his. "Sully?" she gasps.

"Shh, baby—shh."

Mackie feels his hands at the base of her spine where he begins a deep massage, moving his hands slowly up her back. She shudders.

"Just breathe," he says, not releasing the pressure of his thumbs. You're so damned beautiful." His hands come around her waist and he slides her skirt and panties off and kisses her abdomen. She reaches for his jeans, unzips them and there is nothing between them anymore. He reaches across her, opens the drawer in the nightstand and puts on a condom. Linking his fingers in hers, he pulls her on top of him where she waits, breathless as he brushes his lips across hers, teasing her. He kisses her ears, the hollow at the base of her throat and back to her mouth. She feels his tongue in her mouth, tastes him greedily. She feels him lift her onto him and finds herself mindless, taking him deep inside. He turns

her on her back and strokes, plunging deeper until she rises
up to him and they find a rhythm.

"Oh," Mackie moans, "oh—please—yes." And feeling
Sully shudder, Mackie is there with him and finds herself
silently weeping as their heartbeats slow.

Chapter 27

Awake at dawn, she looks at the light filtering through the shutters on the high windows. She remembers falling asleep in his arms and then remembers what came before. The lovemaking. She feels heat rise up from her belly and some feeling she can't at first identify. It is joy followed all too quickly by uncertainty. She feels reborn and unstable.

She looks over at Sully who is sleeping, takes the time to study his face in repose. He is guileless, she thinks. He seems untethered by family, by history—even the ex-wife so easily dismissed, seems hardly to have left an imprint on him.

She is naked and completely unused to it, although the sheets feel wonderful against her skin. This is a kind of decadence that she has never known. I am a wanton woman she thinks. I have a lover. And just as quickly, she feels ridiculous.

She moves as close to the edge of the bed as she can without falling off and leans over to scoop her sweater off the floor. Pulling it quickly over her head, she tries not to wake Sully in the process, but fails.

"Good morning," he says, his voice morning husky.

"Good morning."

"How do you feel?" He says, rubbing sleep from his eyes.

"I'm not sure," she says, truthfully.

"What do you mean?" he says, and clears his throat. "Do you have a Katzenjammer?"

"A what?"

"A hangover?"

"No. It's not that," she says. " It's just that in my vast repertoire of lovers, you are the second."

He grins, broadly, his dimples warming Mackie to her core. "I'm honored, and I won't ask for comparisons."

"I feel like a beginner," she stammers, "For instance, I never had protected sex before."

Sully's deep laughter erupts into the room.

"Sweetheart, these days there is no other kind."

Mackie blushes furiously and says, "Obviously. It's just not something I ever needed, Sully. It's new to me."

"Well, why don't you just mosey over to my side of the bed and we'll practice," he says, propping his head on his arm and patting the sheet.

He is open in a way that Mackie finds disarming. She slides out of bed and picks up the rest of her clothes from the floor. "I'm going to go get washed up and finish dressing," she says smiling. "And then I'm going to go home and gather my thoughts." She kisses him on the forehead and then on the mouth and he grabs her wrist and tugs. She falls into his mouth, wants to stay there forever, but finally she pulls away, afraid of giving so much, maybe too much. She rushes down the stairs.

"I'm not just a one night stand, you know!" he yells out and Mackie feels happiness bubble up inside her.

MACKIE

I'm trying out for cheerleading today. I've made the second cut and this is the big day. I'm afraid I won't be able to do the cartwheel. I have never been able to dive either; something about putting my head lower than my feet, kind of like flying upside down, I'm afraid I'll crash.

If I get chosen the girls will come and kidnap me during the night. If I don't I'm not sure I'll want to wake up in the morning.

Chapter 28

Memorial Day, the unofficial signal for the return of the summer people, finds Mackie trading storm windows for screens and replacing the heavy, lined draperies with crisp, cotton curtains. She remembers the yearly ritual from childhood; the quilts on the beds replaced with chenille, the slipcovers coming off the furniture and the fact that life moved outside to the porch for a few months. From Friday evening until Sunday afternoon Shoreham's population swells and recedes like the tides. The local contractors have more work than they can schedule for the first time since autumn. The town takes on color as paint is refreshed, gardens planted and stores that have been shuttered for the off-season open for business.

Mackie is getting her sea legs. She feels the tug of her girls in California, is anxious that the house will sell quickly and still concerned about money, but the cartons have been unpacked and the house seems to be emerging from some cocoon. Mackie has planted pansies along the front walk and trimmed back the forsythia at the side of the house. Things have always just taken root where they landed before but now Mackie is establishing some kind of order.

She has started to rise early, having coffee only and then walking along the beach for an hour or so, picking up bits of driftwood and sea glass. She can see Sully's lighthouse in the distance and she imagines him there. She imagines him often, spends an inordinate amount of time remembering his body, reveling in the sensations that he brings to her. Like a teenage boy she finds herself aroused nearly constantly. The touch of fabric against her nipples hardens them. She craves him like she used to crave food.

Most nights they sleep alone. His schedule is not regular and Mackie has not yet looked for work. He drops by midday and they make love on the couch in the living room, on the floor in the kitchen, peeling off just enough clothing so that they can fuck and that word has taken on new meaning—not an expletive but an exclamation; visceral, joyful, playful, excruciating. Sully goes on to work and Mackie enervated, doses off for hours and awakens wired. At six pm she feels as if she is just starting her day. She gives him a key and sometimes, half-awake in the middle of the night, she finds him beside her, naked, hard but still cool from the outside air. He comes closer, burrowing into her back. One hand on her breast one on her belly he brings her alive.

Today, decked out in shorts, a t-shirt and running shoes, Mackie drives out to Third Cliff with the intention of walking on the beach. She's read an article about power walking and thinks it might be just the thing to get her back in shape. She's lost a few pounds since she's been with Sully and is determined to be in great shape by the time Emma has the baby, a girl, who Francisco and Emma will name Elena

Katherine after her grandmothers. This piece of news sits inside Mackie, warming her.

She is sitting at the bottom of the cliff putting on ankle and wrist weights when she spots someone swimming toward shore. She lights up a cigarette and pauses to watch the strokes, strong and even. The swimmer emerges from the water, well-muscled body glistening in the sun. Mackie cannot remember paying much attention to men's bodies before Sully, but now she finds herself taking great pleasure in studying the physicality of men. And this man moves with grace up the beach. He pauses, picks up a towel and takes a moment to dry off. Throwing the towel over his shoulder, he slips into a pair of deck shoes and heads toward Mackie.

"Well, good morning, Mary Katherine."

She almost doesn't recognize him and then, she quickly stubs her cigarette out in the sand. "Dr Joy?"

"Graham will do."

Mackie nods and gets to her feet, shifting uneasily in the sand. "I'm sorry. I didn't recognize you without your glasses."

"Ah, well. I finally had that corrective surgery done. Laser, it's quite good really. I got tired of misplacing my specs all the time."

"I understand. I just keep about ten pair of those supermarket readers. They're everywhere. One in the glove compartment, bedside drawer, kitchen drawer, etc.—you get the picture." Changing the subjects she says, "Not many people swim here. This water is freezing."

"Ah, but I'm of tough British stock. Raised in Cromwellian boarding schools, being the lightweight in our football scrums, surviving without centralized heating. I developed rather a thick skin I'm afraid. We believe a good, brisk swim in the Atlantic gets the blood circulating."

Mackie laughs, enjoying yet another side to the good doctor.

"But enough about me." And with that he points to Mackie's arm, a look of concern crossing his face, "I don't think that's a good idea."

Puzzled, Mackie says, "What—the weights?"

"No, I applaud your effort at exercise, but is that not a nicotine patch on your arm?"

Mackie feels herself color.

"And you did just stub out that nasty butt beside you?

"I've been trying to quit. And I'm down to just a few a day."

"Well good. I know it's not easy. Some people seem to have an easier time than others. It took me forever."

"You?"

"Yes. More than one associate put a cigarette back in my mouth and lit it. Apparently I became the doctor from hell."

She nods, "I'd still sell my first born for the morning cig."

"And I understand that impulse." He doesn't smile. "You look good Mary Katherine."

"Thank you." Mackie wants to sprint down the beach, showing the good doctor how truly fit she is beneath it all. Instead she stands anchored to the spot until finally he speaks again.

"Well, I need to get back home. I have no office hours today and I've promised Daly that we'd go to the cinema. It's her favorite thing to do besides the tea parties."

Mackie remembers her girls at that age and thinks

that she will be reliving that sweet ceremony with Elena Katherine in a few years. She has a sudden flash of the good doctor sipping tea from a tiny cup, pinkie raised. She smiles at the vision. "What movie are you seeing?"

He shrugs his shoulders and the corners of his mouth lift. "Something Disney I suppose. I'm afraid I'm not good at the Daddy business."

Mackie thinks, clearly, he is anything but and he is, more than that, a man unaccustomed to smiling.

Chapter 29

"Who knows?" Boo says. "People talk." She is breathing heavily and her face is scarlet as they unroll the sisal rug onto the front porch at Mackie's.

"Just sit down, Boo." Mackie orders, practically pushing her aunt onto the glider. "I never should have let you help me move this stuff up from the cellar."

"Oh right, missy, and what would you have done then? Hauled it up here all by yourself?"

"I could have asked Sully. I guess I should have asked him—but never mind. What kind of talk, Boo? What do you mean?"

"Well, the wife, if there is one, definitely isn't in the picture. And you know—two men living together—" Boo's eyebrows shoot up. "Course I don't believe it for a second, I think you can always spot a homo."

"Boo!"

"It's true, Sweet Pea. 'Cept for Rock Hudson certainly had us all fooled."

"Herbie and Graham?" Mackie says. "That's just ridiculous. Besides, Herbie has his own apartment in the barn."

Mackie shakes her head, exasperated, " And Herbie is Daly's nanny and he cooks for the family."

"Don't get all huffy," Boo starts rocking and the glider protests, squeaking loudly. "Leastwise, I said I didn't believe the rumors. And it's Graham now is it? When did you and the doc get on a first name basis?" Boo says, lighting up a cigarette.

"I just ran into him on the beach the other day, Boo. He was swimming, if you can believe it. I don't know too many people brave enough or crazy enough to do that."

"You need some oil for this thing, Sweet Pea," Boo says, continuing to make the glider groan.

"I'll take care of it," Mackie snaps. "And for goodness sake don't say 'homo', Boo. People don't say things like 'homo' and 'lezbo' anymore."

"Well, Miss Fancy Pants, what do people say these days? God forbid I should be out of touch."

"I'm sorry, Boo." Mackie wants to take back her words. The last thing she wants is to alienate Boo, one of the most accepting people she knows, regardless of her terminology. " I guess the best thing to do is not assign any kind of name. But if you have to say something, gay works." Mackie kisses her aunt on the forehead. "Gay works for everyone."

———»《●》«———

When Sully comes by late that evening Mackie is sitting on the front porch reading. The squeak of the glider has been replaced by the sound of crickets and the croak of frogs talking down in the marsh. Coming up the walk he says, "Hey lady, mind if I join you?"

Putting down the book she walks over and opens the screen door. "Get in here," she says, reaching out to him. He stands two steps down from the door and she is momentarily taller than he is but soon finds herself in his arms, head tucked under his chin. "Working late tonight, huh?"

"There was a bad car accident out on Justice Manor Road. Two kids are dead. Not even out of high school. I swear I never get used to it. Every fucking year."

Mackie hears the tension in his voice. Smudges of gray underline his eyes and she wants nothing more than to make it better for him.

"The airbags saved the driver and the kid in the front, but the two kids in back weren't even wearing their belts."

"I'm so sorry, Sully," she says, hugging him.

"Thanks," he says softly and they just stand together letting the silence build. "Damned stupid kids think they're immortal. Thank God I never had any."

"It's frightening how much you can worry about them and yet have no control—especially when they're teenagers. But I can't imagine not having a family." Mackie sighs, "Don't you worry about leaving nothing of yourself behind, that at the end of the day all there is is you?"

Sully shrugs, "I don't think about it," he says dismissing it. "What are you doing sitting out here, anyway? It's cold."

"I'm layered, she says, pulling at the neck of her jersey, " Turtleneck, two sweaters, jeans, and the ever popular flannel jammies underneath it all."

"Well, that does sound promising."

But Mackie hears the sadness in his heart and not the banter. "How about some cocoa?"

"Can you lace it with brandy?"

"Of course."

"Don't suppose you can hold the chocolate, the milk and the mug and serve it in a snifter?"

"You've got it, mister."

Sully goes over and lights the fire while Mackie goes into the kitchen to get her cocoa and Sully's snifter of brandy .

"Mind if I put some music on?" he calls to her.

"Not at all. The cd's are in that basket by the bookcase. I'm not sure you're going find anything you like, though."

When she comes back into the room she hears Ray Charles singing, I Wonder Who's Kissing Her Now. She hands Sully his glass and without taking a sip, he puts it down on the coffee table, grabs her hand and takes her mug. Putting it down beside his glass he pulls her into his arms he starts to slow dance. At first she feels awkward but soon she finds herself moving with him. The music transports Mackie to another place and another time. Sully holds her so close that they begin to move as one. She doesn't quite know how he manages to turn off the one lamp that was burning, leaving them in firelight. They dance, barely moving, not speaking. Mackie measures their breathing and clings to him as if he is her life raft, afraid to need anyone so much, knowing the consequences. But for tonight, for this moment in time, she loves everything about him. She loves this night. She loves his smell, the geography of his body. She loves his sadness. Maybe his sadness is what she loves most of all.

Chapter 30

"Hey, Hon—you still need to work? If so, I've got the primo job for you."

The voice comes over the phone and at first Mackie has no idea who it is talking and what they could possibly want. She has been up to her armpits in Clorox. On some kind of manic clean up mission she has disinfected every surface in the house.

"Excuse me—who is this?

"Sorry Hon, it's Al—from the bar. "You did say that you're a decorator, a designer?"

"Al? Al Fletcher?"

"None other."

Mackie listens to the voice she knows so well from Turner's. She pictures Al's extravagant earrings and her perfectly manicured nails, sees her flamboyant mop of hair and feels her confidence through the phone.

Peeling off her disposable gloves, she waves the fumes away. "Al, I think I said that I know how to hang wallpaper—and maybe I've decorated a few houses in my time."

"Well, that should work, don't you think, Hon?"

"Work?" Mackie says flustered.

"Time to join the real world."

Mackie hears a soft chuckle.

"Welcome to the working class, Mrs. Kinsella."

"I'm not sure I'm ready. I'm not ready. Maybe I could be ready? Just what kind of job are you talking about anyway, Al?"

"The kind I'm sure you can do before lunch with one hand tied behind your back. Just jump in, Hon. This one is gonna be a gimme."

"What is it, Al?" Mackie pleads, her brain going a mile a minute.

"Just a kid's bedroom. You had kids, didn't you?"

Mackie feels her heart slow. Kids are not scary.

"Are you there, Mackie?"

"Do you know anything else? Is it for a girl or boy? Or is there more than one? How old?"

"Just a little girl. And you had two of those, didn't you, Hon? How hard can it be? I'm thinking Barbie, fairy princess, lots of pink and lavender—maybe some of those little ponies and castles?"

"What?"

"Unless you think Wonder Woman would work?"

Mackie's mind is spinning. When she thinks of little girls, she envisions apple greens, soft pinks, patchwork quilts.

For years Emma and Eileen shared a room, two wildly different personalities trapped in ten by fourteen spaces. One time Emma was into all things exotic while Eileen was into minimalism favoring all things earthy. Mackie, working on a budget, painted the whole room neutral ivory. Going to several import-export stores netted her a fuchsia parasol and a futon. Suspending the parasol upside down from Emma's corner of the room, she placed the futon under it and set up a shoji screen to act as a divider for the girls. On Eileen's side she found a sisal rug, put Eileen's mattress right on the floor and accented it only with cotton pillows in various shades of cream.

Decorating rooms was one of the things that Mackie had enjoyed most about moving. Having a fresh canvas to bring to life, new spaces to define. Doing it for someone else might be fun. Heck it might even be rewarding.

"How did you find out about the job, Al?" Mackie asks.

"Oh, you know how it is here, Hon, everyone talks. Sometimes I feel like a regular clearing house. I guess I should start charging a finder's fee or something." Al chuckles. "I heard about his one from Rod Varney. He does most of the residential painting and stuff around here. But it seems he's booked through September or October and Dr. Joy wants this done for his daughter as a birthday surprise. And I guess that's all of a few weeks away."

"Did you say, Dr. Joy?" Mackie asks.

"Yep. You know him?" Al asks.

"I do, Mackie says, warming at the memory of her last encounter with him on the beach. "And I've seen his daughter. He's smitten with her for sure, but then who wouldn't be. She's just adorable."

"Well," Al says, "From what I hear he's been raising her alone all her life. Seems like Mama wasn't ready to have a kid." Al snorts, "Just imagine, not ready for a kid—like whoever is?"

"Probably why he spoils her to death."

"How do you know about his wife, Al?"

"Not a wife, Mackie. He never married her. She was young, some kind of braniac doing a fellowship or something at Radcliffe or one of those other chichi schools in Boston. I take it that Dr. Joy was the respected guest 'lecturer' when they met." Al imbues the word with anything but respect.

"God, Al—did you get a dossier on the man or what?" Mackie asks.

"People love to divulge secrets to their local bartender, Mackie. It's one of the perks and curses of the job. Dr. Joy's man, Herbie, and a total sweetie he is, is as much of a talker as the doctor apparently isn't."

Mackie is absorbing the information and trying to imagine that she will become a professional anything in the near future.

"I think you should give him a call. Or better yet, just go on out there and talk to the man."

"Thanks, Al. I'll think about it. And thanks for thinking of me." Mackie hangs up the phone and thinks, good lord what am I getting into?

Chapter 31

Mackie is elated as she drives up to Turner's Tavern to share her good news with Al. She can hear the muffled sounds of laughter from the bar as she walks down the corridor. It is a balmy Saturday evening and the restaurant is full of summer people dining on the fresh catch. Mackie looks into the warmly lit room and smiles. It was not long ago that she felt out of place here, but now she feels entitled. She is now two. She has Sully. They are surely a duo, although she does not completely think of them as a couple yet.

To her surprise it is not Al who holds court tonight behind the bar, but Fitzy. The usual coterie of townies anchor their places and Fitzy looks polished, almost dignified with his starched white shirt and creased black trousers in lieu of his normal off–duty jeans and vintage shirts. "What are you doing here, Fitzy?"

"It's my new gig," Mackie. "I've retired from the department. I'm getting too damned old to eat the firehouse chili, my tummy can't take it anymore." He grins widely and rubs his sizable belly. "I'm just going to take over two shifts here for Al and spend the rest of my time fishing. That and keeping my missus happy, which in her case means shopping."

"Wonderful, Fitzy."

"And now, what can I get for you?" he says, polishing a place on the bar in front of her and putting down a napkin.

"Actually, Fitzy, I was looking for Al. I wanted to talk to her—share some news."

"Well, why don't you just run by her place. I'm sure she's home. She was pretty psyched about having time off for a change. You know where she lives?"

Mackie shakes her head, "No."

"Out off Three Mile Road—hellish little driveway too, go right past if you blink. Look for the Big Bird mailbox, bright yellow with feathers."

"Thanks, Fitzy." Mackie thinks how appropriate it is for Al to have a ridiculous mailbox.

"No problemo. You just make sure to tell her just how fine I look here." A collective groan goes up and Mackie smiles, waves and leaves the bar.

⸺◦⟨◉⟩◦⸺

"I hope it's okay that I came by without calling," Mackie says when Al opens the door and quickly realizes that she most definitely should have called. Al's eyes are swollen with tears and she was obviously not expecting company.

"Welcome to Casa Chaos!" Al says bravely, sweeping Mackie into the entry. Mackie trips over a pile of shoes that apparently belong to giants. High top canvas and sandals mixed in with deck shoes. Al pulls her past a room where five or six kids are playing pool and swigging soft drinks. Al rolls her eyes. "Formerly known as my living room," she says, motioning with her thumb. "I'm sorry for the state of the house, but it's the only way I can keep tabs on my kids. Gotta make 'em want to hang out here instead of somewhere else. This way I get to know their friends, tattoos, warts and all."

They travel down a hallway and end up in a kitchen. The phone rings and Al ignores it. "Definitely not for me. Probably one of Bumper's many girlfriends." The doorbell rings and there is the sound of several more kids arriving. "I live in occupied territory," Al says, pulling out a chair and motioning for Mackie to sit down.

"Bumper?"

"Bumper is my seventeen year old, he of the pierced eyebrow. It's just amazing what girls find appealing these days." Without asking, Al takes out two flutes from the cabinet, goes to the refrigerator and pulls out a bottle of Crystal Roederer champagne. She deftly opens it and pours, holding it up to the light, handing Mackie a glass and taking one herself. "When things look bleakest, celebrate life." She sips it and sighs. "This is a little bit of heaven—add a chicken lobster with some drawn butter and I'm there."

Mackie sips and nods her head in agreement. "It's wonderful, Al."

"Bumper's real name is Bradley, but he was a human bowling ball as a baby and unfortunately the nickname stuck."

Mackie smiles. "We called my youngest 'Leenie-beanie-scaloppini', but lucky for her the name didn't stick. Ironically, her sister, Emma became a chef." Mackie sips her wine.

"Champagne is always such a treat." And then, feeling

awkward about dropping in, she apologizes.

"Don't be silly. And don't worry about the tears," Al says. "For some reason today, everything seems like a crisis. Can you believe I got called into the principlal's office today?" Al takes another sip, "Julia, my youngest, is going to have to go for counseling—and me with her."

Mackie frowns. "How old is she, Al, and what happened?"

"She's ten. And, according to the principal and several eye-witness accounts, she's been sexually harassing one of the boys in her class."

"You've got to be kidding!" Mackie says. "At ten?" Her face arranges itself into a mask of incredulity.

"Seems she was taunting him on the playground. And ultimately she gave him a wedgie."

Mackie can't help it when she erupts into laughter. "A wedgie???"

"You know, you grab the back of the underwear and pull? I'm afraid growing up with a houseful of older brothers has made Julia a bit aggressive."

"But surely you can't be serious about them putting her on suspension for that?"

"The school has a zero tolerance policy. One of the sixth graders was suspended for bringing a baby aspirin to school."

"Good grief," Mackie says. "I'm awfully glad my kids are grown now. I think it's a lot tougher raising them these days. And I can't even imagine doing it alone the way you are, Al."

"Some days are tougher than others." Al smiles. "Today was a pisser. But never mind—things are getting better already." She motions to a chair, "Sit down, Mackie. What brings you here, anyway?"

"I stopped by the tavern to thank you for the lead on the job for Dr. Joy."

Al beams, "You got it?"

Mackie nods and lifts her glass. Al takes hers and clinks it against Mackie's. "Congrats, Hon! Well done."

"I can't believe it was so easy, Al. I'm going to take Daly out so that I can get to know her. She's going to be with her mother for a week and when she gets home the room will be done. Graham has no idea what Daly might like and he's pretty much given me carte blanche to do whatever I think will suit her."

"Well, that all sounds good." Al tops up Mackie's glass and her own. "It's a beginning. I'm proud of you, Hon! Just imagine— your own little business!"

"I don't think it's a business yet, Al. I haven't even started the room." But Mackie is touched and hopeful all the same.

"You should get some business cards made up, Mackie. What are you going to call yourself?"

"I have no idea, Al. I'm not even sure it will work out."

"Of course it will. You've just gotta believe in it, Hon. Believe in yourself."

"Thanks, Al."

"For what?"

"Being a friend." Mackie means it. "It's been a long time since I've had a new friend."

"What about Sully?" Al raises her eyebrows.

Mackie grins widely and feels the flush of heat. "I'm not exactly sure I'd call him a 'friend'. Actually—" Mackie stammers, "I'm not sure what I'd call him."

Al studies Mackie's face and then says deliberately, "Are you getting involved, Mackie? I mean, romantically?"

"I'm not sure," Mackie says. "I just mean—I'm not sure what he means to me. This whole thing is new. I only ever had Richard."

"I don't mean to meddle, Hon," Al says. "It's just that I've known Sully for a long time. His ex-wife did quite a number on him and I never want to see something like that happen again. I'd never want to see him hurt that way."

Mackie frowns, "What happened, Al?"

"Olivia Cabot happened."

Mackie raises her eyebrows but waits for Al to continue.

"She was summer folk. Rented Sur Mer, that rambling white elephant of a Victorian out on Third Cliff. You could say that she sort of took the town and the townies, especially Sully by storm."

Al, the ever-attentive bartender fills Mackie's glass once again and Mackie asks, "What did she look like Al? When was this anyway? Sully told me that he had been married but it was pretty obvious that he didn't want to talk about it."

"Sully's like that, Mackie. Not much for history. He's actually kind of child-like in that way. Just takes life one day at a time. And it's been a long time since the divorce." Al pours what's left of the bottle into her glass and continues. "Liv was striking, a raven-haired Boston Brahmin. Her eyes were so pale you could almost see through them. It was downright spooky. And her skin was flawless, never went outside without one of those oversized straw hats and huge sunglasses." Al shakes her head, remembering.

— 194 —

"She arrived just before the fireworks on the fourth of July—must have been ten years ago now maybe even eleven? Amazing how fast time goes."

"Really?" Mackie wonders if Sully has been alone since then. She can't imagine a man as physical as Sully not being with someone in all that time—but then why is she presuming that there's been no one else? It shocks her to realize that she knows almost nothing about him.

"Liv was sophisticated, Mackie. Really out of Sully's league. Kind of Coquille St. Jacques to his clam chowder if you get my drift."

"I'm beginning to."

"She walked with one of those fancy canes—I think it had a duck's head on it or something, phony as a three-dollar bill if you ask me. Story was she had fallen off a horse when she was about eighteen and the limp was a souvenir."

Mackie is trying to picture her, trying to imagine Sully smitten with such an exotic sounding creature.

"They moved into her Beacon Hill townhouse after Labor Day and were married by Thanksgiving."

"Wow," is all that Mackie can say.

"She owned a gallery—or I should say, her family did. They turned it over to Liv as sort of a wedding gift. I think she saw Sully as the next Richard Avedon."

Mackie says, "Not at all how Sully saw himself, I take it?"

"Yep. Liv surrounded herself with beautiful people and I think she saw Sully becoming part of that life. But he hated it. He missed the solitude of the beach—the whole landscape of it."

Mackie tries to imagine Sully in the city, being led

around, urged to be something he clearly wasn't.

"It didn't take Sully long to figure out they were in trouble."

"Didn't he love her?" Mackie asks.

"I think she was more of an addiction," Al says. "And as it turned out she was addicted. Some kind of prescription drugs she'd been getting for years and took with Scotch chasers."

"Wow, dangerous combo."

"Sully started drinking pretty heavily himself to keep up with her."

Mackie raises an eyebrow.

"I think he was hitting the bottle so he wouldn't hit her. She'd become awfully spiteful."

Mackie sighs, hurting for him.

"He came back here after a New Year's Eve party that had gone particularly bad. He only hinted at what had gone on, but apparently some harder core drugs were involved and some—" Al takes a sip of her Champagne and continues, "kinkiness?"

Mackie does not want to know.

"He'd stopped calling her Liv and started calling her Livid. By April the marriage was over."

"Thank you for telling me. It helps me to know a little bit more about him."

"Let's just say he's a work in progress," Al says. "It's taken him a long time to get over her and not all his scars are visible."

Mackie tries to take in the information and give something back to Al at the same time.

"I do care for him, Al. But I'm just not sure if there's

a future there. Believe it or not, I'm kind of a neophyte. A damned old one to be sure, but—"

"Aha." It's Al's turn to grin. "Are you telling me that you're in lust?"

Mackie blushes furiously.

"Of course," Al says. "I should have known. Sully is more than a little attractive."

"Did you ever date him, Al?"

"Nah. That would be almost incestuous. He's more of a brother to me, if you know what I mean."

"I think so. I've had some people like that in my life too."

"Then you know the feeling."

Mackie nods.

"I'd be capable of hurting anyone who hurt him."

"Listen, Al, I was married to Richard for nearly three decades. He was my best friend, my husband, and my lover. We grew up together—passion changed to something else. I think I lost track of where I ended and he began."

Al says, "I'm afraid that's why I married three times. Just that rush—you know?"

Mackie blushes and says, "I do now." She gets up and gives Al a hug, "I'll be careful, Al. Thanks for the champagne—and the referral."

"You're most welcome."

Mackie pauses at the threshold of the door. "You do care for him."

Al nods and runs her fingers through her tangle of curls. "Yes, I do."

They embrace as Mackie gets ready to leave. It feels so good to have a friend here, albeit one who cares more about

Sully than about her.

"Ignore the lecture, Hon."

"Thanks for talking to me, Al. And thanks for the wisdom."

"Don't kid yourself, kiddo, free advice is usually worth about what you pay for it."

Chapter 32

June arrives with a burst of sunshine and temperatures that fool everyone into thinking that it's true summer. Mackie drives out to pick Daly up on a Wednesday morning, armed with a picnic basket and a canvas bag full of books. Mackie, slimmer than she's been in years and wearing cropped linen pants, sandals and a white t-shirt, has pulled her hair into a ponytail. She's planned an excursion to the old spur track, a place hidden deep in Indian Woods. She remembers going there often as a child and feeling at once isolated and cosseted.

She rings the bell to the main house and is surprised when Graham opens the door.

"Well, good morning," Mary Katherine. "I'm afraid that Daly is just out in the barn with Herbie. French today—at least I think it is. She's been bonjouring and merciing me all during breakfast." He looks at his watch. "Do you mind terribly waiting until her lesson is over?"

"Not at all," Mackie says looking around the foyer and up a staircase past a gallery of artwork to an open hallway. The main house is every bit as elegant as Graham's suite of offices. Mackie can see a room dappled with sunlight straight ahead. It is furnished comfortably in muted plaids, the walls painted a soft, café au lait color. French doors are opened out to a patio and Graham beckons her to follow him there.

"We can sit on the terrace. It's such an amazing morning." He covers the space in several long strides and stacking dishes and mugs and folding a newspaper, he says, "Pardon the mess. Have a seat. Daly should be here in a few minutes."

Mackie sits, "You're not working today?"

"Not until this evening. Seems everyone is keeping very well indeed." And he looks her over from head to toe. "Present company included. You look good Mary Katherine. Content."

"Thank you." And she wonders if it shows. She'd once had a business associate of Richard's whisper in her ear that she looked 'freshly fucked'. She had been horrified at the time and had he not managed an engaging smile and had she not known that he spoke the truth, she might have slapped him. He was, of course, a rogue, the kind who played on being outrageous. It was a Christmas party—or a going away party, in Chicago, or was it New York?

"Have you managed to quit the fags?"

"Excuse me?"

"The cigarettes."

"Yes. Finally," Mackie says and adds, "Finally once again that is. It was a whole lot easier this time. But then I was a whole lot younger the first time."

"Weren't we all?" And she sees a gleam in his eye, the hint of a smile.

Daly erupts onto the terrace. She is three and a half feet

tall and forty pounds of boundless energy followed by a two hundred and fifty pound behemoth of a man called Herbie. It is apparent who is in charge.

"Daddy!" she says breathlessly. "Herbie says I am his best student."

Behind her, Herbie stifles a smile and nods somewhat solemnly, hands clasped behind his back.

"And, Daly, might that have anything to do with the fact that you are Herbie's only student?"

Herbie puts his finger to his lips in the universal gesture for silence and Graham lowers his eyes to his daughter's and says, "Tres bien, mon petite chou-chou."

"I am not your little cabbage!" Daly giggles.

Mackie wants Graham to smile and he doesn't. Mackie wants him to reach out and take Daly in his arms, or kiss her on her forehead, or at the very least touch her. And he doesn't.

"Your French improves every day, Daly."

"Merci, Papa." Daly puts the emphasis on the second syllable and Mackie feels witness to a sacred bond. Although they don't touch, she knows somehow that they are connected. The love in his eyes is so apparent that it is almost painful. And, after all, who is she to judge?

"Say hello to Mrs. Kinsella, Daly," Graham says. And obediently the small head turns, flaxen hair gleaming. Mackie can smell fruit coming off the child and thinks, aha one of those watermelon shampoos or strawberry aloe, something that would never sting the eyes. She had used ivory soap herself as a child and her own girls had grown up with Breck and when they got old enough to buy their own, they spent exorbitant amounts on whatever the latest musky or salon-induced product was.

"Bonjour, hello." A tiny curtsy and Mackie is in love.

Graham then gestures to Herbie and makes the introduction. "Mary Katherine Kinsella, this is Herbert, Daly's teacher, our cook, our good friend. Without him we would be adrift, drowning in our own detritus. Herbert, this is Mary Katherine, a new friend. She is going to spend some time with Daly."

Herbie says hello and nods to Graham and to Mackie in turn. "It is very nice to meet you Mrs. Kinsella. Take care with the little one."

"I will. It's nice to meet you, Herb—and she stutters on the ending.

"Herb will do." He hands a book to Daly and says, "For tomorrow you do the three pages." She looks up solemnly at Herbie and he says, " You did well today, Daly. Have a wonderful time with your new friend, Mrs. Kinsella."

<hr />

And they did have a most wonderful time. They shared their picnic, Mackie pointing out some wildflowers and warning Daly about poison oak. She read several stories to her and asked her what were her favorite things in the world to see and do; what did she play, what colors did she like. By the time she was delivering Daly home she had garnered a good idea of what to do to transform Daly's room.

BOO

"She's got her own little business going, Buddy." Boo sits folding laundry and sipping her Jim Beam. She shakes out a tee shirt, lays it flat and proceeds to smooth away imaginary wrinkles.

"It's called—get this—*Go To Your Room.*" Boo chuckles.

"Ain't that a kick? She's decorating, hanging paper and even making furniture for kids rooms."

She runs fragile hands across the shoulders, folds one sleeve in and then the other, folds bottom to top, lifts it to her face and inhales. "I miss you like crazy, Old Fool."

She adds the shirt to a stack of half a dozen other shirts and jockey shorts and walks to the chest of drawers that was a wedding gift from her parents. It is a piece that she has treasured and polished more times than she can remember. It is the repository of her memories.

"She got business cards printed up and everything. Seems she did up that bedroom for the doctor who ain't a homo's daughter."

Boo pulls out the drawer, puts the underwear in and closes it. Pausing to open the next one down, she pulls out one of Buddy's old uniform shirts. This one has never been laundered and still bears sweat stains under the arms, across the collar, in the center of the back. The place that Boo so often found comfort. She loves laying her head against that place where she could feel him even when he was turned away. She loves his smell. Imagines that it is still there after all these years.

"S'cuse me—gay! The word is gay." Boo frowns. "God

forbid I'm politically incorrect. But, Buddy—I miss the days when men were men—if you get my drift."

Boo puts the shirt on the bed and lifts a small package, tissue wrapped and pristine. It is tied with a length of white satin ribbon that was cut from Boo's wedding dress. She thinks she might stop breathing altogether. Taking the package she sits heavily on the bed and unties the bow. Unfolding the tissue, Boo looks upon a small layette; a pair of pale, yellow booties, several nightgowns with drawstrings at the bottom and little cuffs at the sleeves, the crocheted afghan, soft, cotton diapers, a whimsical set of diaper pins shaped like ducks that bring tears to Boo's eyes and yet bring a smile. Dreams, she thinks. Putting everything back, folding tissue, smoothing and retying the ribbon, Boo takes a deep breath. Closing the drawer, she stands straight and mumbles a prayer. Just breathe she thinks. Just keep on breathing.

"So, Old Fool, seems our girl built this kind of miniature house for this child. The safest place in the world—right in Daly's bedroom."

She closes the drawer. "Well, it is her name, her momma is Korean. It means something in that country. Something good I'm sure, something strong."

Boo sips and says, "She's a wonder," and adds, "Not Daly, although she might be, I'm talking about our girl."

"Mackie hung the wallpaper all by herself. It's like a perfect garden, Buddy, picket fence and all. Beautiful flowers that never die, butterflies perching on tree branches. I think she even hand-painted some fairies here and there to surprise the child. It's wonderful. All kinds of bright colors and fluttery things."

Boo is tired. "It's like a doll house only little girl-sized," Boo says. "There are windows and doors and a little staircase that Daly climbs to her bed. Oh, and get this, Buddy, there's even a doorbell that actually rings! Underneath the house is a place for her babies and books and her entire little world."

"I'm so damned proud of her, Buddy. She must have been learning some big lessons all those years away from us."

"And guess what? I'm her first stock-holder." Yes, Old Fool. Can you believe it? She took that money we got for all the junk around here to start up her new life."

Putting the shirt back, she sighs. "I am the C.F.O."

She is tired when she turns off the light and walks wearily to their room. "Ain't it a grand thing, Buddy? Imagine what we've done for her." Pulling back the quilt, she doesn't bother to change into nightclothes. Weary. She climbs into bed and garners just enough energy to turn off the bedside lamp.

"It's Chief Financial Officer, Old Fool," she says before she falls into the dent that Buddy left.

Chapter 33

"You realize of course that Daly is in love with you?"

Graham is at her door. Standing outside on the top porch step where Sully stood not long before. Light filters through the screen. Mackie wipes sleep from the corners of her eyes, runs her tongue across her teeth, and pulls her robe tighter around her waist as she opens the screen door and asks, "Is it Sunday yet?"

Suddenly he presents her with a bag of Dunkin' Donuts and a thick, Sunday newspaper. "All day I believe." And stepping onto the porch he says, "And I am footloose, fancy free and at your service."

Opening the waxed paper bag and peering in, Mackie says, "You already rewarded me quite handsomely for my effort. Pulling out a honey-dipped donut she takes a bite, chews it, swallows and says, " Is this on the infamous 'Dr. Joy's Weight Loss and Sobriety Plan?'"

Taking her hand and lifting it to his own mouth, he looks at the donut, takes a bite. "Mm, he says, "If it isn't, it bloody well should be."

Mackie feels her perceptions of Graham shift. She

surveys the doctor. He is dressed down in khakis and a well-worn sweatshirt. He's taller than she remembers him being and smells different, salty. He looks amazingly younger since he's abandoned his glasses and although he still doesn't smile, he seems somehow more content. Thrusting the donut toward him, she asks, "More?"

He declines but says, " Have you any coffee?"

"Of course. Come on inside."

After their second cup, Mackie says, "I'm so happy that Daly likes her room. I want to thank you for trusting me. I had no business letting you think I was a decorator."

"Why do you always try to categorize yourself, Mary Katherine? It's obvious that you can do whatever you choose."

Mackie hears him and yet can't quite figure out what it is that he is saying. "I'm not sure what you mean?" she says clearing their coffee mugs and turning on the hot water, rinsing them longer than necessary at the sink.

"You seem to question not only what you do, but how you feel, what you should think—"

Mackie shrugs, "And you, Graham, no self-doubts—no agonizing?"

"Oh, I've given all that up."

Mackie looks in his eyes, clear, blue and amazingly intelligent.

He nods. "I'm afraid it's true."

Mackie smiles.

"Bloody waste of time. You know of course that no one is ever really concerned about what someone else is wearing, or thinking, or saying for that matter."

"Really?"

"Yes. Tell me what anyone else was wearing at the last party you attended. Tell me who said what at that little local bar—Turner's Tavern?"

Mackie tries to remember and comes up blank. There is a great silence and Graham bestows one of his rare smiles.

"I think I've spent my whole life worrying and wondering what people think of me. I saw myself and my actions reflected in Richard's eyes for so many years, I'm not sure I ever stop to think of how I see myself."

Graham stands up and says, "Well, perhaps the time has come for you to start pleasing yourself and let the rest of the world take its own course?"

Mackie nods, liking the doctor, liking his philosophy on life and wondering just how he came to be so self-assured. "Do you mind if I ask you something personal?" Mackie says.

"By all means, if you don't mind if I find it impossible to answer."

"Well, it's clearly none of my business, but I was just wondering what happened between you and Daly's mother."

She sees a deep intake of breath, thinks he won't answer and then he says, "Cho, Daly's mother, had a definite agenda and a baby was not part of it. She simply couldn't see herself as a mother."

Mackie waits for more, stares at him, looking for the slightest hint of emotion; anger, sorrow, disappointment, but his face is a mask.

"I, on the other hand, thought a child was a splendid addition to what had otherwise been a fairly selfish existence. I've never regretted having her for one second. In a world that sometimes seems randomly assembled, Daly makes perfect sense."

Mackie nods in agreement. She has this feeling of completeness since finding out about Emma's baby. The fact that she will soon be grandmother seems to make everything that has come before and everything that might come after, right. "I'm learning that, Graham. But it seems that I'm a slow learner."

"Surely there's no problem in that."

"Does Daly's mother see her often?"

"Cho plays an active part in Daly's life. While we are not a 'traditional' family, Daly gets everything she needs—at least at this point in time. We keep the negotiations open."

"Thank you," Mackie says, "I shouldn't have asked."

"You were curious, no?" Graham says.

"Well, yes," Mackie says, "But I am sorry. Your personal life is just that."

"Not to worry. I'm not a stupid man. I know there's a lot of speculation about my circumstances. Shoreham is a small town and idle chat and speculation are the order of the day."

Mackie blushes, thinking of Boo's comments and as if he reads her mind, Graham says, "While Herbie does prefer same-sex liaisons, I am hopelessly heterosexual."

"Of course you are," Mackie blurts out. "Not that it matters, of course." She feels as if she has embarked on a path to conversational hell but continues to babble. "One's sexual orientation—" When the hell did she turn British? She sounds like Margaret Thatcher.

The corners of Graham's lips curve up into a smile that so inclusive, so beatific that it transforms his face.

Mackie is finally, blessedly rendered speechless.

Chapter 34

"Hello Beauty."

Mackie pours her third cup of coffee of the morning and cradles the phone to her ear, loving his voice. She feels the now familiar surge of desire. She thinks that he should sell his voice for commercial purposes. Voice-overs. Not Barry White and yet not quite Donald Sutherland—but the kind of voice that sends one to a different place.

"Sully." Just the word seems sensual. She walks out to the porch and asks, "What's up?"

"Do you want the graphic description or do you want to know what I'm doing?"

Smiling, she decides to ignore the banter. "Would you like to meet for breakfast someplace? I'm staging models at Sonoma Cove, and I've got to go into Boston this afternoon to look at fabric, but I have a couple of hours now."

"Sonoma Cove?" Sully asks. "Are those the ones the King Brothers are doing out on the North River?"

"The same. Ironic isn't it—a little bit of California wine country right here in New England."

"What the heck is 'staging' anyway?"

"I just try to create a little scenario for them. A plant here, a picture there, a little bit of paint. A little bit of set design and voila!"

"Wow, I'm impressed, Mackie. I didn't realize you had such hidden talents."

"Well, there's a lot you don't know about me, yet. I'm a woman of many skills."

"I miss you, career-girl. I think I like you better when you're at loose ends."

She chuckles softly; "And I think I like me better now, Aemon Xavier Sullivan. Here I am, lurching toward maturity just before I'm eligible for my AARP card."

There is a silence and then, "Why don't you come over here then, I'll scramble us something and then you can be on your way. I'm shooting out at Bailey's Shipyard but they aren't expecting me until after noon anyway."

"Okay. Give me twenty minutes to shower and change and I'll be there."

"I'll be waiting."

<hr>

Mackie knows the way to Sully's by Braille. Traversing the road between their houses for weeks, daylight and midnight, she has yet to define their relationship and she has yet to feel the comfort that she felt for so many years with Richard, who just seemed right. Always there, always the perfect fit. Sometimes after she and Sully make love she feels the urgent need to flee. His little house seems alien. Nothing of her past is there. Nothing of her present either. It is his, more totally than Mackie can explain. And in Sully there seems no past and no future. There are no footprints of life. No family photos. No familiar stains or odors. There is just him.

She is a woman on a mission, appropriating time much as Richard must have done for so many years. Her briefcase (a sweet re-gifting and reach out from Eileen, is the one that Richard and Mackie presented her with upon her graduation from UCLA Law School.) The leather now burnished, the shoulder strap softly comfortable, it occupies the passenger seat beside her. She and Eileen now manage good phone conversations. Ironically they seem to connect more over the phone than they have ever managed face to face.

Mackie has traded her Cartier watch for a series of Swatches that she chooses by her mood of the day. She finds them whimsical, but practical and worries that they are somehow addictive. She owns eight of them but has not been gutsy enough to wear the 'Octopussy' model yet with its serpentine wrap-around, faux-gold band. As she glances down at her 'Black Sheep Too' version with its fluffy, cartoon sheep frolicking across the face and the band she realizes that she is going to have to eat and run at Sully's.

Emma's weekly call came in right after she hung up with Sully and they talked for half an hour. Heading into her final trimester, Emma feels wonderful, energized and confident. Mackie will fly out a few weeks before Emma's due date and be there for the baby's birth. Emma wants her to decorate the nursery and Mackie is trying to figure out what she can do with a color palette of black and white, which Cisco and

Emma have chosen to stimulate the baby at her earliest possible moment. No frills or lace for Elena Katherine.

She is barely out of her car when Sully comes out, picnic basket in hand. The wind lifts his hair and Mackie looks at him as if he was a work of art. Oblivious to his bounty, still seemingly untouched by life, he says, "Hello, Beauty." Disarming her, he bends to first take her earlobe between his lips and follows that sweet gesture with a kiss. "I thought we could have a little breakfast picnic out on the jetty."

"Oh, Sully. I'm so sorry." His eyes turn steely ebony. "I'm afraid I only have time for a quick cup of coffee. Emma called and—" she looks down at her watch, "I'm afraid I'm running so far behind now."

She looks at him and sees a petulant look reminiscent of Richard when she was failing him once again in some undefined, miniscule way. And she wants to appease him. "Maybe we can have a latish dinner tonight?"

"I'll check my book."

"Sully?" The same part of her that wants to appease him wants him to stop acting like a child.

"Call me when you get back from the big city." He turns away, walks back to the house and enters, closing the door behind him.

Chapter 35

Laden with fabric samples, wallpaper books and catalogues, Mackie drives home from Boston. Her thoughts have been of Sully off and on all day. He seems resentful that work is taking her time. In fact, he seems to resent anything that interferes with them just being together, anything that worries her. And she has much on her mind these days.

It's not only Emma and Eileen now, but also baby Elena on the way. It's Walter and his aspirations, Francisco and his family, damn it, she even worries about Al now with her unruly brood. And the good doctor, although he seems competent and together, will he be able to give Daly all she needs? And mostly it's Boo. For Boo has become so much a part of her life that Mackie cannot begin to imagine what she'd do without her.

Cursing the commuter traffic and vowing to get herself another cell phone now that she has a legitimate job, Mackie pulls off the highway and finds a payphone in front of a convenience store. Punching in Sully's number she waits as it rings it's orchestrated four times and the machine picks up. "Sully here. You know the drill."

She waits for the beep and breathes into the phone, "It's me. I'm so sorry about this morning." Glancing at her watch she sighs and adds, "I'm crawling home. Please come by. I should be there by seven or so. I'll cook." And hesitating before hanging up the phone she whispers, "Love ya—and longs to hear the old familiar reply—me too."

Mackie gets home at six- thirty, kicks off her shoes, strips off her clothes and runs herself a steaming bath, adding some of the scented oils that Sully gave her. She closes her eyes and dozes off for a few minutes. Dressing carefully in a new sundress, Mackie watches as the clock marches past seven and then eight. Sully does not come by. And he doesn't call. When she remembers to check her answer phone, two calls are from Eileen and one is a hang-up, either a telemarketer or Boo, who often refuses to talk to her machine.

At quarter to nine, Mackie changes into sweats and calls Boo.

"Hi, Sweet Pea, whatcha up to?"

"Did you try to call me, Boo?"

"I don't think so, but now that you're talking to me, how about coming over here for a while. You've been scarcer than fish lips. I miss your face."

Mackie begs off. "I've been in Boston all day, Boo. And I'm still looking at a couple of hours of work tonight. I've got to be at the condos in the morning, but I can take an hour or so for lunch tomorrow. How about it?"

"I'm going to be working around the house tomorrow. I'm sanding down the dory so I can paint it. Figure if I fix it up maybe I can sell it what with summer here at all."

"Do you need money, Boo?" Mackie asks, alarmed that

Boo is selling the boat. Knowing Boo won't take the money from the garage sale back, she's opened a separate account and is adding a little to it each week. She wants to make sure that Boo doesn't ever do without.

"Nah, Sweet Pea, I'm just tired of looking at the damn thing. Figure I'll get it out of the yard and plant a garden there. One of those English cottagey looking ones with all the different flowers. Lots of colors and a little wild, you know the kind?"

"I do. I think that would be wonderful Boo, maybe I can help you with it?"

"Sure thing, Sweet Pea."

"Okay, it's a deal. Listen, why don't I pick us up a couple of lobster rolls at Anchors Aweigh and swing by your place around noon. We can talk about the garden then, okay?"

"Suit yourself," Boo says. "But are you sure you don't want to come over for a while now? Maybe play Scrabble or something?"

Mackie would rather chew glass. She wants to sulk. "Boo, I've got a few more phone calls to make and I'm going to climb into bed early." Part of her holds out hope that Sully will still show up but she's not about to call him again.

"Okay. Sweet dreams, Sweet Pea."

"Goodnight, Boo."

Mackie places the phone in its cradle, goes and pours herself a glass of wine and turns off the downstairs lights, climbing wearily up to bed. She opens the bedroom window, takes a deep breath of salty air, listens to the gentle roll of the ocean and picks up the phone to call Eileen.

"Hi, sweetheart." She misses her girls all the time. It

doesn't take more than the sound of their voices to warm her.

"Hiya, Mom. I just wanted to let you know that they're presenting an offer on the house tomorrow."

"Woohoo!" Mackie shouts into the phone, her spirits suddenly lifted.

"It's just an offer, Mom." Eileen's voice goes down an octave. " Is there somewhere I can fax the paperwork to you? A copy shop or something?"

"There's one in the office at the condos. I'll get the number for you. Hang on."

"Mom?"

"Yes?"

"Don't get your hopes up. The offer might not be what you're looking for."

"It'll be fine," Mackie says, confident. "Leenie?"

"Yes, Mom?"

"I'm going to accept it as long as it's in the ballpark. It's time to get on with it."

"Okay, Mom. I'll make sure you get the paperwork as soon as it's done."

"Thanks for all the help, kiddo. You are my girl."

"Am I, Mom?"

"Oh yes, don't you ever think otherwise. You are amazing, Leenie."

Mackie puts the phone down on the bed and rushes downstairs, grabs the Kings' business card and picks up the extension. She gives Eileen the number and talks for a few minutes about what's going on with her daughter. She hears that Walter has landed a national commercial for toothpaste and has started to write his first screenplay. Leenie tells her that she has made an appointment with her ob/gyn to discuss fertility drugs.

"You know that I couldn't have gotten through the last year without you, Leenie. You are so solid."

"Goodnight, Mom," Mackie hears the quiver in her voice.

"I love you so much, Leenie."

"I know."

And suddenly there doesn't seem anything more to say. Mackie hangs up, goes upstairs to hang up the other phone and says a silent prayer for egg and sperm.

Chapter 36

Mackie calls Sully in the morning, wanting to put an end to the silly impasse. Not waiting for his machine to pick up, she hangs up and calls his cell phone. He doesn't answer and frustrated, she still doesn't leave a message. Screw him she thinks, if he's going to behave like a spoiled child who needs him?

She makes her selections of paper and fabric for the first house at Sonoma Cove, choosing a really nautical theme of navy and crisp white with accents of yellow. It's the smallest of the models and in some ways more of a challenge with its open floor plan and just fifteen hundred square feet of space. She keeps the fabric simple, combining mattress ticking with white duck. She can picture Emma and Cisco moving in with baby Elena, although she knows they will never move east. Cisco has his business and his family. Nevertheless, Mackie decides to create a nursery for the tiny third bedroom. She'll use lots of white dotted Swiss for the curtains and dress a bassinette with pure white cotton. She likes thinking about the kind of people who might move into these houses and thinks that maybe she'll get her real estate license as a backup,

PATTY O'HARA

in case Go To Your Room doesn't work out.

At eleven-thirty, Mackie leaves to pick up lunch and spend some time with Boo. Pulling into the driveway, she sees that the dory is not looking much improved, although it's obvious that Boo has started to sand off the old paint. Mackie tries to remember what color it must have been, seeing now only a faded barn red stripe against peeling once white paint. "Boo?" she calls. And again, a little louder, "Boo!" When no one answers, Mackie decides she must be inside the house.

She climbs the steps, goes into the kitchen and calls again, "Boo?" Feeling tendrils of fear rising in her chest, she goes from room to room looking for her aunt. The house is stuffy; dust motes float around Mackie as she walks upstairs. She thinks maybe Boo has fallen and hurt herself again. Maybe she is unconscious. Or maybe she just went for a walk, Mackie thinks; trying to calm her breathing, slow her heartbeat.

She peeks into the bathroom, then goes into Boo's bedroom where she finds her aunt, face down on the floor. "Boo!" she screams. Mackie falls to her knees and shakes her Aunt's shoulders, "Can you hear me?" Realizing that Boo is not breathing, she flies to the telephone and dials 911. "She's not breathing!" Mackie gives the address, says we're upstairs," and drops the phone, going back to Boo. She tilts Boo's head, lifts her chin and checks again for breathing. Pinching Boo's nose and putting her own mouth over Boo's she gives her two breaths. Hoping she remembers CPR correctly, she puts the heel of one hand locked with the other over the center of Boo's chest and presses down fifteen times and then gives her another two breaths. She keeps up a constant chant of 'please God, oh please, oh please' as she presses and stops only to breathe for Boo. Time loses all parameters. She is willing her life into Boo with every thrust and Boo lies still, moving only to the pressure of Mackie's hands. A few times, she thinks that she feels Boo's breath, soft against her ear, thinks she feels a pulse, but she is afraid to stop.

At first she doesn't recognize the sirens as what they are, a sound so alien in Shoreham as to be almost unheard. Heavy footsteps, strong arms and steady voices lead Mackie away. "We've got her now."

Someone gives her a cup of water. The day becomes a blur. Boo being lifted onto a gurney, being carried downstairs and out the door. The sirens diminish into the night. Sully arrives at the house minutes later and bolts up the stairs. He folds Mackie into his arms. "She's going to be fine," he says. "Fine."

Mackie begins to shake uncontrollably. She remembers the feeling from childbirth, after delivery; teeth knocking together and arms and legs going into spasm. She can't stop trembling. "She was gone, Sully. I couldn't get her heart beat."

Chapter 37

Boo, under observation in the Cardiac Care Unit of South Shore Hospital, calls Mackie several times a day to report in. "Good morning Sweet Pea, I think I'm going to get sprung tomorrow. This place is no place for someone in my condition."

"Is that what the doctor's say, Boo? You're ready?"

"One heart doc says a little surgery, some kind of stint or stent something. Another one says wait and see. Take some pills, exercise and change my diet. The good doctor Joy says that it's really my decision to make. I'm fine. Going to do some rehab—not the Betty Ford kind—some program they have here at the hospital. Out-patient."

"Boo? Are you sure that's the right thing."

"Yep. You saved my life and I figure I should be good for another ten thousand miles or so. I'm not messing around with what I've got. Case closed, Sweet Pea."

"Okay then," Mackie is not going to argue with her aunt at this point. "I'm going to arrange for someone to stay with you for a while, though. Help out with cleaning and cooking and stuff."

"Waste of money, Sweet Pea. I can do everything myself but drive right now. Maybe you can be my chauffeur for a little while."

"Well, of course."

"You coming in today, Mackie?"

"Would you mind terribly if I skip today, Boo? It's the fourth of July—the anniversary of Richard's dying. I'm afraid I don't feel much like doing anything at all. I'd kind of like to be alone."

"No sweat, Sweet Pea. You just do whatever you need. I'll call you in the morning after the doc comes by. Let you know if they're going to let me go home."

"Okay, Boo. I'll talk to you in the morning. I love you."

"Of course you do."

———— ◦《◉》◦ ————

Sadness washes over Mackie in waves. She misses Emma and Eileen terribly on this anniversary of Richard's death. They sent a huge bouquet of flowers in the most cheerful mix and vivid colors, and both of them phoned to talk, but it all just makes her miss them more.

Heavy clouds threaten rain and low tide brings a sulfuric, hard-boiled egg smell wafting up from the beach, adding insult to Mackie's sense of injury. She wonders what she is doing living here, so far away from her children and grandchildren-to-be. She wants to blame Richard for all the moves that took them away again and again. Why couldn't they have stayed put, grown roots here instead of being gypsies? But of course, she had wanted to move too. She had been a partner, not always willing, but locked into it. Locked into Richard's career and all that entailed. Now the girls are settled, their roots in California, three thousand miles away.

Sully calls to check up on how Boo is doing and to ask her if she wants to go to the bonfire at Wade's Beach. She begs off and puts a moody disc in the player and decides to wallow. Melancholy seems the order of the day. She hasn't allowed herself to run through her repertoire of Richard memories in a long time.

They knew each other inside and out, or so she thought. But now there is this question that will never be answered, because whatever Richard did in those last years, and whatever his motivation might have been she will never know.

The music ends and Mackie dries her eyes, goes upstairs and changes into sweats and cross-trainers. She'll take a long walk on the beach. It's a lousy beach day which is perfect; the summer bums will be inside by their fires and the townies won't show up until it's time for the fireworks to start.

MACKIE

Richard paces the floor with Emma. They are both miserable and neither of them knows why. But because Emma can't talk, and no one has slept in two days, Richard and I decide that she is teething. He holds her in 'baby Barcalounger' arms, crooning.

Next comes a series of memories—snapshots in rapid fire: Emma and Eileen, three and one respectively, have fallen fast asleep, one on each end of the living room sofa. Richard sits between them, head bowed, obviously fast asleep and dreaming. I return from a yoga lesson envying their comfort with each other.

Richard is teaching Eileen how to ride without her training wheels.

Fast forward to the four of us playing tag football on the front lawn.

Four years later, we are, all four of us, flying east for my mother's burial. The girls are dressed in somber colors at the wake. Eileen refuses to go into the room with the open casket. We all approach the communion rail and hold our hands out to embrace the host. We are alien mourners.

We are back home and I am falling in love with Richard for the hundredth time, loving the way his two front teeth cross slightly in the middle, thinking his receding hairline makes him look sweet and vulnerable. I love the way he climaxes, shuddering to be inside me. Full, I thank god for my life and fall into a peaceful sleep.

Chapter 38

Having walked on the beach until she felt herself shivering and heard the beginning of the fireworks show, Mackie finds herself at home and lost at the same time. She knows she won't sleep and thinks she must call the good doc to make an appointment to talk. She needs a remedy for this loneliness.

"Graham?" Mackie asks, somewhat shaken by the fact that he has answered his own phone, until she realizes that she has called his home number and not the office.

"Yes?"

"This is Mackie Kinsella—Mary Katherine. I was wondering—"

"Are you all right?"

"I'm ok, thanks. I'm sorry, Graham, I called the wrong number. I'll phone your office in the morning. She figured that the service would pick up and she could leave a message. " I'll make an appointment."

"Are you not well?"

"Not at all. No, well that is—I'm well." She stammers, takes a deep breath and goes on. "I remember that you said before, once—that I could talk to you. And I so much want to talk to someone. Well, not just someone, actually—you. I was wondering if I could talk with you."

"Yes," he says and there is an excruciating silence.

"I'll phone the office and make an appointment, then. In the morning."

"Or you could simply talk to me now," he says.

Mackie feels sorrow and gratitude hold hands and rise up in her throat until she is unable to speak.

"Mary Katherine?"

She does not want to sob. Sobbing is such an ugly, desperate sound. But it renders her helpless as it comes, unbidden from the deepest part of her. She covers the mouthpiece with her hand, hoping that he cannot hear. She gulps, breathes, swallows and swallows again. "I'm so sorry. Thank you. I'm fine." And she drops the phone into its cradle as the fireworks rumble and illuminate the night sky.

She takes a shower and gets into pajamas before she calls Sully. "July is definitely not my favorite month, she says."

"I'm so sorry, Honey. Do you want me to come over now?"

"You're the sweetest thing in the world, Sully, but no. I'm having a cup of tea and I'm going to bed."

"Alone?"

"I'm sorry I've been so inaccessible, Sully. I'm just exhausted. Going back and forth to the hospital—everything. I just need to get through this. Do you understand?"

"I'm trying to, honey. Just do what you need to do. I just miss being with you."

"Can you meet me tomorrow at Turner's?

"Sure."

"Sully?"

"What?"

"I miss my girls."

"Of course you do."

"Sully?"

"What, Mackie?" He sounds distracted, like he wants to just get on with whatever it is he's waiting to do. Maybe head for that bonfire at the beach.

Mackie wants to explain that although being here is her choice, it's not without cost. She wants even more to think that Sully knows that.

"Mackie?" he repeats.

"Nothing. I'm sorry, Sully. I'll see you tomorrow. Good night." Her eyes brim with tears.

"Good night, Baby. Love ya."

But Mackie cannot sleep and she sits on the glider, which still squeaks despite Boo's directives to oil it. The rain, which threatened its presence all day, finally arrives after the fireworks end. It is beating a soft tattoo on the roof over Mackie's head. The air smells sweet, fecund. Mackie still agonizes over Elena's nursery, working and reworking the possibilities of black and white in her mind.

Giving up, she goes on to plan the second condo at Sonoma Cove. This one will be Tuscan, earthy—plump roosters loom in the back of her mind. And copper pots. The heart is the kitchen. It holds a professional Viking stove that has set Mackie's mind spinning. A retired couple will purchase this one. Having traveled the world, they will hone in on Shoreham, wanting the four seasons, wanting enough space to include their three grandchildren and those yet to come. She'll put bunk beds in one of the guest rooms and a trundle in another. Baskets and plants will help fill out the spaces and she'll find an old farm table for the dining room and set it with mismatched dishes and good linens.

She has lost track of the time when she sees headlights coming down the street and knows it must be Sully. But the car is wrong. And the shape is wrong. And it is Graham who is standing once again on the top step outside her porch door. She can't help but smile when she sees him.

"What are you doing here? What time is it anyway?" She unlatches the screen door, letting him in.

"I'm making a house call. Standard operating procedure for a British doc."

"Oh, Graham," Mackie says, you really shouldn't be doing this. She takes his wrist and reads his watch. "Good grief, it's after eleven."

"Apparently so."

"Who's watching Daly?"

"I enlisted Herbie. He seldom goes to bed before midnight."

"I certainly didn't mean for you to come running over here. It's not an emergency."

"Not to worry."

"Well, now that you're here, the least I can do is get you a cup of coffee, or some hot chocolate—or something?" Mackie walks into the house and bids him to follow.

"It's not necessary for you to get me anything at all."

Graham walks through the living room, looks around and says, "You have a lovely home here. Everything is welcoming, nicely done." Going into the dining room, he walks over to the piano and looks at the family photos that Mackie has selected and put in mismatched silver frames on top of the piano. "Your family?" Graham says.

"Yes," Mackie says.

"You must be proud."

"Thank you, I'm more than blessed. Are you sure I can't get you something to drink—or eat? Would you like a brandy, maybe?"

He shakes his head, no and sits down at the piano. "Herbie made stroganoff tonight, and as usual I overdid it." Opening the lid and fingering the keys, he asks, "Do you play?"

"No. It was my mother's. She was good—and she taught. She gave lessons here when I was a child. But I was hopeless at it."

He frowns and directs his attention entirely to the keys as he begins to play something classical. Mackie thinks perhaps it's Haydn, but she is not really that familiar with classical music.

"You play well," she says.

"Thank you." He segues into a Gershwin tune and handles that with equal ease. He pats the bench and says, "Come sit by me." She joins him, feeling awkward but expectant. "You said you wanted to talk?"

"Well, yes. I did." Nervous without really knowing why, she feels her pulse quicken. He starts playing Stardust, and Mackie relaxes, tries to formulate her questions. "Hoagie Carmichael?"

"Yes indeed. Do you like this one?"

"I do. I love it, actually. Do you have any other hidden talents, doctor?"

He stops playing and takes her hands in his just as he did in his office. It is an act of unexpected intimacy and it feels wonderful. She takes a deep breath and begins, "I damaged Boo," she says. And now her heart is at full gallop.

A crease appears between Graham's eyes, "How so?"

Through a fine mist of tears she begins, "Even though I know she wasn't breathing—wasn't responding—I think maybe I did the CPR the wrong way. I could hear a cracking—I broke her ribs. I had so much adrenalin pumping and I was so afraid she was going to die—like Richard."

He gives her hands a squeeze.

"You saved your aunt's life."

"Maybe." And unwittingly she continues. "Today is the anniversary of my husband's death. I guess it's just been weighing on me. I've always felt somehow responsible for Richard's death, you know. As if I should have known something was going on with him."

"How might you have known? Did he have symptoms? Had he been to the doctor?"

Mackie shakes her head. "He had his annual physicals of course, and he was health conscious. He was in the hospital when he went into cardiac arrest."

"Mary Katherine, people die. Sometimes there's nothing anyone can do."

Mackie nods, but she is not convinced at all. "It was after that I learned CPR, the girls and I. It felt like something we could do, something positive."

"And indeed it was. You did precisely the right thing. As for broken ribs, that is a most common occurrence. You kept your auntie alive long enough for the paramedics to arrive and use the defibrillator. She's going to be fine, thanks to your good sense and actions."

She hears him, lets his words sink in to find a corner of her pain. "It's just so terribly hard to see people you love hurt. And I was so completely helpless when Richard died. It was kind of like getting swamped by a tsunami." She takes a deep breath. "It's a good thing I didn't study medicine. I'd make a lousy doctor."

He nods and the corner of his mouth turns up.

"Thank you so much, Graham. I'm so sorry that I bothered you with this."

"You are never a bother." His eyes are quite striking, deep blue and surrounded by lots of crinkles. There is such a kindness about him. Breaking the spell, he gets up from the piano and says, "I've changed my mind about that coffee. Is it too late?"

"Not at all." She gets up and walks into the kitchen, feeling lighter, "Unleaded?"

"Pardon?" he says, following her.

"Decaf," she says, grinning. "Sorry I forgot that we speak different languages."

"Yes. He says, smiling, that's right. I speak English, and decaf would be splendid."

Chapter 39

"Hey, Hon, aren't you looking fabulous!" Al, face aglow, sports earrings that resemble washers, pours a glass of wine for Mackie before she even has time to hop up on the stool.

"Thanks, Al." And peering closer, she asks, ""Are your earrings from a local shop?"

"Nah, Hon, But they're wonderful, aren't they! Bumper made them—can you believe it? I think he may have a real flair for design."

"They kind of look like faucet washers."

"They are faucet washers! Isn't it brilliant! He's making the most amazing jewelry out of all kinds of hardware and stuff." She holds up her sleeve for Mackie to see the cuff.

"Lug nuts?"

"Exactly."

And Mackie bursts into laughter.

"Not really practical for this job, but-—hey, you can't discourage enterprise in action."

Al is taking the cufflinks out and rolling up her sleeves.

"Of course not," Mackie agrees, sipping. "You're giving me the good wine again, Al, aren't you?'"

"It's happy hour. Get happy! Are you meeting Sully here? I haven't seen him in a couple of days."

"Mackie checks her watch," yes, and he should be here any minute. She feels heat buildup at the thought of him.

"Things are going well between you, then?" Al asks.

Mackie just smiles, she feels like Mona Lisa.

Are things okay with them? Mackie isn't at all sure of that. But she has no intention of talking about it here and now. She sits, flanked by the usual contingent; Fitzy and a couple of his off-duty firemen buddies, the Piper twins, and four or five summer people, identifiable by their upscale wardrobe and pallor.

"How is your aunt doing?"

"I brought her home this morning. Apparently she's going to be fine. It's hard to believe."

"She is one awesome character," Al says.

"You don't have to tell me that. She wouldn't let me get anyone in to help her and she's never going to let me forget that I broke her ribs."

"You saved her life, Hon. Who'd of thunk it? I'm in awe, Mackie. I'm going to have Fitzy do a class here, this month sometime."

And then, he is behind her. She senses him even before he wraps his arms around her. He bends his head down to her and she is enveloped by his scent before he touches his lips to her neck. Taking his time, he moves to her ear and whispers, "Hello, Beauty." And spinning her around on her barstool he holds her at arm's length and looks at her face. "Aha, just as I remembered."

"What?" she says. Her voice is thick with wanting him.

"You," he says, pulls her to his chest and kisses the top of her head. "Just you."

"Hey, you two want a room?" Al asks, placing a napkin in front of Sully and grinning. "What can I get you, Sully?"

"I'll have what she's having, Al."

"You've got it." Al pours a glass of wine for Sully and then goes to the end of the bar and banters with the Piper twins.

"So, how was your day?" he asks, sitting down on the stool beside her.

"It was good—very good. I'm having great fun decorating with other people's money. I'm still doing all the paperhanging and painting, but I'm able to farm out some of the labor-intensive stuff, the prep work and the cleanup for instance. And I've found someone who can do the soft furnishings to my specs."

"You're practically a corporation," Sully smiles.

"Hardly, but I think I can take care of myself. At least I'm beginning to feel that way."

"Shhhhh!" he puts his finger against his lips.

"What?"

"I just want to look at you."

Mackie smiles, feeling some of the tension that was between them disappear.

"I'm sorry I haven't had time for you—with you, Sully."

"It's okay." He tilts his head and looks at her. "You have a pretty big life going on, Mackie."

"I guess I do." She thinks a minute, "But you are a big part of that—of my life."

"Well," he nods his head, "That's something, isn't it?" He puts a twenty-dollar bill on the bar and says, "Let's get out of here. If you ask me real pretty, I might even cook for you—later on."

"Much later on," she says and winks conspiratorially.

"Why don't we go to my place? I have a feeling that the sunset is going to be spectacular and with any luck we can watch the sun come up together."

They don't often spend the night together and Mackie wonders if that is part of the reason that things are not as clear with him. How could they not feel separate when they weren't sharing the day-to-day trivialities, for better or worse, but not for real?

"I'd love to spend the night with you," she says suddenly serious.

"Then drop your car off at your place and I'll follow you."

"Great. That'll give me a chance to change and check my messages."

They pull up in front of Mackie's house and she motions for him to come inside. "I'll make it fast, promise," she says as she lopes up the stairs. "Pour yourself something —or put on some music—whatever."

"Okay. No hurry. We've got all night."

"Just give me ten minutes."

"Mackie?"

"Yes?" she yells from halfway up the stairs.

"I've missed you."

"Me too," she says. "Don't go anywhere."

She turns on the shower, stripping off her clothes as she goes. Lays out clean unders and a pair of khakis and a linen shirt. True to her word, wet hair pulled back in a clip, she appears downstairs ten minutes later. Sully is sitting in the middle of the couch, eyes closed, listening to some Nina Simone. The bluesy music suits Mackie's mood for an entirely different reason now. She tiptoes over, straddles his lap and kisses him. Grinding her body into him, she feels him harden against her. He thrusts his tongue into her mouth and they kiss deeply, softly and then with urgency. Mackie feels everything ignite inside her but she pulls away, flushed, wanting to look at him. Wanting to read his face. Wanting more than anything to prolong the feeling.

She smiles and says, "You have missed me, big boy!"

"More than you know."

"Don't ever let me forget how lucky I am to have you, okay?" Mackie says, pushing back, kissing both of his cheeks and his forehead before getting up.

"Where are you going?"

"Just let me check my messages and we can leave, okay?" She walks over to her answer phone and pushes the button.

"Hi Momma, it's Emma. Just wanted to say we miss you. Give me a call when you can. Oooh—before I forget, Cisco and I have decided on red for the nursery—so put on your thinking cap. Love ya."

Sully smiles at Mackie and says, "Me too."

The second message is a hang up and the last one brings Graham's voice into the room.

"Mary Katherine, this is Graham. I just want to tell you that I enjoyed last evening immensely. It's not often I get to entertain someone. And please remember, you can call me anytime."

Sully's face is suffused with color. His eyes narrow into slits and he stands up, confronting Mackie. "Just what the hell is that all about?"

"What?" she says, thinking what it must sound like to Sully but not liking his tone of voice nor his stance.

"Let's see if I have this right," 'a cup of tea and bed?' He shakes his head from side to side.

"You don't understand."

"Damn right I don't!" His voice is going up an octave a minute. "And just when did the entertainment start last night? Too bad I couldn't have been here."

She wants to throw something at him. "You're being ridiculous," she says instead. "Graham is a friend. It's that simple."

"Oh, right, Mackie. I could hear that friendship in his voice. And by the way, when did you and Dr. Joy get on such a cozy, first name basis?"

"Stop it, Sully!"

"Done," he says with steely indifference, as he picks his keys up off the table and heads for the door.

"Of course, just leave! It's a lot easier than talking, isn't it?" Mackie yells at his retreating back, "I needed to talk to someone, Sully—that's all. Graham cared enough to come over."

Sully turns around and she sees the hurt burning in his eyes. "It would have been nice to have the chance to talk with you, Mackie, but I guess you don't think I have much to offer in that department."

"Stop behaving like a wounded child," she says, moving toward him.

"Well, you're certainly used to dealing with those aren't you, Mackie?"

Mackie feels as if she has been sucker punched. Tears spring to her eyes. "Don't you dare question me about my girls, Sully. They are my life, no matter how much it hurts, no matter how much work it takes. It's sad that you can't invest yourself in anyone else. I guess it's a good thing that you never did have children."

"So, that's what you think of me? How neat. Well, thank you for the mini-analysis. And on that note I think I'll say good-night." She follows him out to the porch.

His foot is hitting the bottom step when she yells.

"Okay. Fine! Just keep taking your sterile black and white pictures. Keep living in your isolated tower by the sea. God knows you don't need me in your life, Sully! You damned well don't need anybody."

He pulls away from the house leaving a trail of rubber. The phone rings and Mackie decides to let the machine pick it up when she hears Eileen's voice, " Mom, I'm afraid I've—"

Mackie grabs the phone, "Leenie. It's me. What's going on?" Her heart is hammering and sweat breaks out across her forehead, down her back.

"The offer fell through."

"Damn it all to hell."

"I'm sorry, Mom. I'm not sure exactly what happened."

Mackie sighs. "It's not your fault, honey. I'm just not having a good day. Do you mind if I call you in the morning?"

"Of course not, Mom. Listen it'll work out. Try not to worry."

Chapter 40

She is physically ill and unable to sleep again. Pacing and fretting most of the night, she feels like a zombie in the morning. Throwing on a tee shirt and overalls and a pair of canvas slip-ons, Mackie drives to work, grateful to have a destination—a job.

She vacillates between thinking she is hateful to thinking Sully is a consummate asshole. She replays the conversation over and over in her head, trying to find out when they went from misunderstanding to venom. Finally, she thinks they were both wrong. Surely this is nothing that they can't work through.

Yet, niggling at the back of her mind is the rush she feels at the sound of Graham's voice. The pull she feels to him when he is in the room. She will stop thinking.

Throwing herself into work, she applies primer to the walls of what she has come to think of as her 'Tuscan' condo. She is going to use a combination of glazes and maybe do some stone blocking for instant age. Although there is a constant parade of workmen around the site, she is left to her own devices. It's one of the things she enjoys about the job, this illusion that she is part of a team. She works without stopping for lunch, using graph paper to figure out furniture arrangement and tacking swatches of fabric at the windows, looking for just the right effect.

She hopes that her work here will garner enough attention to bring in some more work. But, knowing that she can't count on word of mouth alone, she's begun to run an ad in the South Shore Sentinel. Go To Your Room, is going to need to start booking jobs in advance if she is going to have the kind of security that she wants.

Feeling pain and stiffness in her back, she stretches, yawns and takes a final survey of the house. It's after five and she is going to drop by Boo's, cook them both a meal and make sure that her aunt is not overdoing it.

She stops at the fish market and picks up some haddock then swings by the fruit stand for sweet corn and new potatoes. Her final stop is at the package store where she drives up to the window and asks for a chilled bottle of Perrier Jouet. She's taking Al's advice and celebrating life, regardless of how badly it seems to be going.

Expecting to find Boo wan and weary but hopefully recuperating, Mackie is stunned when she walks in and sees Boo dressed in a leotard with a flowing shirt over it. Her hair has been pulled into two pathetic little ponytails at either side of her head and she has one of those stretchy headbands across her forehead. She looks utterly ridiculous and perfectly wonderful at the same time.

"Hey Sweet Pea, woohoo! Champagne! What's the occasion?"

"It's Wednesday," Mackie says, putting the groceries

down on the counter.

"You look like the Wreck of the Hesperus, you've got paint all over you!"

"Why thanks for pointing that out, Boo. I hadn't noticed." Mackie empties the bag and goes to the sink, washing her hands and drying them on her overalls. She starts to shuck the corn. "What are you dressed up for anyway?"

"I was doing my work out," Boo says. "It's important to look the part, don't you think?" Mackie looks startled. "Well, not really a work-out. Just some little exercises, the ribs have to heal before I can really cut loose."

Mackie rolls her eyes, washes the potatoes, puts them in a saucepan and finds another for the corn. "I don't suppose you have anything resembling champagne flutes?"

Boo starts opening and closing cabinets and peering in. Finally she shrugs and produces two jelly glasses. "How about these, Sweet Pea?"

"Perfect," Mackie says, smiling. Expertly uncorking the champagne, she pours two glasses and then hesitates, "Is this allowed?"

"I think it's okay—leastwise it ain't fattening," Boo says, taking the glass, lifting it to the light and clinking it against Mackie's. "For every sorrow, cheer."

"Why that's lovely, Boo." They sip simultaneously.

"There's more to it, but I forget the rest." Boo sips hers and Mackie looks at her auntie, so thankful that they are here together, sharing this moment. "I think it must have been one of Buddy's old toasts, God rest his soul. It probably ended with beer—cheer and beer."

They look at each other and laugh.

"God I miss that man! Wouldn't have been the worst thing seeing his sweet face again."

Mackie understands completely. She would give anything to see Richard one more time. "Boo, did you have one of those near-death experiences?"

"You mean like the tunnel and the light and all that stuff?"

"Exactly."

"Nope. I saw nothing, Sweet Pea. Nada. I was working on the dory and I started to feel kind of funny—hard to describe, but anyway, I decided to come in and lie down for a while, figured I might've been getting sun struck or something. Then nothing. To tell you the truth I don't really remember much about the whole thing afterwards either. I know they zapped me good. And I know you did the CPR business before that, but truthfully there wasn't a damn thing mystical about it."

Mackie goes over and hugs Boo, holds her quietly. "I'm so grateful you didn't leave me, Boo."

"I'm okay sweet girl. I'm right here. Not planning on going anywhere for a long time."

"Well, that's the best news ever." They stand there, Mackie feeling taller and stronger than she has ever felt before. And suddenly she feels Boo heave against her. Deep sobs wrack Boo's body and Mackie holds her tighter, so unaccustomed to this role reversal.

Finally, Boo pulls away and says, "You wanted to know about your Daddy."

Mackie looks into her aunt's face and watches as Boo wrings her hands, grabs a kitchen towel and wipes her face, blows her nose. "Buddy says it's time."

Mackie feels her heart expand and contract. "It's nothing, Boo. It's not important." She is afraid, suddenly not wanting to know. "What possible difference can it make now?"

"Maybe none, Sweet Pea—maybe none."

Mackie walks out of the kitchen and into the living room and Boo follows. "I didn't need a father, I always had Buddy."

Boo comes up behind her and locks her in a surprising embrace. "You did have him, Mackie. He was your father. Buddy was your father."

Mackie spins around and stares mutely at Boo. How can that be possible? She can't find her voice.

"It doesn't change anything, Sweet Pea. It's just water under or over the dam."

"Mother and Uncle Buddy?" Mackie says. "How? Why? Boo, that's just ridiculous." Mackie wonders if Boo is delusional.

"It happened, simple as that, Sweet Pea. That's God's own truth."

"Mother and Buddy had an affair?"

"Don't go calling it that—what they had was one night of comfort that led to you."

"You've known this. All these years, you've known?" Mackie is incredulous. "How could you not tell me?"

Boo sits down on the sofa and pats the place beside her. "You never asked before, Sweet Pea. Besides, what good would it have done?"

Mackie ignores the offer to sit and paces the room, stirring up a flurry of dust motes. "Then why tell me now, Boo. Why now after all this time? I don't understand."

"I just figured I don't want to die without you knowing who your father was. You never really asked before, Sweet Pea. Seemed to me it was getting to be real important to you."

"You forgave mother? I can't believe your own sister betrayed you that way."

Boo gets back up and takes Mackie by the shoulders, nailing her with soulful eyes. "I forgave them both, Sweet Pea. Seems to me there was nothing to gain by losing them. Just think about it."

Mackie pulls away again, shaking her head in disbelief and Boo continues.

"This way I got it all. I always knew Buddy loved me. I knew your momma did too. And then there was you."

"Whoever I am," Mackie says, feeling angry and bewildered at the same time.

Boo shakes her head, "Just think what I would have lost, Sweet Pea."

There is a knock at the door and Boo goes to answer it. Tears are stinging at the corners of Mackie's eyes as she sweeps by Graham, almost knocking him over. She runs down the stairs and gets into her car, slamming the door. By the time she starts the ignition, she is sobbing and she takes off not knowing where she is going to, not even knowing who she is anymore.

She finds herself at the lighthouse, the house itself closed and still, the jetty a peninsula of black calling out to her against the setting sun. She's come running to Sully and he's not here. Leaping out of the car, she clambers over the rocks and climbs onto the first giant block of the jetty. Although the surf appears fairly calm by shore, Mackie can see that there are waves cresting and crashing out by the bell buoy. Her body is wracked and her tears mingle with the salt in the air as she hurries out, nearly losing her footing more than once. She reaches the end of the jetty and she crouches down, anchoring herself between two huge slabs of granite, she lets the water drench her. She doesn't know how long she huddles there, but finally there are no more tears to shed.

"Mary Katherine?" The voice is strong against the wind and Graham squats down beside her and says, "Boo is terribly worried about you. She had me take off after you. I must say you drive like a bat out of hell. I was afraid I wouldn't be able to catch you. By the time I parked here you were halfway out on the jetty. I was afraid if I yelled after you, you'd pitch yourself into the ocean."

She looks at him and says, "I don't know who I am anymore."

His arms come around her and they just sit there on the rock, bodies pressed together, holding on to each other until their breathing becomes synchronized. She has no knowledge of how the hug becomes something more, a continuation, his mouth comes down to hers in the softest way, and she falls into him. And then there is no thought and no intrusion, just the rush of blood as the kiss deepens. They rock together, locked in soundless communion, until she eases away. "Graham?" shaken, she tries to make sense of what is happening and turns away.

But he turns her face back to his and kisses her again. Then a wave almost knocks both of them into the sea. He pulls her up. "This is dangerous," he says, drawing her hand to his mouth, he kisses it. "Come on. We need to get on dry land, Mary Katherine. He leads her back off the jetty and they are both shivering and soaked through when they get to her car.

"Graham," I can't do this. "I'm just so confused." She turns her back to open her car door but he turns her fully around and brushes his lips against hers, kisses her eyelids, and comes back to kiss her deeply. He wipes salt water from her face and smiles.

"Just this," he says. "This is all I want."

Chapter 41

"I still have a hard time believing that you could all keep the particulars of my birth a secret from me," Boo.

They have just left Boo's cardio-rehab and linger outside the door. Boo is in turquoise tights and is wearing a Centipedes t-shirt. A pair of athletic socks puddle over red, high-top converse sneakers. There is always an odd assortment of people there: all shapes and sizes; the ones who look as if they should never have had a heart problem and the ones that look like heart attack on a plate. They go through the motions and there is an aura of thank you that surrounds them.

"We made a pact, so to speak," Sweet Pea. "And, believe it or not, that was the end of it. Period. The three of us just carried on living. End of report. In those days we didn't have any television gurus to tell us how to fix our lives." Boo charges out the door of the clinic leaving Mackie hurrying to catch up.

"I'm beginning to understand why mother always seemed so unhappy. I must have been just one living accusation in her face every day." Mackie unlocks the car door with her remote control and Boo climbs in.

"Don't flatter yourself, Sweet Pea. Life just goes on, you

know. Your Momma had plenty of good times and she did love you, no matter what you think. Of course we all did. Don't turn into little Ella-cinders on me now."

Mackie sighs, starts the car and says, "Buckle up, for God sakes Boo. The last thing I need is you dying on me again." Her life has become one, irreconcilable mess. Questions swirl around in her brain and there is no one willing or able to answer them. Just thinking about her mother making love with Buddy makes her cringe. How could Boo just accept it? Her own sister! So much for her mythical father, the long lost dead one. Her mother should have been a novelist not a piano teacher.

And then there is Richard and the unexplained financial mess. She is beginning to feel like the biggest buffoon in the free world.

She wants to talk with Sully but all she has of him now are dreams. When she sleeps she sees him hurt and vulnerable and alone. And then she wakes up in the middle of the night knowing that he is wrong, so completely wrong. Wrong in his judgment of her. How could she think he could be part of her life?

"Thanks for the lift, Sweet Pea," Boo says. "You're turning into one fine chauffeur."

"You're welcome, Boo."

"Listen, I can call Charlie Pickett the next time I need to see the good doc. I know you're missing work and stuff."

"No, Boo. Just let me know when you need to go. Call me."

She goes by Sully's that evening and sees his car still sleeping on the gravel drive. No lights shine out from within, save for the beacon in the light tower. Her fists pound at the door and her voice goes hoarse from shouting for him. She sits out on the jetty crying until she is too exhausted to cry anymore.

Days turn into weeks and there is only the absence of Sully. It is Shoreham, a small town by any measure and yet their paths don't cross. She's given up trying to talk to him and it is obvious that he will never talk to her again. She longs for the touch of his skin against hers. She imagines the back of his hand softly on her throat, his lips catching her pulse, lingering there.

She rarely goes to Turner's Tavern because Al doesn't look at her the same way. The good wine still arrives. There is banter about Bumper and the rest of her kids, but something has changed. There is an elephant in the room. And the elephant is Sully, conspicuous by his absence.

Things begin to go disastrously wrong at Sonoma Cove and Mackie feels her world falling apart again. The third condo has a monstrosity of a floor plan that sets Mackie reeling. Soaring ceilings and a series of anonymous rooms, random walls. She thinks whoever designed this one was on some kind of bad trip. She begins by painting the whole interior what she thinks will be a soft blue. But when it's finished it's more of a GI gray. It's dismal and Mackie spends the next three days repainting it a safe antique white.

Sketching ideas and discarding them almost as fast, nothing is happening. The King brothers are pressuring her to finish as the real estate market is taking a downward turn and they are trying to move up the opening date. They cut her budget for the remaining two houses.

Chapter 42

Mackie sits, thumbing through an issue of Architectural Digest in Graham's waiting room. She is praying for inspiration for the last two condos. She's been chauffeuring Boo around and is surprised that she actually enjoys the down time it gives her while she waits.

The door to the examining room opens and Boo comes into the waiting room. Graham stands behind her. "Hello, Mary Katherine. It's lovely to see you." He walks to the desk and asks Nancy what time his next appointment is. Checking his watch, he excuses himself and goes back into his office.

"I'm ready to drive my own car again, Sweet Pea. And the doc says that he's 'over the moon' with my fast recovery."

Mackie smiles for the first time in days. "Wonderful, Boo."

"Ain't those Brits a kick, 'over the moon'—I just love to listen to that man talk."

Nancy stifles a laugh as they leave.

Mackie drives Boo home and turns down her offer of lunch. "I've really got to get back to work, Boo." She kisses her cheek and promises to take a rain check.

She now has a mobile phone for the business and her calls are automatically directed from her home phone. She wants to take no chance on missing Sully if he should call. She's pulling into the parking lot at Sonoma Cove when the phone does ring. Her heart rises hopefully in her chest as she answers it. "Mackie Kinsella."

"Mary Katherine," Graham Joy here. "I hope I'm not disturbing you."

"Not at all, Graham. Is something wrong?"

"No, definitely not. I was just wondering if you might like to have dinner at the house this evening? Daly has been missing you and I thought it might be pleasant."

Mackie hesitates. "Well, Graham…"

"Herbie is ready to impress you with his culinary skills."

And she thinks, why not? "I'd like that. What time should I be there?"

"Say seven?"

"Seven is fine. What can I bring?"

"Not a thing. We look forward to seeing you." And after a pause, "I look forward to it, Mary Katherine."

It will be good to share a meal with someone besides her aunt. Sitting at Boo's kitchen table is losing its appeal. It is almost as off-putting as Mackie's solo dining in front of Wheel of Fortune and Jeopardy.

Back inside the 'house from hell' as she has come to think of condo three, it occurs to Mackie that she must simply take one room at a time and hope that something evolves. She starts with the powder room where she begins to imagine a series of guests preening in front of it's over lit vanity mirror. When she sees her own reflection, she is startled, not recognizing herself. She is thinner for sure, her face more sculpted. Fatigue shows in her posture and she inhales, squares her shoulders and sees an immediate improvement. She bends over, touches her toes, shakes her head and rakes her fingers through her hair. Upright again, she looks in the mirror. "You are one fabulous broad," she says. And then, running cold water, she splashes her face and whispers, "Someone will be along soon to lock you up."

Home at five, feeling discouraged by her lack of progress on the house, she showers, cuts her leg twice while shaving and abandons the idea of wearing a sundress. The dog days of August have arrived and the evenings, usually cool at the beach are holding the mugginess of the days. Given the grandeur of the house, Mackie imagines that dinner at Graham's will be a formal affair and so she tops her white linen trousers with a tank top shot through with gold threads and finishes with gold sandals. She adds gold hoop earrings and her Octopussy watch, pulls her hair into a French twist and hopes for the best. Uncomfortable with the thought of arriving empty handed, she stops to pick up something for Daly.

Graham and Daly are waiting at the door as she walks up. "Hello, Mackie," Daly beams.

"Mrs. Kinsella," Graham corrects.

"It's fine," Mackie mouths putting a question mark in her eyes.

"Very well, then. But I shall continue calling you Mary Katherine if you don't object."

"And I shall call you Mackie!" Daly says emphatically.

Mackie takes the gift bag from behind her back and says,

"And this is a little something for my favorite four year old."

Daly looks at Graham, questioning. He nods and she takes the bag from Mackie with a little shiver of anticipation. " I love getting presents."

"I do too, Daly. Especially 'just because' ones."

"Just because?" Daly says wrinkling her nose.

"Just because I wanted to—no birthday, Christmas, holiday—just because."

Daly opens the bag and pulls out a bottle of dishwashing liquid and another of Karo syrup. "Thank you." She is clearly puzzled, but too polite to say anything else.

"Do you know what that is, Daly?" Mackie says, looking from puzzled daughter to indulgent father.

"Well, I think this green one is soap—but I don't know what this other one is?"

"Well one is soap, Daly and the other is Karo syrup, but when you mix them together with water you get—" And Mackie produces three intricate wire wands from her purse; one shaped like a frog, one a heart and one a star. "Magic bubble juice!"

Daly is clearly enchanted. "Oh thank you, thank you. Let's go make some. You can help me Mackie." And she bounds off to the kitchen shouting, "Herbie, Mackie's here and we're going to make magic bubbles!"

Graham warns, "Slow down, Daly, no running in the house. And to Mackie he says, "That was kind of you. I'm afraid we'll be enlisted to help now. There will be no peace until she plays with this." He leads the way to the kitchen where Herbie is setting a table with oversized plates, red-checkered napkins and thick goblets. A huge bowl of salad sits on a granite island and two enormous pots are under fire on the stove. "Hello, Herbie. It looks like you're cooking for the emerging nations."

He smiles, " Not at all, it's simply lobster and some native corn. It's such a hot night." He takes the edge of his apron and wipes his brow as if to prove it. "Sorry to intrude on your kitchen, Herbie. But Daly is anxious to try out her new bubble wands."

"How can I help?" Herbie asks.

"Well if you can just lend me a cup or a jar, preferably plastic I'll be out of your way in a jiff."

"I think I have the perfect thing," Herbie says going to the recycle bin and taking out a wide-mouthed bottle that once held ice tea. He rinses it in the sink and Mackie comes up behind him.

"Great," she says. He stands aside and she fills the bottle nearly full with water, adds a couple of squirts of the dish soap and a bit of the Karo syrup. She puts on the cover and shakes it gently. "Voila!" she says, handing it to Daly. "Magic bubble juice!"

"Out in the garden, Daly," Graham says. "Mary Katherine and I will be right out to watch you." She walks out through French doors, carrying her bubbles as if they were liquid gold. "Would you care for an aperitif? A sherry perhaps?"

"What are you having, Graham?" she says, hoping it's not sherry as she tasted it once and thought it tasted like nail polish remover.

"A beer," he says, surprising her, as has nearly everything about the evening so far.

"That sounds perfect." And without saying a word,

Herbie pulls three frosted mugs out of the freezer, opens the refrigerator and takes out three bottles of beer and pours for all of them. Handing Mackie hers first and then Graham's he finally lifts his own and hoists it, saying, "Cheers!"

They share dinner around the table with Daly making a great show of trying to crack her lobster without help. Watching Graham eat lobster and buttery corn on the cob does away with any illusion Mackie had of him being formal and 'stuffy'. She insists on clearing the table and loading the dishwasher while Herbie goes upstairs to supervise Daly's bath followed by Graham who will read her nighttime story.

Mackie takes her coffee out to the garden where a breeze coming off the river has finally taken the edge off the heat. She sits, listening to crickets and watching fireflies when Graham comes out with his own coffee and takes a seat beside her.

"Herbie says to thank you for the help in the kitchen and to tell you he enjoyed the evening."

"How sweet of him," Mackie says. "Won't he join us for coffee?"

"No." He smiles, "By the time he's gotten Daly to sleep he's ready to retreat to the barn. She's fairly labor intensive, as you can see."

"She's wonderful," Mackie says, meaning it.

"That too."

"You are doing a great job with her, Graham. It can't be easy raising a child on your own."

"I'm hardly alone in it," he says. "I have the luxury of sufficient money and I have Herbie's invaluable help. And Cho, for whatever her limitations, certainly contributes to Daly's life.

"I'm sure," Mackie says. "So, you've always been the great gentleman, bachelor," she says and watches as his eyes crinkle and a smile softens his face.

"Hopefully always a gentleman, Mary Katherine, but not always a bachelor."

Mackie sits, waiting for him to continue.

"I was married for many years." He puts his cup down on the table and laces his fingers together. "My wife died of ovarian cancer."

"I'm so sorry," Mackie says. "I had no idea."

"Of course you didn't," he says. "She's been gone nearly twenty years. Pamela and I met in school and married immediately after." He smiles, stands up and takes a few steps. "I still miss her."

Mackie walks up behind him. "It must have been horrible for you, being a doctor and not being able to do anything."

"I had no idea she was ill. I was completely involved with my practice in those days. We'd tried, unsuccessfully for years to have a family and I simply imagined her symptoms were more of the same problems. Alas, by the time we got a diagnosis there was nothing to be done."

She sees his back stiffen and goes to him, encircles him in her arms and holds him tightly. "I can't imagine it." But of course she can. "With Richard I just felt I should have known something was wrong. But with all the drama of the girls—with whatever I imagined I should be paying attention to, Richard was just flying under the radar."

He turns around. "You are so lovely, Mary Katherine."

"I am so not," Mackie says. "I am just lost, Graham. I can't remember feeling this adrift since I was just a kid. And even when I should have been a grown-up, all those years when I was supposed to be the responsible one, I kept thinking I was playing a part in some bizarre reality show. But you know what, nothing of it seemed real at all."

"What do you mean?"

She looks away sees the chair at the table and sits down. She wants a glass of wine, or a brandy. She wants to not be here with this man who is emitting signals that she's not sure how to interpret.

"My life seems to be some sort of fairy tale gone awry."

"And you are Cinderella, missing her glass slipper? Or Gretel lost in the woods and about to be thrown in the oven—or Little Red Riding Hood about to be eaten by the big bad wolf?" Graham pulls her up from the chair and holds her at arm's length.

"I am all of those."

She feels as if she might just collapse. She is so beyond tired and so ready to have someone, anyone write the end of the story.

"And you are not. You are none of those. You are so strong, Mary Katherine. If you could simply learn to trust yourself."

She throws her arms around him and finds his mouth, his skin. The whiskers chafe against her face and she wants nothing more than to be lost in him. The kiss is rough and then sweet and she feels him pull away.

"What?" she asks. The air turns cool between them.

"It's been a lovely evening. You are quite wonderful."

"And?" she asks, feeling the curtain closing on the second act.

"And it's time to say good-night. I'm afraid I have a full

schedule tomorrow and I'm sure you must too."

She is at once rebuffed and excited and she reaches for his crotch and feels him hard against her hand. His head comes down to her neck and he whispers, "Thank you." And taking her hand away, he brings it to his mouth and kisses it. "Good night, Mary Katherine. It's been lovely."

She can't really breathe properly. She has just made a pass and been rebuffed. Trying to gather her dignity back or what might be left of it she says, "The lobster was fantastic. Thank you for the dinner, Graham." And now I will go home and die of mortification. Mary Katherine Kinsella and her raging hormones.

Chapter 43

She wants more than anything to talk with someone about what she's feeling for Graham and for Sully in his absence. She thinks, hysterically for a moment that she wants to talk to Richard. How absurd is that how insane anyway. This is all is fault.

Why couldn't she be one of those lonely women, who wonder if anyone will ever be interested in them again? Or better yet one of those widows who sally forth, happy to answer to no one. She should have taken up skydiving, or joined a group hosteling through third world countries. Or barring that, she should have adopted cats and learned how to garden. Instead, she fled home and now seems locked in behavior more appropriate for an adolescent than for a woman in the September part of her life.

She has been given a shot at a new life in the most awful way and now she is screwing it up royally. It's obvious that she can't talk to her daughters about this and she can't talk to Al, the closest thing she has to a girlfriend. Sully laid claim to that friendship long before Mackie came on the scene. Besides, Al seems already to have chosen sides.

And of course there is Buddy—Daddy. Wow, she still finds herself tearing up thinking about what she might have done had she known. Of course, as Boo said, he was there all those years for her, in a way. She is trying to figure out a way to tell the girls about this turn of events, but knows that it really won't have much of an effect on them. They are more in line with Boo's thinking on past events being almost instant history. And she doesn't think it's the kind of thing a phone call will take care of. She is learning to compartmentalize her life and there is too much present to deal with without lingering on the past.

It is surely an act of desperation when she finds herself at Boo's table early the next morning. "Boo?" Mackie asks, savoring the coffee that is, Starbucks be damned, the best coffee in the world.

"What can I do you for, Sweet Pea?" Boo offers her some whole-wheat toast with fruit spread. "Don't come close to a Dunkin' Donut, but ya get used to it," she says.

Mackie shakes her head. "I was wondering if I could talk to you about something, Boo—actually about someone."

"This ain't about Buddy again, is it, Sweet Pea, cause frankly I closed the door on that one."

"No, Boo. I understand that—at least I'm trying to."

"Okay, shoot," Boo says, taking a bit of toast and chewing thoughtfully.

"Well," Mackie starts slowly, "It's Sully. We had a pretty major fight a few weeks ago and he won't talk to me. He won't take my calls and when I go by he won't answer the door."

"That's 'cause he ain't there, Sweet Pea."

Mackie looks puzzled.

"Leastwise I don't think he's back yet."

"Back from where?" Mackie asks, wondering why Boo knows where Sully is and she doesn't.

"Al told me he was off on one of his little road trips." Boo sips her coffee and continues to eat her toast. "Maybe if you went by the tavern once in a while, you'd keep up with what's going on."

"Well, damn it, Boo, why didn't you mention it to me? Did you think I wouldn't care? Oh shit, Boo. I've been worried sick about him."

"No need to curse, missy. I think he rented one of those camper thingies and he's driving all around the country."

Mackie can't believe what she's hearing.

"I just found out about it. I tried to call you last night and tell you, but I guess you were elsewise occupied—or not answering your phone." Boo snorts at her own humor.

Mackie has an instant replay of being in Graham's arms last night and she feels guilt rise up in her throat like bile. Her face is burning. "I had dinner with friends, Boo."

"Mid-life crisis if you ask me."

"Me?" Mackie asks, wondering if that's the explanation for her recent behavior, mid-life crisis, such a cliché.

"Not you, Sweet Pea, Sully. Next thing you know he'll be buying one of those Harleys. Listen, I don't know what's been going on between you two, but I'm telling you nine times out of ten, you give a man enough rope and it's noose time."

"Did Al happen to say when he'd be back?" Mackie asks, looking at her watch as if it might be any minute.

"Nope."

"Okay, fine." Mackie sighs and opens the back door, "I've got to get to work."

"How's that going, anyway?"

"About as well as the rest of my life," Mackie says and trudges down the stairs.

The condo from hell beckons. Knowing that her budget has been cut way back, Mackie begins to think more economically. After all, for many years she and Richard had little disposable income and yet she managed to make homes for them, warm inviting, often quirky, but always somehow 'homey.'

She drives out to South Shore Plaza to the mall. One part Architectural Digest and one part mall she thinks she can do it. Starting at the print shop, hoping for a bolt of lightning, it happens. She is struck by the Rete prints. His extravagant costume designs so indicative of the Art Deco era seem perfect for the condo. She purchases three of them and has them framed in clear Lucite. As she's heading back to the car, she realizes that she can flea market for other pieces. There are dozens of shops along the coast, treasure troves of memorabilia. With any luck she might pick up a Bakelite piece or two and one of those stylized martini pitchers with glasses would be perfect just set on the living room floor. If she can find a coat rack and some vintage thirties clothing and maybe a boa she can get on to the fourth and final house. She feels her spirits lift.

She is headed back to Shoreham with her purchases when her cell phone rings. She hates trying to talk and drive, so she puts on her directional for the next exit as she pushes the send button. "Mackie Kinsella."

She sees a strip mall to her right and is pulling in, ready to take the call when she hears, "I love you." Almost running over a woman walking with a child in tow, Mackie feels the tears erupt from her eyes. There is no other voice like his. "Sully?" It is not a question, but a sob. "Where are you?"

"Too far away."

She sits, calming herself. Turns off the engine. "What does that mean?"

"Anywhere that I can't reach out and touch you," he says.

She sees him so clearly it's painful. "Sully, God damn it, tell me where you are! I didn't even know you were gone until this morning. I kept calling you and going by the house. Why didn't you call me? Why in hell didn't you let me know you were leaving?"

"I didn't bring my cell phone. I haven't checked my messages."

He sounds elated and she wants to yell at him, to wipe the smile she can feel off his face. "Sully, you've been gone for weeks! How could you do that—just take off like that, without even telling me. I've been sick with worry."

"I've been everywhere, Mackie. And now I'm outside of Chicago."

"Why Chicago? Sully, you can't just take off for nearly a month and then call and tell me you love me—and you're in Chicago for God's sake."

"I haven't called you because I wasn't sure what to say. I'm calling now to tell you that I'll be home in a couple of days and that I love you."

"Talk to me Sully!" she says pounding the steering wheel

with her fist.

"I've been an ass. I don't deserve you in my life."

She wants answers. She needs them and she is speechless.

"We'll talk when I get home," he says.

"But Sully, we need to talk now."

"Not now, baby. I don't want to do this over the phone. I need to see you. I'll be home day after tomorrow."

"Sully," she pleads.

"Everything will be fine Mackie. I'll be there. I promise."

And he's gone. Mackie sits holding the phone. No apology. No explanation, just the declaration of love. And love is a thousand miles away.

Chapter 44

Mackie is beside herself as she pulls into Turner's Tavern. She still has no way to get a hold of Sully and there are so many unanswered questions in her mind. Damn him anyway. Chicago? What's that about? She can't believe he's been driving all over the country for weeks and hasn't called her until now. And he practically hung up on her, albeit gently. How on earth is she going to get through the next two days?

Mackie gets out of her air-conditioned car and the mugginess hits her. She feels her clothes begin to stick to her just walking from the parking lot into the Tavern. It's just a bit past five o'clock and the bar is nearly empty. Al is listing specialty cocktails on the chalkboard; M is for: Mojitos, Margaritas, and Mango Daiquiris. She's wearing her usual crisp white shirt but has traded the black trousers for white shorts. Her hair is pulled back from her face with a bandanna and she looks impossibly cool. Looking up she sees Mackie and says, smiling, "Well look who just washed up on shore." And, laughing at her own joke, she continues, "Long time no see, hon. You look like you're about to expire. Pull up a stool and I'll make you a Mojito."

"What's a Moheeto? Mackie asks, distracted and still upset.

"It's a Cuban drink. It'll cool you right off."

Mackie sits down and Al begins crushing mint leaves into sugar syrup. She adds lime juice, rum, lots of ice and finally splashes in the soda water. "What have you been up to, hon? My two favorite people disappear within weeks of each other. First Sully takes off and then you do a vanishing act. I might get a complex if I didn't know you better."

"I thought you were upset with me Al—because of Sully."

Al frowns, "Now why would that be?" She pushes the drink across the bar to Mackie, "What on earth are you talking about?"

"His leaving!" Mackie takes a sip of her drink

"Nothing new about Sully taking off once in a while," Al says. "But, I must say this is the longest I've known him to be away."

"You mean he does this—he just leaves?"

Al nods. "Yep."

"Why didn't you tell me that?" Mackie says, suddenly annoyed.

"You didn't ask me, Mackie." Al polishes glasses, seemingly unaffected. "And then you just stopped coming in. I figured something was going on in your own life, what with Boo's heart attack and all."

Mackie sighs, "I don't believe this."

"And then Boo showed up yesterday and his name just came up."

"How can he just take off like that?"

"Why not?" Al says. "I'd do it if I could. Like I said, I was getting a little worried though. I can't remember that he's ever been away more than a couple of weeks before."

Mackie shakes her head. "Have you talked to him?"

"Not since before he left." Al crosses her arms, "And just why should I be upset with you, Mackie? What does this have to do with you? I thought we were friends, girlfriend?"

Mackie , feels heat diffuse her cheeks even through the coolness of the drink. "We are friends, Al—and I'm sorry I've stayed away. I guess I've been reading all kinds of messages into things. Sully and I just had a" —Mackie fumbles for the words—"a misunderstanding."

Al arches one eyebrow. "And you had no idea he was leaving?"

"None," Mackie says.

"And you still haven't heard from him?"

"He just called. He said he was in Chicago."

"Chicago?" Al is clearly curious.

"I have no idea what he's doing there, or where he's been for that matter. All I know is that he's on his way back, Al." And Mackie feels her heart sink, wondering if she's betrayed him with Graham—even though there was nothing there. Yet another missed signal, good lord is she ever going to start getting her act together?

Just then a crowd enters the bar, up from the beach and dying of thirst. Al gets to work. Mackie leaves a ten-dollar bill and her drink on the counter. She catches Al's eye and mouths, "See you soon," and she heads home.

Chapter 45

The house feels like an incubator, closed up all day, it smells of stale coffee and moldy facecloths. Mackie kicks off her shoes at the door. Peeling off the rest of her clothing, she ascends the stairs and goes into the bathroom, turning on the taps, dumping in some of Sully's magic gift oils. She goes into her bedroom and throws the windows open, praying for a random breeze. The ocean is silent, not a good omen. Pulling on an oversized t-shirt, she goes downstairs and pours herself a glass of wine. She goes through her music and finds a sound track from The Big Easy. Zydeco music always makes her happy. She is prepared to launch herself into a better mood. Putting the disc in the player she turns up the volume and climbs back upstairs. She lights one of her spa candles for good measure and strips off the t-shirt, sinks into the tub, turning off the water only when it threatens to overflow. She soaks until the water becomes almost cold. Climbing out, she grabs her terry cloth robe, slathers herself with moisturizers, pulls her hair into a high ponytail and heads downstairs. She does not expect hunger, yet finds herself standing in front of the refrigerator looking longingly at the contents. Grabbing a block of cheddar cheese and the bottle of chardonnay, she refills her glass and goes to a cabinet where she pulls out a box of crackers. She gets a plate from the dish drainer, cuts a hunk of the cheese and puts it on the plate adding a dozen of the crackers. Looking around she spots the fruit bowl and grabs a bunch of seedless grapes and an apple for good measure.

The heat refuses to subside and Mackie goes out to the porch with her bounty. She puts the plate on the glider beside her and rocks. She's traded the Zydeco music for blues and drifts into reveries of Sully and their last time together. As many times as she replays the scene, she cannot decide who is wrong and who is wronged.

The sun goes down and Mackie can't be bothered to turn on the lights. She puts the plate on the sisal carpet and curls up on the glider, hoping to escape into one of her dreams of Bette or Liz. Hoping that when she awakens things will fall into place.

She senses him before she sees him. Next comes the incredible scent. And she knows she must be dreaming him. Dreaming Sully. She rolls over and nearly falls off the glider. But she is caught, enveloped and she is not dreaming anymore. "Hello, Beauty," he whispers. "I've missed you so much."

"Sully?" she says breathlessly and tears come to her eyes. He pulls her gently onto the floor, pushing the remnants of her meal away, making a back rest of the glider, arm around her shoulders.

"I see you're still dining al fresco," he says chuckling.

"How can you be here?" she says. "What time is it?

Have I lost a day somewhere?"

"It's somewhere around five a.m." He kisses her fore-head, hugs her, and sighs. "God, you feel good."

"But you were in Chicago!" she says doing the math and suddenly reactivating the anger that she has held for so long. She punches him and then punches him again, pum-meling his arms. "Where were you? How the hell could you just take off like that and not even call me?" She gathers her robe around her and lurches to her feet. "You can't have been in Chicago. You couldn't have gotten here this fast."

He gets up and follows her into the house. "I was in Indiana actually. Not far from Chicago, but on my way here. Once I heard your voice I knew I had to just keep driving until I got to you." He grabs her and kisses her tentatively. She feels his whiskers against her and she pulls away. She shakes her head, "It's not that easy, Sully. I want to know where the hell you've been for weeks and how you could just leave me worrying and sick about you."

"I'm here now, Mackie and I need a shower," he says, peeling off his shirt. "I feel like road kill."

She is speechless. He holds her again and whispers, "I'll tell you everything when I come down. The important thing is that I'm here and I've thought about little else but making love to you for the last fifteen hours." He slides his hands inside her robe and she feels herself respond. She feels her nipples harden under the touch of his thumbs. "But, he says," pulling away and heading upstairs, "First to the showers."

"Just get the hell out of here," she yells. Feeling tears leak down her face. "Go!"

He picks up his shirt from the glider and shakes his head. "You really want me to leave?"

She nods. "You can't just do a disappearing act and then come back like nothing ever happened." She pushes him toward the screen door.

Sully turns back and smiles wryly.

"What the hell are you smiling at?" she hisses.

He shrugs his shoulders, "You know, Mackie, somehow I thought that you, of all people, would understand."

"Understand what? Just what the fuck should I understand?"

"Flight," he says and goes out, letting the door slap shut behind him.

Chapter 46

Mackie is making coffee in the kitchen when Sully appears outside the screen door. Anger still simmers within her, but she wants explanations more than she wants to rant. If he were a dog his tail would be hanging between his legs. He's showered and changed into sweats but he still looks road weary and haggard. "I'm a total shit," he says.

She opens the screen door and motions him in. She doesn't speak but slaps two mugs down on the table. He stands in the corner with his arms crossed protectively across his chest.

She doesn't trust herself to speak, doesn't know if she will scream or cry.

"I've been alone too long," he says. "I haven't had to answer to anyone, care about anyone—until you." His face is etched with fatigue.

She pours the coffee and takes a sip of her own before asking, "What did you mean by I should know about 'flight'?"

"Just that you should. You're the one who ran away from home and landed here, aren't you?"

She thinks about this, frowning. "I don't think I was

running away from home, Sully—I think I was running to it." She motions for him to sit down and she takes a seat herself. "Besides," she says, feeling her voice get stronger. " I didn't scare people to death. I didn't leave them wondering where the hell I was or if I was ok. I had no idea where you had gone. Can't you understand how horrible that was for me?"

He sits down and grabs his mug in two hands. "I didn't think."

"That's not good enough," she says. "You were gone for weeks! Where the hell were you? What were you doing?" She wants to punch him; she wants to hold him.

He rakes his hair back from his forehead. "I've always hit the road when I needed to think," he says. "I truly lost track of the time. I just wanted to get away from here—away from you. I couldn't think." His eyes are moist and Mackie finds herself crying softly too. "I was hurt. You needed something—you needed someone and you turned to someone else."

She reaches across the table and puts her hand over his.

"I wanted to be the one you needed. I still want to be the one you need."

Mackie gets up and paces. "The night I called Graham was the anniversary of Richards' death. I'd had a dreadful, day. I'd thrown a huge pity party for myself and decided that what I really needed was to be alone, to go to sleep and just have the day over with."

"I didn't know that," he says.

"I know," she says.

Sully lets her continue and she says, "When Richard

died there was absolutely nothing I could do. It still takes my breath away to think about it. When Boo had her heart attack and I was there you cannot imagine how abjectly terrified I was to feel that her life was in my hands—in my very breath."

He nods his head. "That must have been awful, Mackie, but wonderful because you saved her. You saved her life."

"I kept her alive long enough for the paramedics to save her," Mackie says factually. "Anyway, I don't know exactly what was going through my mind on the fourth, but I had all these emotions. Fears, expectations and memories just started to surface; Richard's death, doing the CPR for Boo… everything seemed to collide. I thought I was going to have some kind of breakdown."

Sully sits at the table listening hard.

"I thought I'd make an appointment to see Graham."

Sully looks at her, questioning.

"He's my doctor, Sully—and my friend." She can feel the heat creeping into her face and wonders if Sully can sense something. "Anyway, I called his home number by mistake. It was late and I thought I'd just reach his service. Instead Graham answered the phone and I just lost it."

She sees sympathy in Sully's eyes.

"I told him I'd make an appointment in the morning. And then I couldn't sleep at all. Graham just showed up. I think he was worried about me." She sits back down across from Sully. "He was kind. He is a kind and caring man."

"I said a lot of things that night I left," Sully says. "A lot of things I didn't really mean."

"I think we both did," Mackie says.

The weariness settles on both of them. "I'm going to go home and sleep for a while," Sully says, pushing back from the table. He stands in the doorway, framed in sunlight.

Mackie nods, "And I have to go to work, but I should be able to finish up early." She stands and puts the mugs into the sink. She wants to touch him but wants to hold herself apart—at least for a while.

"Will you come by the lighthouse when you finish? Sully asks.

"Yes. We'll talk some more then. Go home. Sleep."

He steps onto the back porch, lets the screen door shut. "One more thing, Mackie."

"What?" she says.

"You were wrong about me."

"When?" she says, puzzled.

"When you said I don't need anybody."

She can't see his face through the shadows on the screen but she can hear him clearly.

"I need you."

Chapter 47

Mackie drives down the coast stopping at one antique shop after another. She doesn't find any Bakelite at the first two but she discovers a wonderful pair of bronze bookends. They are nudes, lounging against seashells and they stand about ten inches high. Mackie hopes she can find some books from the thirties or forties to put between them.

The solitary drive is giving her time to think, about life and about Sully. Everything about him is such a mystery. Everything about him seems so unpredictable. But she has learned that life can veer out of control at any moment—and he makes her happy. And she enjoys the fact that he's unpredictable after all. All those years she thought she knew Richard inside and out and yet she really didn't know him at all.

And Graham? He seems a dear friend, one that she has just humiliated herself in front of, but the person who seems to have offered her more comfort and consolation than anyone else since she arrived back in Shoreham. His kisses had been tender and touching and she did wonder what other secrets she might find within the good doctor. But, dear lord, whatever was she thinking?" Touching his crotch. She feels as if she has suddenly become the Harlot of Shoreham?" She will change doctors immediately. Maybe she can avoid ever seeing him again. And she knows she will never tell Sully about the foolishness.

Mackie stops for lunch at a small restaurant on the Cape. She calls Eileen, gets her recording and leaves a message. If the house in Citrus Valley doesn't sell soon she's going to have to consider renting it. Although she has some money from Richard's life insurance, it won't go that far with a mortgage eating away at it. She doesn't want to be a landlord and she really doesn't want to saddle Eileen or Emma with managing the house in her absence. She's considered burying a statue of St. Joseph upside down in the front yard to facilitate a sale, but knows that the girls will think she's gone around the bend if she suggests it.

She sits staring out at the ocean, sipping lemonade and poking at her salad and finally calls Emma, feeling immediately connected. "Em, sweetie, how are you feeling?"

"Like a cross between a beluga and the Pillsbury Dough Boy. I can't believe I've let this happen, Mom—do you think it's too late to change my mind about the baby?"

Mackie chuckles. "You're almost there, sweetie—just two more months, isn't it?"

"Take off the just, I can't sleep—I can't see my feet anymore, Cisco has to tie my boots for me."

"When are you going to stop work, Em?"

"You remember Cisco's sister, Laura?"

"Yes, the one who's going to start culinary school in January."

"Right"

"Well, she's a 'sweat equity' partner now. She's helping out tremendously, Mom, and she'll run the place completely while I'm gone. I'm going to work until the end of September and then take off until after the wedding."

Mackie's heart leaps, "Wedding!" she yells, grinning from ear to ear. Several people look her way and she mouths 'sorry' and lowers her voice. "Sweetheart, that's wonderful. Tell me, when—what kind—I need details."

'Well, we thought Christmas time would be perfect. That way we can get you back out here, hopefully. I know you're coming to do the nursery and be here for Elena's birth, but you should be here for her first Christmas too, don't you think?"

"Of course." Mackie doesn't hesitate.

"Great. The wedding is going to be small, Mom. We haven't worked out the details yet, but the important thing is that we'll be 'official'."

"Well, congratulations darling! I couldn't be happier. I'll be there with bells on."

"I'm so happy, Mom."

"That's what matters, Emma. It's the most important thing in the world to me."

"And Mom, I hope you haven't been giving the red nursery too much thought."

Mackie smiles, "Actually, I've been kind of preoccupied. I haven't given it much thought, Em."

"Great, because Cisco and I are thinking pink."

"Pink?"

"Yes. But not girly pink, if you know what I mean."

Mackie nods her head although Emma can't see her. "I'll work on it, Em."

"You're the best, Mom. I know you can come up with something. Hey, how are your houses coming along? You must be nearly finished?"

"Getting there, Em. Who knew your old momma would have a little business up and running?"

"I'm proud of you, Mom."

Mackie basks for a second. "I'm happy, Em. Take care and I'll talk to you soon."

Mackie visits a few more stores and just as she's ready to give up, she spots a sideboard. Not in perfect condition, but art-deco in its lines, she bargains for it and gets not only it, but also a unique, tall glass pitcher and two glasses with the glass stirrer still intact. Palm trees etched on the front make Mackie smile.

"You like that art deco stuff?" The owner, a man obviously able to remember the period asks.

"Mackie pulling out her credit card," says, "Truthfully, no. I'm staging some houses for a builder and I'm just kind of running with this theme now."

"Hang on, miss, I'll be back in a sec."

He disappears behind a set of swinging doors and comes back out a few minutes later with a cardboard carton. "Feel free to go through this stuff and take anything you want," he says.

Mackie looks at him questioningly.

"My wife took this stuff in some time back. Someone came in with it. My guess is an estate sale. Leftovers, junk mostly. Frankly, I didn't see any way to sell the stuff, but as I said, you're welcome to it."

Intrigued, Mackie starts to shift through the box. And he's right, it is mostly junk, but she manages to unearth a couple of Bakelite bracelets and a pin, shaped like a pineapple. At the bottom of the carton she finds three art deco neckties, badly wrinkled from their resting place, but unstained and made of pure silk. The stark, geometric designs and brilliant colors are distinctive. She sets them aside, smoothing the ties with her hand, "How much for these?" she asks.

"On the house," he says. Running her card through the machine. He hands it over to her. "Glad to have them out of here. You sure you don't want anything else?"

"Thanks, no," Mackie says, already envisioning one of the ties draped over a bedpost, the jewelry left on the bathroom counter and the martini pitcher and glasses on the sideboard downstairs. She knows it must have been a wonderful party. Knows that people stayed far too late and drank too much and laughed too loud. And after they left, her couple cleaned up the detritus from the party and danced in the kitchen to their own music. They kissed, remembered why they were together and discarded clothing on the way up to bed.

Mackie sees a strappy high-heeled shoe on the bottom step, a laundered shirt, a belt, a soft, silk blouse. But, not sure that Shoreham is ready for a trail of discarded clothing from living room to boudoir, and knowing that she is in the throes of Sully, she snaps out of it.

Tomorrow she'll buy some bright red lipstick and an old-fashioned powder puff, a double-edged razor a wonderful brush and with any luck she can find some shaving soap in a mug—Old Spice, in case her daddy or God is watching.

Chapter 48

Finished for the day, Mackie forgoes home in favor of getting back to Sully. The sun is beginning to lower when he comes out to meet her. He opens her car door and tentatively leans down and kisses her on the cheek. "Good day at the office?"

She gets out of the car and stretches, working out kinks she didn't know she had. "I went on a scavenger hunt."

He tips his head back, "And how did you do?"

"I won," she says, straightening up. "And how about you, did you sleep?"

"I did," he says.

He holds her at arm's length and stares at her.

"What?" she says.

"I have something to show you, but first let's take a walk."

"All right. Is everything okay, Sully?"

"I hope so."

He takes her hand and together they navigate the huge rocks that make up the jetty, Sully finding the footing first and leading her along. The sun is almost sitting on the water and they pass a couple of kids fishing. They continue on out to the end of the jetty by the bell buoy and Sully sits down, pulling Mackie down beside him. It looks as if someone has strewn a rhinestone net across the water. Seagulls, circle and swoop and a few lobster boats make their way back to the pier in the distance.

Sully just sits, squinting into the distance for a while. Finally, he says, "I thought this would be a good place to talk."

"Of course," Mackie says.

He picks up her hand, brings it to his mouth, and kisses the inside of her wrist. "I love you, Mackie."

"I know you do, Sully. And I love you."

"We haven't had a lot of time to get to know each other and I know that you're still getting your sea legs—what with being back here and everything. You're making all kinds of adjustments and the last thing in the world I want to do is crowd you."

She nods. "And I thank you for that, Sully. I haven't always been clear in showing you that. You're important to me too, you know."

"I guess I know that. And I also know that you have led a whole other life that had nothing whatsoever to do with me."

"That's true," Mackie says. "But that life is not what I have now. Everything has changed."

"I know you miss your daughters," he says. "I wish there was something I could do about that Mackie. But I'm way too selfish to want you to go back."

"I don't want to go back," she says. This is where I belong now—I know that. I love everything about living here; the way the air smells, the seasons, being near Boo, being on my own. I feel like I have potential, Sully. I feel new."

"I guess what I'm trying to ask you is if there's a place for an old, renegade photographer in your present, and maybe your future?"

"Oh, I hope so Sully," She throws her arms around his neck, breathes him in savors the place, the moment, the size and shape of him. They sit there together until the sun begins to dip and the temperature starts to drop. Finally, he stands up and pulls her along.

"Good," he says, "That's all I needed to know."

Mackie gets up, "You're a good man, Aemon Xavier Sullivan."

"I'm working on it, Mary Katherine Swan Kinsella."

They navigate the rocks back to land and as they approach the door. He stops Mackie, says, "Close your eyes."

"What now?" she says.

"You'll see, just do it," he says and she hears a quickening in his voice. She puts her hand over her eyes and hears him open the door. Leading her inside he says, "Okay, you can look now."

At first she doesn't know what he wants her to see. The room is lit with candles, shadows dance, and music plays softly. He's set the trunk up for dinner and clearly something is cooking, as she can smell garlic, oregano, maybe rosemary.

Then she sees the walls. Gone are the landscapes and seascapes, in fact all of Sully's artwork is gone, replaced by the most startling gallery of black and white portraits that Mackie has ever seen. Her hands fly to her mouth as she walks first to one and then to another and another. The largest of the prints is an extreme close up of a pair of baby feet, toes curled under, the legs of the jeans just apparent at the top of the frame. It is at once sensitive and stylized. There is a headshot of a man who has obviously lived life as a full frontal assault. A long braid falls across his shoulder as he props his head up on his hands and his battered eyes seem to say to the camera, 'yeah—what the hell do you know about it?'

Mackie is nearly speechless, "Sully," she sweeps the room with her eyes and her arm, "These are just painfully good."

He beams at her. She goes to a picture of two boys about four or five years old. They have each other in the kind of brotherly chokehold that might have turned into a skirmish moments after the shutter closed. He's put them off center in the frame, leaving a good deal of white to the side. It's effective. It's a technique he's used over again in quite a few of the portraits. There are women of all ages, truck drivers, bikers at a rally somewhere. "I had no idea you could do this."

"Well, that makes two of us," he says, crossing his arms and looking around the room with such obvious satisfaction that Mackie feels her heart soar for him. "It's what I've been doing—why I ended up being gone so long." He goes to a stack of five by sevens and starts to shuffle through them. "I have a lot of work left to do, Mackie, I shot hundreds of rolls of film. Thousands maybe." He hands her a picture. An old couple sits on a bench at a bus stop. Her legs are crossed at the ankles. He sits with both feet planted on the ground. They are looking off in opposite directions, each apparently lost in their own world until you look closer and see that they are holding hands. They must be eighty years old at least and there they are holding hands.

"I took that one in a place called Manhattan, Kansas, Mackie."

"It's a great shot, Sully. They've been together forever I guess."

"Actually they're newlyweds." Sully nods his head, "It's true. Buck and Margaret. I don't remember their last name. They met in a nursing home and have been married only a few months. They looked so brave to me—so optimistic and yet there they were holding onto each other, like the teachers used to make us do on field trips. Remember the buddy system?"

"Of course I do." She hears the excitement in his voice; sees the sparkle in his eyes. "It was just an amazing trip. A journey. And I have you to thank, Mackie. I met so many people along the way. You know, everyone has a little story. It's just right there waiting to be listened to."

She goes to him, hugs him. "I wasn't fair about your work, Sully."

"It's ok, Mackie. You let me change. Maybe you even made me change."

"What exactly do you mean by that?"

"Well, sometimes I think you have to get away from your life to find out where you are. To find out where you're going." He steeples his hands together and continues,

"I know it was wrong for me to be away from you for so long, but there's no doubt that something was happening to me out there."

"I was afraid I'd never see you again," she says.

"That's never going to happen again, I promise."

"Are you going to do something with these, Sully?"

Mackie says, feeling warm.

He shrugs, "I don't know. Right now it's enough just sharing them with you. Down the line—who knows?" And he gives a little shiver, "Maybe you're not the only one here with potential, Mackie Kinsella."

Chapter 49

She decides that she must talk with Graham. Clarify what did or didn't happen between them. But life is busy and full and there is Sully and the rest of her life.

She finishes the third condo and is working madly on the fourth, getting ready for the opening, which is now scheduled for mid-August. This model is her favorite. It's not overly large and has a reverse floor plan with a great room upstairs that combines the living, dining and kitchen areas around a central fireplace. Upstairs also holds a powder room, the master bedroom and bath and has decks completely around, allowing views of the ocean, the cliffs and even a peek of Sully's lighthouse in the distance. Downstairs there are two additional bedrooms and a full bath, along with a family room and another fireplace. Mackie thinks this would be a good house for almost anyone; a young couple with growing kids could find privacy in their upstairs retreat, an older couple could accommodate the kids coming home from college for breaks or houseguests coming down for a week at the beach.

The builder has used hardwood floors throughout and

used other natural materials, the fireplaces are fieldstone, and the counters are granite. Because of its views Mackie thinks of it as an outside/inside house and she starts there with her staging. Placing four canvas director's chairs around a glass topped table, she sets it with colorful placemats, napkins and tumblers and mugs. She imagines the owners having morning coffee and juice out there on the deck and later in the day cocktails and dinner. She decorates the house for summer, but knows it would work equally well in winter with the fireplaces ablaze and afghans draped across the furniture.

For now she has rented furniture; two overstuffed white canvas couches and a huge marble coffee table. The master bedroom is done with whitewashed pine furniture, anchored with a king-sized sleigh bed and an armoire. Mackie finds a hotel supply outlet and orders a dozen thick, white towels and a couple of guest robes and fits the bathrooms with them. Placing thick, French soap on all the sinks, she adds scented votive candles, instant room freshener. She is accessorizing with seashells, driftwood, starfish and other beach bounty. She steals her own sea glass collection and fills an apothecary jar with it and it becomes the centerpiece for the coffee table.

She knows that she might get some interest in her services once the models are open for viewing, but in the interim she's made up a flyer and posted it on local bulletin boards. She also went around to the local real estate brokers, telling them that she had once been in the business and what she is now doing. She explains that after marketing dozens of her own properties, she can facilitate sellers showing their property to the best advantage, simply by getting rid of clutter and arranging their own things in an appealing way. She neglects to tell them that her own house, in California, has been on the market for months and is approaching orphan status.

She and Sully are together almost every night at one or the other of their places and Mackie thinks it is about time she tells her girls about the burgeoning relationship. But she is not at all sure how they'll feel about their mother being with someone and she doesn't see how she can tell them about Sully over the phone. Perhaps she'll wait until October when she goes out to do the nursery. Maybe Sully will even fly out with her and spend a few days, meet her girls. She'd like that.

She stops by Boo's on her way home. "What the heck you got there, Sweet Pea?"

"It's a watermelon, Boo."

"Well, ya, that's obvious, I guess. Whatcha plan on doing with it?"

"I'm going to give you half and bring the other home. I'll cut it into cubes for you. I've got some fresh blueberries in the car and some cantaloupe too. I'll make a nice fruit salad before I leave."

"I guess that means you're not honoring me with your sweet face at dinner?" You've been scarce, Honey."

"I've been busy, Boo. And to tell you the truth, I've been having dinner with Sully almost every evening." Mackie bites her lip, "I guess I might as well tell you—we're kind of an 'item'."

"Woohoo!" Boo claps her hands in glee. "I was hoping you two would get it on."

Mackie blushes, "I'm sure it's going to be common

knowledge soon, at least around Shoreham. I haven't said anything to the girls yet though, I don't think they're ready to see their mom with someone."

"Everybody has to live their own life, Sweet Pea. Both your girls have found someone to be with." Boo opens a cabinet and gets out an earthenware bowl, finds a carving knife and hands it to Mackie. "Just because I never found no substitute for Buddy, don't mean you shouldn't get on about your business."

Mackie goes to the sink, washes her hands, "So, do you think Buddy would approve?"

Boo comes up behind Mackie and gives her a bear hug, "All my Buddy ever wanted was for you to be safe and happy."

Mackie gets misty, squeezes her eyes shut and grabs a dishtowel to dry her eyes and then her hands. She spins around to face Boo. "I miss him, Boo. I miss my father."

"He's worth missing, Sweet Pea."

Chapter 50

Mackie has the keys to the condos and she is showing Sully around. The grand opening is scheduled for the next day at ten and Mackie is anxious for Sully's imprimatur on the project.

She imagines that he'll just do a token walk-through, but he surprises her, spending time in every room and every house. Mackie opens the doors and then stands back, hands locked behind her back. She longs to explain the thinking that backed up each and every choice; the colors, the fabrics, the vignettes that she has set up. But she stands mute, trying to see it all through his eyes. They walk from one condo to the next and Mackie longs to ask him what he's thinking. His face is a mystery. She hasn't felt this nervous since Sister Philomena did fingernail inspections.

They are standing on the deck of the fourth condo and Sully surveys the horizon. "Amazing," he says and Mackie is not sure if he means the view or her work. "You've done such a thoughtful job, Baby. It's like each one has its own character. They're great!"

And she shines from within. "You like what I've done?"

He just nods his head. "I guess all those moves you made over the years trained you for this job."

She thinks about it for a moment. "You're right, Sully. I guess we lived in just about every kind of house over the years; apartments, ranches, capes, townhouses, colonials—good grief! I hadn't really thought about it. It was just always my job to be the 'homemaker'. I guess that's what I've been doing all these years." Mackie has never realized just how descriptive the word is. She used to resent writing it in the space for occupation, but it always seemed preferable to housewife, which invoked visions of indentured servitude and house arrest.

Sully leans against the railing and squints his eyes, "Aha, I can see home!"

"It's great, isn't it? I love the wrap around balcony on this model."

"Kind of a modern widow's walk," Sully says and realizing the connection, pulls Mackie close and says, "Sorry."

She hears his heartbeat, holds him tight. "It's okay, Sully. I'm not watching for my sailor to come home—he's already here."

"You've done such a good job, Mackie," Sully says, easing away. "But what are you going to do with the walls in this one?"

"That's part of the reason I wanted you here," Mackie says. "Sneaky, I know and I don't mean to sabotage you, but do you think we could borrow some of your photographs; the old and the new? The seascapes would be perfect and I can see the portraits hung for emphasis and surprise."

He rolls his eyes.

"I promise nothing will happen to them, Sully—and the black and white is just so perfect for this space. We won't frame them or anything. Just mount them and I'll let you decide what goes where—oh, please say yes."

"You need a good telescope on a tripod—"and he takes her hand and pulls her back inside, finds a spot behind the sofa in front of the French doors, "Here—where you can see the lighthouse. Can you get one by tomorrow?" And then he says, "Never mind, I'll get one for you. Just let me have the keys to the kingdom, okay?"

"You'll do it then?" Mackie is smiling like a Cheshire cat.

"With a proviso."

"Anything," Mackie says.

"I will hang everything myself. No assistance needed. No sneak peaks. You'll just need to trust me to do the right thing here." He looks at her, questioning.

"You mean I won't get to see it before the opening?"

"Exactly."

"Deal."

"Deal," he says and gives her a high five.

————)(())(————

Mackie wakes up to the sound of rain on the roof. Typical of New England weather, they have gone from heat wave to cold snap. The sky is heavy gray and forbidding. Nevertheless, she is excited about the grand opening, excited to see how Sully has hung his pictures. She showers; dresses in black linen pants and a cotton sweater, slip-ons and takes time with her hair and make-up. She sits having coffee on the front porch. It's too early to call the girls and the opening is set for ten o'clock. The King Brothers are pleased with what she's done but she wants to take a last look at everything before the doors open to the public. Sully is going to meet her there at nine-thirty. She keeps checking her watch every ten minutes, willing the time to pass and finally she gives up and calls Sully. "I know it's only eight, but I can't wait any longer."

He chuckles. "I'm surprised you haven't gone ahead over. I halfway expected to see you come back last night."

"I want to be with you when I see it," she says.

"Okay," she can hear the smile, "I'll meet you there in ten minutes, okay?"

"You've got it." She hangs up, grabs the keys and runs down the steps thanking God for Sully and her life.

She sees his car when she pulls into the parking lot but there is no sign of him. Thinking he must already be at the house she hurries down the path, passing the other three condos, breathless by the time she arrives at the door. "Up here," he calls and she climbs the stairs to the great room. "You must have flown!" she says, going to him, kissing him, taking him in.

"I was already here," he said. "I finished hanging them last night but I wanted to see them by daylight—such as it is."

She begins to look around, spots first the landscapes and seascapes that he does so well. Some he's hung above the fireplace and others are simply propped on the mantle to great effect. The telescope he wanted stands on its tripod aimed out to sea—aimed at the lighthouse actually. "That was a great idea," she says, pointing to it. "Where did you find it?"

"It's Duffy's. He wants credit for," Let's see—I think he called himself an assistant decorator." Mackie laughs, "Well, be sure to thank him for me. I'll make sure he gets it back unharmed."

"The photos are perfect, Sully." She looks at him, "Thank you so much for helping. Did you hang any of the others— the portraits?" she asks.

"I did. I put a few downstairs in the family room and I mounted some of the five by sevens for a collage in one of the bedrooms."

"Oh let's go look," she says.

"Wait, Mackie," he all but shuffles his feet, "First there's something I want to show you. He takes her hand and leads her into the master bedroom. Beside the armoire hangs a portrait of two young women. Propped back to back, both in black turtlenecks, arms crossed across their chests, they smile out past the camera. One is blonde; hair blowing in the wind, the other dark and full, but the lineage is unmistakable.

"Oh my God," Mackie says, tears brimming at her eyes, "Emma and Eileen—how? I don't understand." She turns to Sully. "You saw them? You know them?" She is shaky and Sully comes to her, embraces her.

"I made them promise not to tell you until I could surprise you with this. They're wonderful girls, Mackie, wonderful women," he corrects himself. "You must be incredibly proud."

Not knowing whether to be angry or elated, Mackie

pounds Sully's shoulder. "How did you find them?"

"Well, I remembered that Emma's place was called Regular Joe's. It wasn't difficult, Mackie. I explained that I was a friend of yours and just driving cross-country on a photo shoot."

Mackie shakes her head, still trying to get used to the idea that Sully has met the girls, and that they have managed to keep it from her.

"Surprisingly, they seemed to know I existed," he says. "I was happy for that."

"I can't believe they didn't tell me about this."

"Aw, Mackie, don't be upset with them. I made them promise. They thought you'd be happy with the surprise. We thought you would be."

"It's a treasure, Sully. Honestly, I'm just in shock."

"Emma got a hold of Eileen and we shot a couple of rolls of film on the beach by the coffee shop. I've got lots of snaps to show you, when you have time."

She can't take her eyes of the picture. "They are beautiful, my girls, aren't they?"

"Yes. But consider the source, Mackie." He smiles, "Maybe you'll let me take your picture someday?"

Mackie nods.

"Emma made me promise to shoot from the waist up, but we took some profile photos for your eyes only. She said she doesn't want to be remembered as a full blown incubator."

"That's my girl." Mackie looks at her watch. "It's nearly show time, Sully."

He squeezes her, "Break a leg, Baby."

Chapter 51

Sales are brisk at Sonoma Cove with only a few houses available by the end of September. Mackie knows that she's going to need to start putting money aside for the inevitable slow holiday season as well as her trips to California. She's studying for her real estate license and can't remember how she used to fill her days before this. There is never enough time, but she is happy. The California house is finally in escrow and scheduled to close by mid-October. Although not a windfall, it will be a nest egg for the winter and she'll even be able to pay Boo some 'dividends'.

She's walking up and down the aisles of the drugstore, absentmindedly tossing travel size toothpaste, hand cream, Q-tips into her basket when someone touches her shoulder. Spinning around she sees Graham standing there. Her face immediately flames. "Mary Katherine," he says.

"Graham!" Having effectively pushed him out of her mind she can't believe that she's face to face with him now.

"It's been a while. It's lovely to see you."

"I'm sorry I haven't been in touch. I've just been incredibly busy."

"I understand," he says. "Are you going on holiday?" he asks, looking at her basket.

"Actually, I'm going out to California for the birth of my first grandchild. I'm going to take some time, decorate the nursery and visit with both my girls."

"Wonderful," he says.

"How is Daly?" she asks, lurching to safer ground.

"She's good, Mary Katherine. She's starting horse riding lessons, keeping Herbie and me quite occupied—as always."

Mackie nods. 'Please say hi to both of them for me."

"Have you time for a coffee?" he says. "I have a free hour and I'd enjoy catching up with what's happening in your life."

"Well," she says, "Of course I do. Let me finish up here. I'll meet you—where?" she asks, flustered.

"Why not the coffee shop across the street?" he says, tilting his head towards the front of the store.

"Great," she says. "I'll see you there in ten minutes? All right?" Thinking, maybe I can just beg off, tell him I have a sudden appointment or something, good Lord what am I going to say?

"I'll be there."

Mackie picks up a few more things, chewing on the inside of her cheek, pays for them and crosses the street. She is silently practicing opening lines. Graham, I'm so terribly sorry if I led you on in some way, Graham, I don't think you know this but I've become quite serious about someone— Graham, of course you had no way of knowing that I was involved with someone and we were having this huge fight, or at least I thought we were and he was gone—Graham, I'm fond of you and there is no denying that there was something happening there, but—

He's sitting in a booth by the window and he smiles through the glass at Mackie. She goes in and takes the seat across from him. No Starbucks, they have a choice of coffees, regular or decaf. The waitress comes over, flips their mugs over and pours for both of them. "Anything else?" They shake their heads simultaneously and she disappears behind the counter. This is the kind of place where conversation is never interrupted by service.

Mackie adds cream, a little sugar, takes a sip and smiles. Her hand is shaking and Graham reaches across the table and calms it with his own. She finds herself staring across the table into his eyes. "It was just a kiss, Mary Katherine." And that simply, he defuses the situation. He sips his coffee. "And it would have been truly lovely if it were more."

She blushes furiously and can't think of what to say.

"I would say I regret it, but that would be untrue. I could be clinical and say it was a typical 'transference' but I don't enjoy labeling behaviors."

Finally she clears her throat and says, "I'm involved with someone, Graham."

He laces his fingers together and nods at her. "Yes, I suspected that might be it." He squints, "The photographer from the paper?"

"His name is Sully," she says. "I wasn't sure he and I were together when I came to dinner, Graham. But—we are—together that is." She shifts in the booth and forges ahead. "I want to apologize for—" she bites her lip and rolls her eyes up, swallowing hard.

"The grope?" He says.

She covers her face with her hands and drops her head to the table. Hearing the sound of laughter, she looks up and sees the sparkle in his eyes.

"It might have been nice to take that a bit further, actually," he says. She has no idea what to say and so she simply smiles back at him, the pink gradually fading from her cheeks. "Perhaps another time?"

"Graham—I don't know what to say."

"Then don't say anything at all." He smiles at her and she gets a glimpse of the man he is. "I'm happy for you Mary Katherine, perhaps even a bit envious."

She feels lighter, breathes easier.

"I hope this won't preclude our being friends?" he asks.

"Of course not," she says. "I care for you, Graham. I care about you. And of course I'd love to keep Daly in my life."

"Very well," Graham says, smiling. "We shall be friends with a brief yet wonderful history."

"That would be nice." Mackie looks at her watch, "Oh God, I've got to run. I've got a list as long as my arm of things to do before I leave."

"Well, thank you for joining me for coffee, Mary Katherine. You won't be a stranger anymore?"

"No, I won't. I promise."

"Good luck to you. And good wishes for a healthy grandbaby."

Sliding across the booth, she stands, bends over to him and kisses him on both cheeks in the chaste, European fashion. "The kisses were splendid, Doctor Joy."

BOO

Up in her attic, Boo sits, rocking and smoking. "I didn't want to do this without talking with you, Buddy, but I found someone who can make it safe." She sips her Jim Beam. "I am not going to talk about the smoking, Old Fool. Dammit, they got me doing cardiac hooha twice a week and eating all kinds of healthy. I haven't had a clam roll since my heart attacked me."

"So, this young kid—well not that young, but he has his own little business with carpentry." She inhales, closes her eyes. "Stop interrupting!" She takes another sip, "Mackie told me about him if you need to know, Mr. two-cents worth. Guess he helped her with some of her jobs at that chichi place she was decorating."

She gets up, pulls the sheet off the crib and runs her hand lovingly along the wood, unused, yet beautifully aged. "So I want your go-ahead. I think it's time. This will make a safe place for Emma and that Cisco the Kid's baby."

"Our girl is going out there tomorrow. Decorating the nursery up. I told Mackie that I wanted to give Emma a crib, but I didn't tell her it was this one. Lord, she doesn't even know about the baby we lost."

"Well, I'm going to explain it. Put it all in a little letter," Boo feels her chin quiver, and she sniffs. "He's picking it up this afternoon."

"Of course it will get there in time, Old Fool." She kisses her fingertips and touches the crib. "He says he can have it back here in two days." Then you and me are going to send it UPS by air."

"You know, those guys in the brown shorts and shirts? Apparently they're considered sexy these days." She stubs out her cigarette. Fans the air, and coughs.

"Course they don't hold a candle to you, Buddy, just my opinion. But don't go getting all smug up there, you know I never could resist a man in uniform."

Chapter 52

Sully drives her to Logan and they say good-bye. "Kiss and fly," she says. "I'm afraid we're going to be doing a lot of this, so no big farewells."

He nods, "Gotcha, Baby."

"I'll be back just as soon as I can and I'll call you constantly."

"I'm counting on it."

"And you'll miss me desperately."

"That I will." He grabs her suitcase out of the trunk and brings it to the curb for check in.

Folding her into his arms, he kisses her, long and deep, "Now get the hell out of here," he says and she sees his eyes glisten.

She is so excited about the baby, about seeing her daughters and she is so sad to be leaving Sully. It is the price. He waves without looking back and she stands in line, breathing in Boston, watching Sully navigate the traffic until she can't see him anymore. The skycap takes her bag, driver's license and itinerary and she hugs herself, surveys the sky and listens carefully to the noise, saving it up.

She and Emma work on the nursery together. It is more of Emma watching and suggesting and Mackie working. Not surprisingly, Emma and Cisco have changed their collective minds once again and pink is out. "We don't want Elena to be locked into anything gender specific," Cisco explains.

Emma just acquiesces. "Whatever, Cisco wants. I just want her out." With just three weeks left to her due date, Emma is suffering all the typical late pregnancy miseries; lack of sleep, swollen feet, inability to breathe and mood swings.

Mackie keeps all opinions to herself and just goes along with the plan of the day. Cisco is working long hours with the business and studying nearly all night. He hopes to get enough credits toward his degree to graduate in January. Mackie knows that all this sleep deprivation will hold them in good stead for when the baby arrives. Cisco is solicitous and just a little aloof. Mackie, as a mother-in-law in training, tries to give them as much privacy as possible given the dimensions of the apartment. She is sleeping, unsoundly, on a cot in the baby's room.

As promised, she calls Sully late every night. Just hearing his voice fortifies her. "How about a little oral sex?" he croons one night, sending her into fits of giggles which she stifles for fear of waking everyone up. "Tell me what you're wearing," he whispers seductively. "Sully, stop it!" she hisses. She's wearing an oversized t-shirt and a pair of pajama bottoms, wanting to be covered in deference to Cisco and their nocturnal passings in the hallway. "You have no idea how strange it is to be staying with your grown children in their place. It feels so odd. I'm trying to feel comfortable, but I feel like an intruder," she says. "Not that they don't want me here, I know they do, it's just incredibly awkward."

"Well, Baby, it won't be long until you're back here and I can't tell you how excited it makes me to think of having sex with a grandmother."

"You are incorrigible," she says.

"Yet, loveable."

"Yes."

"Go to sleep," he says. "Dream about me."

———◦(◦)◦———

Mackie applies a second coat of sage green paint to the walls and tries to decide if gingham is gender specific or not. She pans on making bedding for the crib that Boo is sending but it has yet to arrive. Emma is out shopping for what she'll need for herself when the baby comes, nursing bras and blouses, one of those wrap around pillows that the baby can lie on to feed, a small supply of infant sized diapers and a few other things that she didn't get at her baby shower. Cisco left the house before seven a.m. and said he wouldn't be home until late, after classes. Mackie decides to treat Emma, Eileen, Walter if he's available, and herself, to a dinner out at whatever restaurant appeals to Em by evening.

The phone rings and Mackie decides to let the machine pick it up when she hears Emma's voice, "Momma, pick up the phone if you're there."

"Em?" Mackie is breathless after lunging for the phone.

"I'm on my way to the hospital. My water broke in the middle of Toys R Us and I'm having gang-buster contractions." Emma sounds much too calm. "I already called Cisco. He's swinging by to get you."

"Oh my God, Mackie says, "It's not time, Em."

"Apparently Elena has other ideas," Emma says and then there's a sharp intake of breath. "Listen, the paramedics are here and the store manager insists they take me to the hospital. I'll see you there, Momma."

"Oh, Emma!"

"I love you, Momma. Hurry."

Cisco and Mackie arrive at the hospital to find Emma ensconced in a private birthing room that more resembles a hotel suite. The lights are dim, music is playing and Emma, already in a hospital gown, lies back, hooked up to a fetal monitor. This bears so little resemblance to the labor that Mackie knows that she thinks there must be some mistake.

Cisco goes immediately to Emma, kisses her forehead, rubs her arms and just says, "Well, look at you."

"I'm already dilated five centimeters," Emma says. Mackie sees pain etched in her daughter's face, but also sees a slight relaxing as Cisco continues to touch her.

"Hi, Momma."

Mackie's hands fly to her mouth, "I don't believe this is happening now."

"I'm fine. The baby's fine. I'm going to get an epidural just as soon as the anesthesiologist gets here."

Mackie approaches the other side of the bed, "Are you

all right, honey?"

"I'll be better when he shows up," Emma says and manages a wry smile. "It will still be a while before things get interesting, so if you want to go ahead and get something to eat, or whatever, do, Mom. I'll be okay now that Cisco is here."

There are few incontrovertible facts in life, but no one will dispute that above all, birth is a miracle. It is after midnight when Emma and Cisco deliver their baby. The doctor sits at a stool between Emma's legs, asks for one final push and the baby is with them. Tears stream down Mackie's face as the doctor clears the baby's mouth and nose, lays it across Emma's belly and says, "Oh, my we've got a shy one." Disputed by a lusty wail followed by a round of laughter, Mackie stands in awe as Cisco cuts the cord that connected mother to son for so many months.

BOO

Dear Baby,

You don't know me, but I am your great Aunt Boo. And that's not patting myself on the back—just what they call us old aunties the second time around.

Once upon a time (yes, like in the fairy tales) I was going to have a baby as beautiful as I'm sure you are. But something happened and the baby couldn't be here—there are rumors of workers needed in heaven, but who knows?

Anyway, the important thing is that Buddy and me wanted you to have this place to keep you safe and loved, of which there is no doubt you are and will be.

Even though I've never been on a plane, I'm not too old to learn new tricks and I'm going to try hard to come and visit you out there in California (even though it's a whole different world than Shoreham). In the meanwhile rest assured there is a guardian angel watching over you at all times.

Across the years and across the miles,
Grandpa Buddy and Boo

Chapter 53

Emma, Eileen and Mackie all sit on Emma's bed with their backs propped against the headboard. Baby, Richard Francis nurses at his mother's breast and they have all four fallen into a sort of numb reverie.

"I can't believe with all the ultra-sounds and gizmos that they didn't know the baby was a boy," Mackie says. "For Daddy and me, you were both total surprises, but I thought that now they were able to really pin down the sex of the baby ahead of time."

"So much for the miracle of modern medicine, Mom," Eileen says. "For all those docs know, I guess there might be a higher power at work."

"Daddy would have been so pleased, Emma, to have a namesake."

"It's kind of sad and happy at the same time, Momma—isn't it?"

"Oh yes, Em. I'm dealing with a lot of bittersweet things these days."

Eileen scoots closer to her mother and says, "Like finding out that your uncle was actually your father?"

"That was pretty huge, Leenie."

"Big time," Emma says. "Can you even imagine Mom having an affair with Daddy's brother—if he had one?"

"It wasn't actually an affair," Mackie says. "At least that's what Boo tells me. It was more of a onetime mistake, that unfortunately ended up with me."

"Well, no, Mom. Not unfortunate—here you are and so are we—and even baby Richard," Emma says. "So not unfortunate at all."

"And Boo forgave both of them?" Eileen asks.

"She's a pretty amazing person," Mackie says. "But you know, I'm still not sure why she kept it a secret for all these years. And I'm not sure that I'm one hundred percent ok with that."

"What do you mean, Mom?" Emma says.

"Well, all those years my mother was so hard on me. Insisting that I be so perfect. Of course I never felt I measured up. I think I can understand now how she felt I had to be better than anyone, anything. But at the same time it was so hard being her daughter."

"Is it ever easy?" Eileen says and Emma echoes her.

"Yeah, momma. Is it ever easy?"

"I guess you're right about that—on both sides. It's no piece of cake being a mother either." Mackie smiles, "I guess we just keep learning and hoping to do the best we can with what we have. Just look at you, Em. I think you're going to be a great mother. And Cisco will be a great Dad too. You were lucky to find such a good man."

"I hope that Walter and I can be the kind of parents you and Daddy were, Mom. That is if we're ever lucky enough to have a baby."

Mackie gives her daughter a hug, "I'm sure it will happen, Eileen—I feel it. I'm so proud of both of you. You've accomplished so much more than I ever did. I know I haven't always let you know how much I've relied on you—both of you. You are my great girls."

Emma takes a sleeping, satiated Richard off her breast and lays him gently in the bassinette beside her. "Ok, you two. Enough of this mutual admiration and love-fest, I'm going to nap while the baby does. Out with you both!"

Sitting in Emma's tiny kitchen, Mackie and Eileen sip tea and munch on cinnamon toast. "This feels like old times, Mom," Eileen says. "I remember when Daddy used to make us breakfast to give you a 'sleep in morning.'

Mackie smiles at the memory. "You know, Leenie, I'm finally able to think about Daddy without that dreadful heaviness. There are lots of those little memories that crop up. We had a good life together."

"Too short," Leenie says.

"Too short." Mackie agrees.

"Mom?" Leenie says.

"What, honey?"

"I think I know what happened with Daddy and the money. At least most of it."

Taken aback, Mackie says, "You do?" Her heart is pounding and her hands tremble. She's not sure if she wants to know what Richard did. Maybe it's better not to know. Things are going so well now, what can it help?

"It's taken me a while to figure this out, Mom," Leenie says, getting up and pacing the kitchen. "I believe that Daddy took the money from the second on your house and started doing some day trading."

Mackie raises her eyebrows, questioning.

"Basically, Daddy was going on line and buying and selling stocks in the same day. It's hugely speculative. It can be lucrative, but also devastating."

"And Daddy was doing that—day trading?"

"Yes, I think he was banking on making a profit on those short-term fluctuations." Eileen frowns. "It got out of control."

Mackie shakes her head. "So basically he was gambling?"

"Exactly." Eileen brings the kettle to the table and adds water to their mugs. "And at first, at least, I think he was doing well with it."

"And then?" Mackie fixes her own tea and wonders at this smart woman who is her daughter.

"Then—things went south in a hurry and I think that's where the Vegas trips came in."

"Talk about gambling!" Mackie says.

"I think he was trying to recoup the losses and instead he just ended up compounding them." Eileen says.

Mackie sits absorbing the information and feels sadness wash over her. Not for the money but for the fact that Richard hadn't shared this with her. "He must have felt so ashamed, Leenie." Mackie feels tears, "And alone. I should have known something was wrong."

Leenie comes to her mother and embraces her from above. "You had no way to know, Mom. And I'm sure he thought he could fix it. He was so good at fixing things—always. You both were."

Mackie feels relief and sorrow settle on her. "Thank you

so much, Leenie, for keeping on this." She stands up and enfolds Eileen in an embrace and this time there is no resistance. They stand in the kitchen locked together, finally on even footing.

MACKIE

I stand in my bedroom, nineteen years old and full of wonder. I've designed my own wedding gown and saved my salary for months to have Rhoda of Egypt make the dress for me. Rhoda is not an exotic beauty, but actually a middle-aged, balding man who took over his wife's tailoring business after her untimely death. But his vision is mine. I am wearing an A-line dress of raw silk with covered buttons down both sleeves and the back of the dress. There is no lace. I am a no frills kind of girl. The pillbox with veil might have been a mistake, but that is hindsight.

I've been working in personnel at the Prudential Insurance Company for a year and a half and I feel like the rock of Gibraltar, but not quite as solid. Richard has been offered a job in Virginia and we will be leaving Shoreham for Arlington right after the wedding. I wonder if Virginia is true south.

Buddy is downstairs, standing in the kitchen drinking a beer for courage. He won't sit for fear of creasing his tuxedo. He's also told me that he's not giving me away. Apparently I'm to be 'on loan' to Richard. And God forbid he doesn't take care of me, never mind the degree from Boston College. Buddy has slathered on an extra helping of Vitalis and his face is baby soft and smells wonderfully of Old Spice.

Boo is in the kitchen dressed in turquoise lace and overseeing the food that we'll serve to the hundred people who've accepted our wedding invitation. She's been cooking for days. Our fridges are filled to the brim. We've resorted to borrowing fridge space from the Murphy's next door and the Sawchuck's across the street. A dozen coolers are in the garage. They are filled with beer, soft drinks and wine.

I've ordered lavender roses for Boo and my mother that I will give them after Father Flaherty pronounces Richard and me husband and wife. Mrs. Richard Kinsella awaits me.

I've always felt as if I have two moms. Boo with her unconditional love and food, mother with her great expectations.

The summer chapel is only two doors away from our house and no one has ever been married there before. It is plain. The kneelers are not padded and there is no air-conditioning. On the practical side, we won't need limos.

My mother comes into the room and I think I must look at her, as if it might be the last time I see her, or maybe even the first. She has the same green eyes as I do. I look and see her life trapped inside, so secret, so inaccessible. And I think about my own life, so uncharted, so hopeful.

Chapter 54

Three days later after tearful good-byes and promises to return at Christmas with Sully and Boo, if she'll fly, Mackie boards the plane for her flight home. The idea of the combination wedding/christening that Emma and Cisco are planning makes Mackie smile. She takes a pillow and blanket from the overhead storage and climbs into her window seat. She's sad at leaving, but anxious to be back in Sully's arms by dinnertime.

She's tried to store up the feel of baby Richard's skin, his clean baby smell, the contentment she felt each time he fell asleep against her heart. She doesn't know if it's wishful thinking or simple truth that the baby looks a little bit like Richard. She knows that he would have loved being a grandfather. But she is Nana Mac and that is enough. She will fly to see him and he will be a tiny traveler too, coming east to her. Eileen and Walter have promised to visit. Her house by the ocean is big enough to hold them all, after all, her children and her grandchildren and all those yet to come.

They'll learn about the seasons and sea glass and snow. There is magic.

CPSIA information can be obtained
at www.ICGtesting.com
Printed in the USA
FSHW011606271018
53326FS

9 781977 202345